CITY
UNDER
ONE
ROOF

CITY UNDER ONE ROOF

Iris Yamashita

BERKLEY

New York

BERKLEY
An imprint of Penguin Random House LLC
penguinrandomhouse.com

Library of Congress Cataloging-in-Publication Data

Names: Yamashita, Iris, author.
Title: City under one roof / Iris Yamashita.
Description: New York : Berkley, [2023]
Identifiers: LCCN 2022021601 (print) | LCCN 2022021602 (ebook) |
ISBN 9780593336670 (hardcover) | ISBN 9780593336687 (ebook)
Subjects: LCGFT: Detective and mystery fiction. | Novels.
Classification: LCC PS3625.A672227 C58 2023 (print) |
LCC PS3625.A672227 (ebook) | DDC 813/.6—dc23/eng/20220525
LC record available at https://lccn.loc.gov/2022021601
LC ebook record available at https://lccn.loc.gov/2022021602

Printed in the United States of America
1st Printing

Book design by Tiffany Estreicher

For Kayoko Yamashita

1928–2005

CHAPTER ONE

AMY

"AND WHEN DID YOU FIND THE BODY"—OFFICER NEWORTH paused for a moment before adding—"parts? When did you find the body parts?"

It was a hand and a foot, to be exact. Or at least Amy thought there was a foot. She hadn't bothered to look inside the boot, but since Officer Neworth said "parts" instead of "part," she assumed there must have been a foot—a bloated, sawed-off, purple-blotched piece of flesh that would have made her dry heave at the sight.

"Yesterday, around eleven a.m.," she said. She was pretty sure she had mentioned this detail at least six times that very day. She'd thought getting pulled out of algebra class would be fun, but now she was having second thoughts.

The boot, she remembered, looked fairly new. It was covered

with mud and grime, but the treads weren't that worn and the laces hadn't frayed yet. She hadn't told any of this to Officer Neworth, though. Up until then, she'd tried to say as little as possible, sticking to answers like "Yes," "No," and "I don't know."

Amy Lin stared at Officer Neworth and his receded-to-an-island hairline and decided that he was not someone who could be trusted. For one thing, he was wearing a gold watch. Any man who wears a gold watch is a little shady. Second, anyone who asks you the same question over and over expecting a different answer does not trust you, and therefore you should not trust them. And last of all, Neworth was from Anchorage, and Point Mettier people tended to keep their mouths shut around any of the "otters." "Otters" is what the kids called people outside Point Mettier because it kind of sounded like the word "others."

"So, tell me again, who were you with?" he asked.

Amy sighed internally and gave him a glare. Did she look like a caged parrot that would keep repeating the same thing over and over again?

Officer Neworth shifted in his seat and adjusted his leather duty belt, which sagged with the weight of lethal equipment—a baton, cuffs, a magazine pouch, a flashlight, a Taser, pepper spray, and, of course, a Glock pistol. But despite all his protective gear, Neworth looked uncomfortable under the glare of a seventeen-year-old who was barely five foot two. He finally turned his eyes away and looked down at his notepad. "Celine Hoffler and Marco Salonga?"

"Yes," Amy finally answered as if his question was somehow offensive.

"And what were you doing at the cove?"

"Just getting out." Amy wasn't about to tell him the real reason they went to the cove, which was to smoke pot. Even though marijuana was legal in Alaska, they were still minors.

IT WAS A Sunday, and there was a break in the rain, so they had all bundled up in their neoprenes, parkas, and ski caps and decided to paddle their kayaks out to Hidden Cove. On sunny days in summer, Sanders Glacier across the inlet would look brilliant against the sky, with blue and white ice caps like a giant slushy spilled onto a mountain valley. Tourists would come in flocks during the high season to Point Mettier. Even though, Amy knew, the real pronunciation of "Mettier" was probably the French way, rhyming with "get away," everyone butchered the name and said it in a way that sounded like "dirtier." The otters always wanted to see the glaciers in the sound and paid top dollar for cruise ships and yachts to take them up close. Amy wasn't sure why. She'd been up to a few of the glaciers, including Sanders, and had come to the conclusion that they were prettier from afar. On that Sunday in October, though, there had been dense clouds hanging low over the cove and Sanders just looked like a looming gray monster behind the mist.

Since tourist season was over and the thrum of motorboats and Sea-Doos was gone, it was pretty quiet on the water. Just the *dwop dwop* sound of their paddles dipping in and out, and the kittiwakes screeching overhead. Once they got to the beach, they loitered around, passed a joint, not really talking or doing anything specific. Celine hopped on a fallen log and balanced across the length of it like a high-wire act. Her sandy blond hair floated behind her in the wind, the way you see in the movies. Amy had always been envious of Celine's hair, because hers was just a dull black. She wanted to dye

3

it platinum blue, except that her mother would probably kill her—literally. Marco was skipping rocks, or maybe he was throwing them at birds; she couldn't remember exactly.

Amy started combing the beach for mementos to add to her collection: fish skeletons and coins, jewelry, and other odds and ends left behind by careless tourists. It was about this time that she noticed something on the south side of the cove—just a little shimmer, like a Morse code of light—and headed over toward it to investigate.

It was sunshine reflecting off the rubber toe of a hiking boot. She didn't realize then that it was anything more than a boot. Kind of a shame, she thought, that someone had lost a perfectly good boot. But when she bent down on the gravelly shore to take a closer look, something else caught her eye. Something she had almost stepped on.

It was a severed hand, half-buried in the sand. Or at least it looked like a hand, but it was green and almost translucent, the way glow-in-the-dark stickers look when the light is on. She could see the lines of the joints on the fingers, but the entire hand was swollen and greasy-looking. It felt as if a whole minute went by while she just stood there, staring. In reality, it was probably more like ten seconds before she finally blinked and found her voice.

"Guys," was all she could muster. The others immediately stopped what they were doing and came to see what she was pointing at. Celine was the one who actually screamed—a high-pitched, earsplitting almost wail of a cry that echoed across the valley and sent shivers down Amy's spine.

"AND WHAT DID you do after you found the parts?" Officer Neworth interrupted her thoughts and continued with his interrogation. At least it felt like an interrogation to Amy, even though it was just a witness account.

Amy wanted to reply, "What do you think we did? Hang them up for Halloween decorations?" But instead she said, "We went back to the Dave-Co and told Officer Barkowski."

"The Dave-Co?"

Amy sighed. "The building we're sitting in now. The Davidson Condos." The condos were supposed to have been named after some general who served in World War II, but she had heard a rumor that the buildings were actually named after Randolph Davidson, a famous Alaskan con man who set up a fake telegraph office through which he took money for sending blips and beeps that never went anywhere except into a wall.

Neworth laughed at the name. "Is that what you call it? So, how long have you lived here . . . in the Dave-Co?"

Amy knew this question had nothing to do with the body parts. "Fourteen years," she replied.

"Holy cow," he said with a kind of pity in his voice.

People from Anchorage tended to look at Point Mettier kids as charity cases. "It's always shittier in Point Mettier," they would say. It wasn't just about subzero temperatures and eight months of practical winter. The thing that really made otters believe residents of Point Mettier were batshit crazy was the fact that they all lived in one building . . . in the Dave-Co.

There were 205 full-time residents in Point Mettier. The Dave-Co had a post office, a church, an infirmary, and a general store that also acted as a gift shop, selling the same touristy tchotchkes since the nineties—Sanders Glacier mugs and cork coasters with pictures of moose, bears, or kittiwakes. The school was just an underground tunnel away.

Back when the city was a military outpost, the Walcott Building next door had a bowling alley, an auditorium, a movie theater, and even an indoor pool, but that building was practically destroyed in the big earthquake of 1964, and now it was just an abandoned skeleton of itself. The Dave-Co, on the other hand, didn't have any of those cool amenities, not even a barbershop or salon where people could get a decent haircut.

For a seventeen-year-old, it was boring as hell. It was more of a prison than a home, really. If it weren't for the Internet, Amy thought, she would have killed herself over the lack of stimuli.

Most families who came to live in Point Mettier left after a year or two. Nobody was actually from there and nobody liked to stick it out for too long. Celine had come about two years ago from Minnesota. Marco Salonga's family had come from the Philippines. Amy and her mother had probably come from the farthest end of the earth, but they belonged to the longtimers club because Amy had been only three when they arrived. She didn't know any other kids who had lived in Point Mettier that long. Even Spence Blackmon and his younger brother, Troy, didn't arrive with their mom until much later, when Spence was ten and Troy must have been six.

People had all sorts of reasons for moving to the city. Some said they fell in love with the scenery or that they liked the isolation or that they liked living in a close community. Amy didn't believe any of their stories, though. She knew the only real reason people moved out there was because they were running from somebody or something. Why else would you live in a backwater hole of a place where everyone lived in one building and your eyelashes could actually freeze? In fact, Amy had only just found out the real reason why Ma had moved the two of them out there to run a restaurant serving stuff even she knew was barely passable as Chinese food. Again, though, she wasn't about to spill any of this info to Officer Neworth.

THERE WERE JUST two police officers in Point Mettier: Chief Sipley and Officer Barkowski. Amy had watched enough television to know that the police station she was sitting in now was just a tiny locker room compared with what other cities had. There were the main reception area with tiny squeezed-in desks, the "interrogation room" closet they were sitting in, and a one-cell jail. Whenever there was a suspected "major crime," like when a tourist tried to kill her husband by stabbing him repeatedly with a dinner knife at one of the restaurants on the pier one summer, Anchorage police were called in, which was why Officer Neworth was there, questioning her about the body parts.

There was a knock at the door and Officer Barkowski poked his head in. "You almost done, Officer Neworth? Or have you just discovered that Amy Lin is a maniacal serial killer?" He gave Amy a friendly wink, and she smiled, despite herself. Officer Barkowski had started working in Point Mettier a year ago. He was always talking to the kids, pretending like he was one of them, making friendly conversation. Amy knew that it was an act, but at least he spoke to them like adults instead of uneducated third-world charity cases. Overall, Amy thought he was one of the good guys, but that didn't mean she was going to let him in on any secrets. Chief Sipley, on the other hand, had been in Point Mettier longer than anybody. She wasn't sure exactly what his story was. He looked kind of like a bald and drunken Santa Claus on the outside, but even though he appeared jolly, Amy knew that on the inside, he was the kind of guy who was much smarter than he let on and was always calculating something.

"Chief Sipley just radioed from the cove and says everything's been bagged and cleared out there," Barkowski reported.

Officer Neworth closed his notepad as if he had just been idling away his time, waiting for this cue. "I think we're done here."

Barkowski eyed the pad like he was just itching to take a look. "We hear there's been a lot of these cases popping up on the coast. Is that true?"

"Yeah, we've heard there've been a few in Canada and Washington as well," Neworth admitted. "This is the third set in Alaska in a year."

"Any leads?"

"No." Officer Neworth stood up from his chair. "There's speculation that they might have been suicide jumpers, or people who accidentally fell off ships."

"Jesus, that's sad."

Officer Neworth nodded. "The plastic in the boots makes them float up and carries them to shore. We don't get too many hands, though, so it was a bit unusual." He chewed on that for a moment. "Well, we don't have all the answers, and I doubt we ever will. But since we can't identify the bodies or prove any foul play, we can't exactly investigate them as crimes."

Officer Barkowski peeked over at Amy. "School's still in session, if you're done questioning Ms. Lin."

"Oh, right." Officer Neworth suddenly remembered the third person in the room. "You can go now, Amy. Thanks for your cooperation."

Amy got up slowly and a sense of relief washed over her. She exited the office into the maize-colored concrete hallway and felt like she had just cheated a lie detector test. Well, perhaps she hadn't *really* lied. She had just omitted a few facts about who was there. In the end, did it really matter if there were three or four witnesses, especially now that she knew it probably wasn't even a murder, just some depressed tourist who maybe jumped off a cruise ship?

CHAPTER TWO

CARA

THE WINDSHIELD WIPERS OF THE CHEVY SUBURBAN FLAPPED in double time, trying to cut through the vaporous shroud of fog that had cloaked Sanders Glacier Road. The radio repeated its announcement that "a severe early-winter weather system" was headed toward Point Mettier, but Cara planned to be in and out before it hit, just long enough to see if there was a case to reopen.

It wasn't the detached foot that caught her attention. She could buy the running theory of suicide victims, and buoyant shoes causing feet to detach from their decaying bodies. But that didn't explain how a hand washed up next to it, and that was why she was compelled like a moth to a flame on a sojourn to the sequestered town.

The not-unpleasant drive took her along a scenic highway that rimmed Cook Inlet—a finger path of water off the Gulf of Alaska pointing toward the majestic Kenai Mountains. For a moment, she even felt a sense of freedom on the road, with glimpses of civilization-devoid vistas that lulled her out of heavy thoughts. But then she remembered the task at hand and the possibility of a foul murder, and she sobered back up.

She finally reached a sentinel tollbooth from which was monitored what came in and out of the Point Mettier Tunnel. A Native with a reflective neon green jacket and a Seahawks baseball cap ventured to stick his head out of his heated box. He looked to be in his fifties, his forehead weathered with worry lines, his hair slivered with gray, and settled brown eyes peering over reading glasses.

"Little late for the season," he said. "Most places have closed up shop 'til spring."

"Not a tourist," Cara responded. She pulled out her badge from her jacket and flashed it just long enough for him to get a glance.

"Investigating the body parts?"

She nodded.

"Wasn't there just a team from Anchorage here the other day?"

"I'm the follow-up team," Cara responded.

The tollbooth operator scrutinized her for a beat. "Hold on." He pulled his head back in and Cara heard him get on the phone to say, "We've got a Smokey coming in."

Cara tapped her fingers on the steering wheel, wondering who needed to know this on the other end.

The operator finally stuck his head out again. "Tunnel will switch to eastbound in five. Just wait in Lane One 'til the light turns green." Then he waved her through.

The narrow one-way artery burrowing through the mountain

switched directions every half hour. During tourist season, there would have been a line of cars waiting to go through, but it was early November, so her navy blue SUV was the sole vehicle headed in.

When the red-striped traffic arm lifted, Cara drove into what looked like an A-frame ski chalet embedded in the rock, but once she was inside, it felt more like a mining cave, with naked lights strung on a wire above, and craggy walls weeping with moisture. The voice on the radio reduced to a static hiss, and underneath, the tires on the railroad tracks made a steady *kachunk kachunk* sound. Or perhaps it was the sound of her heart beating louder. The darkness stretched on and she wondered for a moment whether she was actually driving through a tunnel or falling into an abyss.

Cara had never been good in closed spaces, but she had learned to tamp down her claustrophobia and no one was the wiser. After a two-and-a-half-mile stretch, pale, grayish light finally streamed through the windshield, and the truck emerged as if breaching the surface of water. She exhaled and was able to breathe normally again.

She drove through a harbor filled with docked fishing boats and recreational yachts. Some had already been winterized, sitting dormant on the asphalt like a disarrayed pod of beached whales. There was a smattering of empty cafés, bars, and restaurants lining the bay. A woman was posting a CLOSED UNTIL MAY sign on one of them. Her pickup truck in front looked like it was already loaded up for whatever her off-season destination was. Nearby stores were already dark. Clearly, this was a town going into hibernation.

Moments later, Cara saw on the horizon a behemoth of a building, wider than its height, casting a shadow over the town. She knew this must be the infamous Davidson Condos.

So, this is it, she thought, driving up to the asphalt lot in front.

This is where the entire town shutters away for the winter . . . at least those who are willing to stay.

ONCE INSIDE THE building, Cara wandered the hallways of the ground floor until she found a green door with the words "Police, Point Mettier, Alaska" stickered on. She wondered about the impermanence of the sticker, as if law and order were only a temporary facade here.

She knocked but entered without waiting for an answer. Inside, there were two people, who glanced up from their gray metal desks. Cara assumed the elder man to be Chief Sipley. He got up and had to scoot his wide frame around his desk. Sixties, Cara guessed, given his brown-fading-into-white beard and bald crown.

The other officer, she fathomed, must be in his late twenties or early thirties. He was tall and fit with a kind of awkward, Mayberry-like charm. He nearly stumbled out of his chair as he also got up to greet her. His dark, almost black hair made her wonder if he was a mutt like her: a mix of Anglo, Native, and Italian.

Cara addressed the elder first. "Chief Sipley? I'm Detective Cara Kennedy."

He put his large hand out for a shake. "Lost the bet to come here, didn't you?" Cara left his jest unanswered, but he was undeterred. "Well, let me tell you, Detective Kennedy, there's pluses and minuses to living here. The minus being that at the end of the season, the whole town clears out and it's just the two hundred of us. The plus being that the whole town clears out and it's just the two hundred of us." He laughed at his own joke. It was a deep, wheezy, congestive laugh. Then he turned to his younger cohort, who had kept silent. "J.B., say hello to the detective. But don't get too close. There's a ring on that finger."

Cara subconsciously moved her hands behind her back.

"Joe Barkowski," the young man said. "J.B.'s less of a mouthful."

She nodded to him and his face flushed red for no good reason.

"So, any local missing persons reported that might connect to the body?" Cara asked, pulling out her notepad.

"Straight to business, huh? No batting about," Chief Sipley said rather pointedly.

"Sorry, I'm not good with the niceties."

Chief gave another raspy laugh. "Well, you'd fit right in here, then. And no, he's still a John Doe."

"Definitely not from Point Mettier," J.B. chimed in. "And no one who stayed at the inn appears to be missing."

"I thought APD had this all wrapped up. Probably just another suicide jumper, didn't they say, J.B.? Like those other body parts they've been finding." Despite his casual demeanor, Cara sensed that Chief Sipley was covertly assessing her.

J.B., on the other hand, didn't seem quite convinced about it either. "Pretty odd, though, to find those extremities washing up like that."

"Is there a reason why they're sending you back here? They've already bagged the evidence. Nothing criminal is what they made it seem like." Sipley set himself back behind his desk.

"We want to take a closer look at this one," Cara said in as matter-of-fact a tone as she could manage, and she didn't elaborate. She didn't want to waste any time on chitchat, so she added, rather impatiently, "Can you take me to where the floaters were found?"

Chief Sipley turned to J.B.

"Sure . . . sure thing," J.B. said.

J.B. AND CARA hopped into his patrol car and headed toward the harbor. She had already loaded her camera and investigator's tool kit in the trunk.

J.B. attempted some small talk. "So, how long you been a detective?"

"Seven years in the force, four years as detective," she answered. It was only a partial lie.

"I've been thinking of following that path myself. Mind if I watch? Learn the ropes?" He was an eager beaver.

"No problem."

"Your, uh . . . husband. He in law enforcement too?" J.B. tried to be subtle.

"No. He was a manager at a biotech firm." There was a moment of silence—a mental record scratch. Cara knew the "was" needed to be elaborated upon. "He died a year ago, along with my son, on a hiking trip," was all she added. With time, she'd learned to say this with a succinctness and devoid of tears.

"Oh Jesus, I'm sorry," J.B. said, and he seemed genuinely sorry, because he grew quiet.

He slowed to a stop as a large figure crossed the road, seemingly drifting in with the fog. It was a moose, shaking its fan-shaped antlers as it lumbered to the other side of the road. Then Cara noticed it had a collar and a leash, and there was a person holding on to the leash. It was a woman who was probably in her late twenties, but her frumpy style made her look older, dressed as she was in a plaid parka, thigh-high boots, and a chestnut-colored beret that was too large for her head. She sported polarized sunglasses and short cropped hair and paused for a moment to give Cara an uncanny glare before she led the moose all the way across.

"That's Lonnie Mercer," J.B. said, nodding toward the woman. "She and Denny are longtimers here."

"Denny's her husband?" Cara asked.

"Denny's the moose."

THEY BOARDED A vessel marked COAST GUARD AUXILIARY UNIT, so Cara assumed there wasn't enough funding for a dedicated police boat. J.B. handed her a regulation neon-orange personal flotation device before taking the wheel and puttering out of the harbor, carving up water wakes behind them. On the way, they passed a ribbon-like waterfall and a colony of kittiwakes that shrouded the cliffs above. Ten minutes later, they arrived at Hidden Cove. Stepping off the craft with her camera around her neck and lugging the kit case, Cara stopped for a moment to admire the glacier-covered mountain directly across.

"Once tourist season is over, you get this all to yourself." J.B. smiled.

For a moment, Cara contemplated how nature could sometimes be both beautiful and terrifying at the same time. It could give and take away in the same breath. She tucked her thoughts away. "Lived here long?" she asked.

"A year and two months. Got recruited out of Montana." He continued talking while leading her across the beach. "There are a couple of people who were born here, but most of the people are like me—transplants. They come from all over the lower forty-eight, and even places like Samoa and Lithuania. Some stay. A lot of them leave after a few years."

"Can't take the isolation?"

J.B. deliberated on his answer. "Since all of us live in the same building, you get to know everybody real well and that's nice. And then after a while, you get to know each other more and it's not so nice." He chuckled to himself. "Over there." He pointed to a sheltered spot on the cove.

As she headed toward the spot, Cara mentally compared the evidence photos in the police database to the lay of the land. Images flashed in her head—a hand half-buried in the sand, and the boot, covered in grime, lying a few feet away on its side. She put the kit down on the ground, then uncapped her digital Nikon and began to document the scene.

J.B. stood where he was, trying to stay out of her way. He made small conversation. "Chief Sipley told me about a couple of elderly ladies—widows—who lived in the Davidson Condos and were really good friends. Like sisters. Even lived next door to each other. Then one day, they fought about something. Nobody remembers what. Didn't speak to each other for two years. Can you imagine that? They passed each other in the hallway, rode the same elevator, and just refused to even look at each other."

Cara snapped photos of the water, the shore, the surrounding foliage, then went farther down the beach, hunting for something the Anchorage team might have missed.

"Are you looking for anything in particular?" J.B. asked, as he started scouring the ground with her.

"No, nothing particular," she responded, while continuing to snap photos. "So, they still live here? The ladies, I mean."

"These two ladies eventually made up and were the best of buddies again, and when one of 'em finally moved out of town, the other bawled like a baby. I guess that's kind of how you'd describe a lot of relationships here. One minute, best of friends, the next minute, mortal enemies, and then back again."

A glint of metal caught Cara's attention. It was a silt-covered syringe. She pulled on a pair of rubber gloves and took a plastic bag from her kit.

"We see a lot of those," J.B. commented. "You know how it is. Oxy, meth, whiskey, weed. You name the addiction, we got it. Just a shame they gotta treat the wilderness like a garbage dump."

He was probably right. Nothing of significance, but Cara dropped it into the baggie and labeled it regardless. As she continued to scour the beach, she spotted a group of unusually shaped rocks. Charcoal-colored, long, and thin, they protruded from the ground like pyroclastic fingers reaching out from some sort of hell beneath. She pocketed a couple of them. Not for evidence, really, but more as a memento.

Just then, a cascade of rocks and other debris tumbled from up by the tree line, and Cara whipped her head toward the noise. She saw a flash of color and another mini avalanche set off by someone or something scurrying up higher into the trees, followed by the sound of branches snapping deeper in the foliage.

"Hey!" she yelled, putting down her kit and running up the beach toward the fog-obscured trees.

J.B. followed her. "Who's there?" he yelled, but there was no answer.

Cara huffed after the figure into the thicket, wet spruce needles thwacking at her. The dense snarl of tree branches hindered her passage and whatever she was chasing got too far ahead, until the sounds of movement could no longer be traced.

She backtracked to a clearing and bent over with her hands on her knees, trying to catch her breath while she waited for J.B., who was still somewhere below.

"Did you catch him?" he yelled.

"Negative," she said, wiping her wet hair back from her face. But then something else caught her attention. Cara headed over to a dark patch in the ground, toward what looked at first like a formation of ant lines. Boot prints.

Cara lifted her camera and took a series of shots.

J.B. finally caught up with her and peered over her shoulder. "That's interesting," he said. "Think it belongs to our voyeur?"

"Don't think so," she replied as she tried to discern a trail. Most of the prints were too faint to use for evidence, and they seemingly disappeared into the thicket. "Looks like these were made maybe a few days, possibly a week or so, ago. And they're nowhere near where our intruder was running."

"It rained about five days ago," J.B. added. "So the prints couldn't be older than that."

She found a good print, almost intact, placed her L-shaped photo-macrographic scale next to it, and snapped some more photos. Satisfied, she straightened up.

J.B. glanced down at his watch. "Speaking of weather, there's supposed to be a system rolling in and it'll be snow this time. You'll want to get back before it hits, and definitely before the tunnel closes; otherwise you'll be stuck here."

Cara looked up toward the angry clouds gathering above. Almost as if on cue, a low rumbling sound echoed across the cove—a warm-up practice for its coming opus. "I'm ready to head back," she agreed.

They found their way back toward the motorboat. "I bet it was just some nosy kid coming up from the hiking trail. We don't get a lot of body parts washing up onshore around here," J.B. offered.

Cara nodded as she scanned the shore for other boats or kayaks, but there was only the coast guard vessel they had come up in.

"I suppose you see a lot of dead bodies on the job. You ever get used to it?" J.B. asked.

The first time Cara saw a corpse on the job was long before she had moved up to detective rank. She had been called in for a traffic accident. It turned out a drunk driver had driven into a light pole and the car had wrapped around it in a gnarled mess of metal. The victim was dead before she got there. What struck her the most was that he didn't look real. He could have been just a wax doll. Funny, she thought, how a body's physical appearance alters once it's without a soul.

Over time on the force in Anchorage, she supposed she did become numb to looking at the dead. Another case. Another job. Something that needed to be objectified.

But all that changed when she saw the remains of her own husband and son—a jigsaw of scavenged bones scattered in pieces and covered in soot. The photos of what was left of them stung her like a thousand needles seared in fire. She could never stop seeing them. She could never stop feeling the pain of it.

"No," she finally responded. "You never get used to it."

CHAPTER THREE

LONNIE

PEOPLE WERE ALWAYS TALKING ABOUT HER BEHIND HER BACK.
Lonnie knew it. Like the lady in Room 706. Lonnie imagined the
words in her head. *Bitch. Whore. Witch. Hussy. Dumbo. Crazy. Loony.
Stupid.* The lady was talking about her behind her back because Lonnie came from the Institute.

Lonnie didn't like the Institute. There were lots of scary people there.
Watching her. They were always watching her. Giving her pills. Pills
she didn't need. And there were cameras and bells. Bells that went off
at night. And people running down the halls. Scurrying like dogs chasing cats. Making lots of racket. Lonnie hated the noise. *Clatter. Clang.
Uproar. Yelling. Racket. Discord. Wailing. Screaming. Crying. Bang. Thud.
Quiet.*

It was a good thing she left. She knew she didn't belong there. She had to go.

She had to go get Denny. Denny was her moose.

Denny's fur was nice and soft. Not like a dog's or a cat's. It was thicker and harder, but Lonnie liked the feel of it when she ran her hand across Denny's back. She especially liked that space on his muzzle below his eyes. She gave him a good brushing every morning and fed him oats, just like a horse. She'd never had a horse, but she was pretty sure having a moose was almost the same. She kept Denny warm at night and put blankets on him and gave him water. When she was with Denny, she felt calmer and things didn't upset her as much.

Lonnie found Denny one morning when she was out in the woods following rabbit prints in the snow. Lonnie didn't do any hunting. Chief wouldn't allow her to have a gun, but she liked looking at animal prints. She knew all kinds of animal print patterns— rabbits, foxes, elk, bears, moose, and, of course, human prints. There were plenty of those that day. Men going hunting. When they pulled the trigger, it made an awful *boom. Bang. Pop. Crack. Thunder. Jolt.* It shook the snow off the trees, made all the animals skitter and tremble.

She saw the men. She didn't recognize any of them, so they must've been tourists. They dragged Denny's mom out, leaving a line of red in the snow. It reminded her of when her mama's head got cracked and the blood poured out and made a line on the floorboards.

Denny's mother was dead. Just like Lonnie's mother.

People were always talking behind her back.

LONNIE HAD LOTS of berets—blue ones, yellow ones, purple ones, but she decided to wear her brown beret. She got Denny and they walked over to their regular spot. The Chinese restaurant. It was always open during tourist season, but not as much when the tourists were all gone. She wanted to get fried rice. *Rice-A-Roni. Rice pudding. Pudding cakes.*

Lonnie crossed the road with Denny. There was a car on the road. She thought all the tourists had left already, but it wasn't a tourist car; it was a police car. Lonnie didn't like police cars. Their sirens reminded her of the lights at the Institute. Always flashing and blaring. So much noise and screaming and yelling. They were always spying on her. Watching her.

J.B. was driving the car. Lonnie liked J.B., but there was a strange lady sitting next to him. Why was there a lady sitting next to him? The lady gave her a stare. She knew that the lady must be saying things about her behind her back. Talking about her. *Whore. Bitch. Stupid.* Lonnie wanted her gone. *Away. Distant. Absent. Left. Departed.*

Lonnie glared back before taking Denny across the road. Then J.B. and the strange lady drove off.

Lonnie tied Denny to the post outside the Chinese restaurant. She was going to eat a bowl of fried rice.

There were Amy and Mrs. Lin. Lonnie liked Amy and Mrs. Lin.

"Hi, Lonnie," Amy said. Amy knew her name. Amy knew that Lonnie liked her table in the orange booth in the back. Amy didn't ask for her order because she always got the same thing. The food there was terrible. Like cardboard. Cardboard cutouts. "Cut that out! Cut that out!" Mama yelled at her. Mama was dead. Lonnie got sent to the Institute.

The food at the restaurant was terrible, but better than it was at the Institute. Amy brought a large pot of jasmine tea and a bowl of fried rice to her table.

Lonnie looked at her watch. Chief had given her the watch. "Watch what you say," he always told her. "Watch who you talk to." "Don't tell anyone our secrets." They had lots of secrets.

Lonnie looked at her watch. People were always watching her.

CHAPTER FOUR

CARA

THERE WAS A HEAVY DARKNESS DESCENDING AND SNOW had already begun to fall in blustering swirls. All in all, Cara was glad to be departing from the bleakness that shrouded Point Mettier.

"You have my number," J.B. said once they arrived at the parking lot of the Davidson Condos. "Just let me know if you need anything else."

"Thanks, J.B."

"Anything at all . . ." There was a tinge of desperation in his voice, which sounded both sweet and sad to Cara.

"Yup," she said, climbing into her SUV, and gave him a smile devoid of encouragement. She looked down at her hands on the steering wheel and the ring on her finger. It wasn't just that she knew she would probably never see J.B. again, but also that it felt wrong to ask anyone to accompany her through the depths of the darkness she was wading through.

Despite the year that had passed, in her mind, her husband, Aaron, was still alive somehow, even though she had watched as his remains were lowered into the ground. Even now, she sometimes smelled a pungent burst of his cologne as she walked into the bedroom, or felt his presence on the living room sofa, where he used to take his weekend midafternoon naps. Their boy, Dylan, was still alive too. She still heard his little feet come plodding down the hallway, or saw him on the swing set outside where the metal chains creaked with his weight, even if others could see nothing but the wind kicking up fallen leaves. There were no final goodbyes, no last hugs, not even a hint that she would never see them again, so those remains she saw lying in the soot could not possibly have once been the vibrant lives she had loved and nurtured. As Cara pulled out of the lot and headed back on the single main roadway, she wiped away a tear and turned on the defroster.

Her headlamps coned a path through the curtain of snow along Curve Back Road, headed toward the tunnel. Ten minutes out, she screeched on the brakes and her heart sank when she saw yellow-painted gates barring passage to the parking area for the tunnel. It was still early in the evening—too early for the tunnel to close, but the signage declared HAZARDOUS CONDITIONS. ROAD CLOSED.

"Shit!" she yelled to the air. For a moment, she contemplated just barreling through the gates, which didn't look very substantial, made of easily breakable wooden posts. But the thought of getting stuck in the dark, unmonitored tunnel beyond deterred her. She had to admit that her claustrophobia seemed to have worsened since the death of her husband and son. So she made a U-turn and headed back with a mixture of frustration and unease at having to spend the night in Point Mettier.

Somewhere along the way, she spotted J.B.'s patrol car. They both rolled to a stop and J.B. scuttled out, wrapping his coat tight around him. The temperature must have dropped twenty degrees once the sun had set.

"I got radioed about the road closure. Tried to give you a buzz, but phone signals tend to crap out once you pass the pier," he said, leaning toward her window.

"Thanks," Cara responded. "Is there another way out of here?"

"Ferry stopped running last month, so the tunnel is the only ticket out, unfortunately." A wind gust suddenly picked up, sending snow in horizontal streams. "Probably a smart bet to stay in Point Mettier and ride out the storm, anyway," he said. "Winds through the passage here can rip your car doors right off."

"What time does the tunnel open tomorrow?" she asked.

"Normally at six in the morning, but with this system, it'd be best to call and check first."

Cara nodded. Things were already getting grimmer.

"We've got rentable suites at the Dave-Co. I'll show you when we get back there." J.B. was almost beaming, despite being the harbinger of bad news.

ONCE THEY GOT back to the Davidson Condos, her first stop was at the general store to pick up necessary toiletries and an oversize T-shirt. The African American clerk had a flowing gray lumberjack beard and wore a felt baseball cap. Engrossed in his newspaper, he barely acknowledged Cara's presence until she brought her items to the counter. Behind him, a display of taxidermied wildlife stared out in frozen-in-perpetuity stances—a red fox perched on a log, a gray wolf with teeth bared, and decorating the wall, prized heads of antlered elk and a moose.

J.B., who'd waited outside the store, then led her to the gray, fluorescent-lit metal elevators. He pressed the button for the ninth floor, and as the elevator squeaked and jolted upward, the eerie enclosed space sent a chill through Cara that had nothing to do with the weather outside.

On the ninth floor, immediately in front of the elevators, there was an apartment converted to an office with a plaque that read THE COZY CONDO INN. The door was slightly ajar, and they walked in to find a squat woman in her sixties wearing a red bun wig. Her makeup was overdone, with blue eye shadow, parched painted lips, and too much rouge, but she was clearly one who prided herself on her appearance. She wore an oversize knitted sweater decorated with hearts. In her hand she carried a pair of binoculars. *Odd,* Cara thought, since it was dark outside, until she realized that they were equipped with night vision.

"Welcome to the Cozy Condo Inn," the woman said.

"This is Ellie Wright," J.B. added.

"Cara Kennedy," Cara said, nodding toward her.

"After you're done here, I can show you where to grab a bite," J.B. offered.

"Thanks, J.B., but I'm not hungry." She almost felt sorry to disappoint him.

He looked down at his shoes. "All right, well, give me a holler in the morning and I'll show you where to get breakfast. You do eat breakfast, don't you?"

Cara smiled back at him, and now it was a smile of genuine gratefulness. "Yes, that would be nice."

AFTER J.B. LEFT, Ellie slid some forms over the counter for Cara to fill out. "I've been expecting you," she said.

Cara wondered why Ellie would be expecting her, since she hadn't made reservations in advance, and then remembered the binoculars. "You always look out for all your guests?" Cara asked.

"I like to watch for whales," Ellie said with a bit of a grin.

Cara gave her a skeptical look. "Unless those whales are in the parking lot, you're not going to have much luck with this weather system."

Ellie ignored her comment and flipped through her reservations book. "I can put you in the Harbor Room. Got a real nice view just like this one, exceptin' like you said, you won't be able to see much through the storm." She had an almost Southern twang in her voice. "Complimentary coffee and tea. Not sure if the Wi-Fi is working. I asked Ron, our handyman, to work on it, but I don't think he's been able to get to it yet."

"That'll do just fine," Cara responded. She didn't care one way or another. It was just a bed for the night. Ellie ran her credit card through an old-fashioned imprinter. Clearly, there was a pay-in-advance policy.

"Investigating those body parts, aren't ya?" she asked.

"Word travels fast."

"Hard to keep secrets around here."

"Well then, maybe you might have an inkling of who the John Doe is? Any male guests, single or otherwise, appear to be missing?"

"Not that I recall," Ellie replied, "and everybody who checked in checked out in one piece."

"Mind if I get copies of your registry for the past couple of months, just the same? It's possible that he died after he checked out."

"Absolutely." Ellie Wright smiled. "Just need to see the warrant."

Despite Ellie's friendly facade, Cara had the impression that she was mocking her. "Solving this case would be better for business, wouldn't it?" she suggested.

"Ms. Kennedy—"

"Detective Kennedy," Cara corrected.

"Detective, guests who come here treasure their privacy, so I don't want them finding out I gave up info unless I had to. And so far, all I've heard is that some poor fellow committed suicide. Maybe jumped off a cruise ship, is what I hear."

Cara sighed, as she couldn't argue with this. Ellie served up another smile and handed her the keys.

"You're in Room 12. On the fourteenth floor. Oh, and it's going to be a howler tonight."

"A *howler?*"

"When it's windy, air comes up the elevator shafts, and you'll hear the building 'talk' to you. If it bothers you, turn up the radio, or—just a minute . . ." Ellie disappeared into a back room and re-emerged with a stack of record albums. *Record albums!* "Your unit's got a record player. Normally, I'd ask for a deposit for these. But I trust you, seeing as you're police."

Cara took the albums out of courtesy more than desire. "Thanks."

CARA WAITED FOR a lift to arrive back at the bank of elevators. The sound of wheels skittering on the thin carpet alerted her to a young girl of about eight on a scooter, schussing down the corridor. Up and then back down the other way. The hallway, apparently, was her indoor playground. She wore jeans, a pink T-shirt with a giant, glitter-speckled butterfly, and white Keds. At least there was one advantage to being confined to the world of a temperature-controlled building, Cara thought—being able to wear a T-shirt year-round. The girl's wavy brown hair was held back with a white hair band. She looked at Cara with inquisitive brown eyes, then finally rolled up next to her. "Hi. I'm Susie," she said.

"Hi, Susie," Cara chimed back. "I'm Detective Kennedy."

"What are you doing here?" the girl asked with genuine curiosity.

Cara didn't want to frighten her, so she gave her an answer without specifics. "I got stuck here because the tunnel is closed."

"Oh, yeah, I guess we're all stuck here," Susie said, satisfied with Cara's answer. "You get used to it," she said, smiling.

Cara was glad to see the young girl's cheerful attitude, despite the bleak surroundings.

"I'm going to visit my friend Joseph," Susie declared, apparently having had enough of her solo scootering, and now waiting with Cara for the elevator.

"What floor does Joseph live on?"

"He lives on the twelfth floor. I don't know if he'll see me, though."

The elevator doors finally clattered open and Cara stepped in, followed by Susie. Cara pressed the fourteenth-floor button, and the twelfth-floor button for Susie. The metal death trap jolted them upward with an ungodly mechanical sound, but Cara held her breath and managed to look calm on the outside for Susie's sake.

"Bye, Detective Kennedy," the little girl said as she exited on Joseph's floor and scootered away.

CARA FOUND HER hotel suite among the oddly numbered doors that didn't seem to follow any standard of numbering. The room itself was a converted apartment with a kitchen, a living area, and a bedroom. The tiny footprint, dark drapery, and mismatched, oversize furniture made the space look cramped, and the decor made it feel as though Cara had come to visit someone's lonely grandmother. A green felt couch occupied most of the living area, complemented by dark waxed tables, faux plants, and doilies galore. Despite the NO SMOKING sign, a reek of tobacco mixed with the stale stench of stifled air permeated the space, probably permanently settled into the fibers of the furniture.

Cara set the stack of records down on the coffee table and unpacked her laptop, which she was glad she had thought to bring with her on the road. She flipped it open and connected her camera to the USB port to inspect the photos she had taken earlier in the day.

Any tourist would have focused on the glacier across the cove, the picturesque water horizon, or the beach itself, but her photos were unromantic scenes of the shoal, charcoal-colored boulders, and background foliage. To anyone else, they would have been unremarkable, but to Cara, every leaf bend, every rock disturbance, and every depression in the sand could be relevant—part of a bigger story that was yet to be unfurled. Immediately, she was jarred by a fuzzy image she hadn't previously noticed, taken amid the trees elevated over the shoreline. She zoomed in to make sure it wasn't just a trick of the eye. There, decidedly, was a person in a brown jacket and white knitted ski cap, blurred in the act of movement, heading away into the woods. It was nothing in the way of evidence, but Cara moved the photo into the "hot" folder.

Cara continued on to examine the set of shots of the footprint. She had already downloaded evidence photos of the actual boot taken from the cove by Anchorage PD, and now she could compare them to the print. She had earlier suspected this, when she snapped the photos, but now there was visual proof that the print was a match, in both tread pattern and size. Cara also spotted something she hadn't noticed before in the evidence stills of the boot. She zoomed in to a dark spot wedged into the treads. It was a piece of something like charcoal lodged in the boot. Cara pulled out the rock that she had picked up as a souvenir and felt a sense of vindicated elation. If the relatively fresh print and the boot were a match, it would mean the detached foot was not the result of months of decay in the sea. This, hopefully, would be enough information to get the case reopened. More important, although she didn't have a name for the John Doe, she was certain that whoever he was, the victim had recently been alive in Point Mettier.

CHAPTER FIVE

AMY

STAR ASIAN FOOD WAS THE NAME OF THE RESTAURANT AMY and her mother ran in the block of tourist shops and eateries along the pier. Amy supposed the lackluster name matched the boring fare they served: egg rolls, lo mein, fried rice, and chicken and fish dishes smothered in a gelatinous soy sauce. The fish was probably the best bet because they got that locally. Otherwise, everything was defrosted from the big freezer. Of course, no one was going there expecting high cuisine or anything, especially during the off-season, when most other places on the dock were shuttered and the only other option for outside eating was the Salty Pub next door.

Amy acted as waitress, bus girl, and cashier. Her mother usually stayed in the back doing the cooking. When Amy was at school, Ma handled everything alone, which worked out okay during the off-season. During the high season, she hired extra help. That was when Point Mettier swelled with summer people. "Summer people" was what everyone called the temporary shop owners, tour operators, and staff who hustled visitors out of their vacation money. Summer people weren't exactly otters, but they weren't really Point Mettier residents either. About a dozen of them rented apartments in the Dave-Co, where they stayed for the season, while others commuted from Anchorage. The one good thing about winter was that when the summer people and curious tourists cleared out, there was a shorter wait for the elevators.

Amy was mindlessly surfing the Internet on her cell, exploring faraway places and daydreaming about one day escaping her parent-induced serfdom to hightail it out of this nowhere town. A tinkle of the bell above the entrance door brought her back to reality.

"Amy! Lonnie here!" Ma yelled at her, peering through the narrow slit between the kitchen and the dining area, as if Amy couldn't see this with her own eyes.

Lonnie came most days. The kids called her Moose Lady Lonnie. Although they all thought she was weird, everybody kind of looked out for her, especially after a couple of scares when the town thought she had gotten lost and was probably going to be found dead and frozen in the snow, but in the end, she'd come trudging back with Denny as if nothing had happened. Chief Sipley got her a watch with a GPS tracker after that in case she ever disappeared again. The tourists loved taking photos with Denny, so in a way, Lonnie and her moose made for good business.

Ma waved to Amy as if she were fanning an invisible coal with her hand. That was her way of saying "Go get to work!" and it annoyed the shit out of Amy.

"Hi, Lonnie," Amy said.

Moose Lady nodded and headed straight to her usual booth toward the back.

Amy set out a napkin and a spoon for her, then poured her a cup of jasmine tea. She didn't bother bringing a menu. Lonnie always got the fried rice. She also didn't make eye contact. It was a secret they had all figured out. Talk to Moose Lady, but don't make eye contact. If you looked at her too long, she'd start shouting at you for no good reason.

Lonnie wore a different-colored beret every day in no particular order, so Amy and the other kids sometimes put bets down on what color it was going to be. Amy had bet on red that day, so she knew she would have to pay up because it was brown.

Amy's cell phone came to life with spastic vibrations in her apron pocket, so she pulled it out before she headed back to the register, where Ma could see. She knew it was Spence before she even looked at the caller ID. His text read, "meet me @ the city." The City was the nickname they gave the Walcott Building, because back in the sixties, when Point Mettier was an army port, people referred to it as "the City Under One Roof." The City was where all the good stuff had been when the military was there, but now it was just an abandoned building.

A few of the kids had discovered the underground passage to the City when Amy was nine, around the time that Spence arrived. The tunnels had been constructed by the military to get between places without having to go aboveground, but then some of them flooded. Plus, the building was falling in on itself with debris and asbestos, so they'd just boarded up the whole system, tunnels and all, for safety reasons. Barbed-wire fencing went around the City's circumference, making it look like a giant, empty, soot-weeping prison, except instead of keeping people from getting out, the barricades were supposed to keep people from getting in. But that didn't stop kids from finding one of the tunnel entries, prying off the wooden seal, and exploring. They found that the tunnels were pretty dry, especially during the summer. During the winter, the water level would rise, but as long as they avoided certain areas, they were traversable with the right footwear. At first, Amy was scared going through the black void of musty-smelling passages, but she wasn't about to let the others know she was a chickenshit. They'd gone down with their flashlights and rubber boots and used spray paint on the walls instead of bread crumbs to help navigate their paths until they finally found a route to the City. If any of their parents had found them sneaking around in there, they'd have been toast, but that was part of the fun.

Spence and Amy were the only ones left who knew how to navigate the tunnels and where the secret entrance was, and by some unspoken code, they had just decided to keep it as their own little secret.

"CU in 1 hr," she texted back to him.

"Amy, no cell phone!" Ma yelled from the kitchen, startling her.

Amy swore that woman must have eyes that could see through walls.

AMY MADE HER way carefully to their usual meeting place—the old movie theater—bundled up in thermal layers, mittens, and a muffler. The cold turned her breath into tiny clouds. Outside, the wind howled like a dog in heat, sending shivers up her spine. If she had to be honest, she didn't like meeting in the City. The ambience wasn't exactly "romantic" in a corpse of a building with blown-out windows, missing doors, and floors filled with crumbling wood and debris. Some people said it was haunted, and she had heard plenty of strange noises that had scared the bejesus out of her in the past—a loud bang or the sound of water running through nonfunctioning pipes, and once, she swore she heard the distinct sound of footsteps. The beam from her flashlight bounced off the walls, which were either graffiti covered or plaster-cracked with gaping holes. She reached the theater, which Amy supposed had once been filled with orderly rows of seats and played old-timey black-and-white movies, but now it looked like a tornado had swept through there, and the felt-covered seats were upside down, missing, or rat eaten.

"Spence?" Amy called out, a bit too anxiously, and there was no answer. She'd taken out her cell phone and was checking to see whether she had enough reception for a text (which of course she didn't) when a gloved hand covered her mouth from behind. She let out a muffled cry before a giggle gave Spence away. Amy spun around and swatted him lightly. "Spence!" she yelled in exasperation.

"Did I give you a good scare? Had to make up for Halloween," he said, laughing. Spence was referring to the subdued celebrations they had had for All Hallows' Eve that year. The discovery of the body parts had out-ghouled any idea of scary fun at the Dave-Co. While the kids were still allowed to go on their door-to-door trick-or-treating, any decorations that hinted of death were quietly put away, and even the planned costume party in the school gym had been kiboshed. Amy secretly appreciated the effort everyone in the building had made and was glad that she didn't have to look at skeletons, fleshy monsters, or bloody anythings in the hallways that would remind her of the gruesome parts.

Spence continued to laugh at her, but it was hard to stay mad at him for long. When he gave her that look of desperation and hunger, it was a deadly combination. Amy wrapped her arms around his neck and kissed him in the weak light that emanated from the phone in her hand.

"Damn, it's cold," he said, coming up for air.

"It's always cold," Amy whispered back.

He found a perch on a still-intact arm of one of the theater seats and sat down, pulling Amy into his lap and holding her. She loved the feel of his warmth and the way he buried his face in her hair.

"So, I heard there's some detective lady here," he finally said.

"I thought they were all done with that," Amy responded. "I've already answered all their questions and they said it was an accident or a suicide. Wonder why they're back again."

Spence lit a blunt. The sour smell blended in with the must. He passed it on to Amy, who took a hit.

"Yeah, not sure why they're back. But if the lady starts asking questions, don't mention I was there."

Amy looked at him skeptically. Spence didn't want his mom to know he had been out at the cove because he was supposed to be at home that day, watching over his younger brother, Troy. Troy was thirteen, and he wasn't a special-needs kid or anything, but he'd always been a little odd. He was very standoffish and hardly ever said a word. Amy wasn't even sure if he had any friends. Spence said his brother was going through some "anxiety issues," and Mrs. Blackmon, being a helicopter mom, would go ballistic if she found out that Spence had gone to the cove instead of staying home with Troy while she was out buying supplies in Anchorage. Mrs. Blackmon, besides being Spence's mom, was also Amy's history and English teacher, and Amy thought all the kids at the cove would be in trou-ble, so she had lied to Officer Neworth and not mentioned Spence's being at the cove. But now it almost didn't seem worth the lie. Spence should just come clean to his mom. Lying to the police seemed like it would have far bigger consequences. But she just nod-ded. "I won't say anything." And after a beat: "I wish I'd never found them."

"Don't worry. You're just a witness." He looked at her sheepishly. "But hopefully, she won't even have to ask you any questions, since they already have your statement."

Suddenly, there was a shift of weight and a creak in the floor-boards. Amy jumped out of Spence's lap, flicking her flashlight toward the sound.

Spence was clearly spooked too. "Hey!" he called out, but of course, there was no answer. Spence quickly put out his joint. "This place is falling to shit," he said, but there was a slight tremor in his voice.

When Amy said, "Let's go back," Spence didn't argue.

CHAPTER SIX

CARA

CARA DONNED AN OVERSIZE "I HEART POINT METTIER" T-SHIRT she had picked up downstairs in the general store and washed her face in the basin in the bathroom. She paused for a moment to look at herself in the mirror. She had thick chocolate hair that looked almost black most of the time, but under the light, its auburn tones would come through. She had worn it long and loose when she was younger, then kept it tied up top or in a ponytail when she'd joined the force. When she finally grew tired of having to fuss with it, she sheared most of it off until there was nothing below her earlobes. Her husband, Aaron, had not been happy with that decision, so she had grown it back to a compromise bob. Now she kept it at an easy-to-manage just-above-the-shoulders length. Around her olive-colored eyes she saw a hint of crow's-feet she hadn't noticed before, and there were bags under her eyes. The stress of the past year's events had clearly taken its toll, and it didn't help that she had lost some weight, adding to the overall fatigued look of her five-foot-nine frame. She stared at the bottle of Xanax sitting on the counter, hesitating for just a moment before popping one of the blue pills, then climbed into the saggy-looking bed, hoping she'd be able to get a good night's rest.

Ellie hadn't lied about the wind. It made an ungodly sound whistling through the hallway and rattling the doors. It was as if a hundred banshees were singing in chorus, warning of impending death. The whole building moaned and creaked in agony.

A surreal, metallic groan like that of a giant ship listing in the wind finally made her sit up and throw off the sheets in frustration. She got to her feet and headed over to the living room to find the stack of record albums that Ellie had given her and picked up whatever was on top. Oddly, the cover featured a picture of a Japanese woman in her late forties wearing a sparkly, oversexified-for-her-age outfit. Cara couldn't make heads or tails of the kanji characters on the cover, but curiosity won her over, so she set the disc on the turntable and gently set the needle on it. She cranked up the volume to drown out the building noises.

The smoky voice of an older woman sang a bouncy jazz tune in Japanese. Occasionally, Cara could make out the English words "old-time jazz" in the refrain.

She climbed back into bed and closed her eyes.

The Japanese melody actually did help to drown the howls of the wind, but just as Cara started to drift, from the building came a loud crack that sounded like metal splitting and jolted her awake again. She sat up, feeling like she was in some kind of cobwebbed haze. The Japanese melody sounded distorted, as if it were emanating from somewhere underwater. Did she need another blue pill? Or was it already one too many? She got up out of the bed anyway and headed for the bathroom.

She switched on the light and gasped when she saw herself in the mirror. There were blood splatters mottling her T-shirt, neck, and arms. Her skin crawled at the sight. The pasty yellow light above the sink flickered. Then she noticed a trail of blood on the floor—a congealing line of red leading toward the bathtub. Fear and anxiety hit her at the same time, as if she were being seared with a scorching fire and chilled to the bone with frostbite all at once, her breath coming in staccato intakes of air.

"Mommy?"

Cara spun around to see Dylan standing there in his jammies. Her son looked pale and frozen, with icicles hanging from his sandy blond hair. His blue eyes looked almost pleading.

"Dylan?" It came out like a simultaneous sob and scream. Her fear and anxiety shifted to grief and guilt. "I'm sorry I didn't find you in time," Cara said, tears streaming. "Baby, will you ever forgive me?"

His eyes were unblinking and Cara reached out to her son, trying to wrap her arms around him, but instead was met with empty air and a sensation of falling. The depth of the void was impossible to fill.

CARA BOLTED UP from the bed with a gasp. A dream like all the others, though her tears were real. She glanced at the clock. It was two in the morning.

The wind had abated, but she could still hear the building creak, a little less angrily now. The record had come to an end, with only the *click, pop, click, pop* of the needle on the rotating disc.

She was still catching her breath from the nightmare when she heard a loud bang at the door, causing her to stir again, but a little more cautiously, wondering if she was still in the dream or if the bang was another wind-related phenomenon.

At the door another rap, which sounded distinctly human, made her get up and grab her jacket to wrap over herself. She went to answer the door, but not before reaching for the pistol she had kept beside her on the table.

"Who's there?" she asked and peered through the peephole. There was no answer and no one she could see in the hallway.

She racked the slide on her Glock into the cocked position and took a deep breath before unlocking the door and twisting the handle. But it didn't open. The panicked sensation from the dream returned.

"Hello? Who's out there?" she demanded, trying to hide the tremor in her voice. She twisted the knob again and pulled harder, but still it didn't budge. She pounded on the door with the flat of her hand. "Hey! Open this door!"

She peered out again through the peephole, but there was no one there. She could guess only that it was either a ghost holding on to the knob or some kind of lock on the outside.

She pointed her gun at the door, determined to shoot her way out, but then wondered if she was still in some vestige of her dream. It would be pretty embarrassing if she damaged hotel property without due cause, so she relaxed her hold on her gun and decided to give J.B. a ring instead.

"I'VE TOLD ELLIE a hundred times she needs to fix this doorjamb," J.B. said from the hallway amid the sound of an aerosol spray directed at the lock. "It's the suction from the wind. Makes the lock stick."

44

The door finally opened with a *whoosh*. J.B. stood there, his hair messed and eyes red, holding a can of WD-40.

"I won't ask where you were planning to go this time of night," he added, and Cara suddenly felt guilty.

"I thought I heard someone in the hall," she explained.

"This place'll do that to you when you're not used to the noises."

"I swear there was a knock." Even Cara thought she sounded crazy.

"Some people say the building's haunted," he said in a tone that didn't sound like he was joking. He handed her the can of WD-40. "You can keep this with you."

"Thanks," she said. "And thanks for coming up. Sorry I woke you."

"Not a problem. Just don't make a habit of it." But he smiled, letting Cara know he didn't really mean it.

IN THE MORNING, Cara headed straight for Ellie's office.

Susie was back on the floor with her aluminum scooter, furrowing little white wheel lines in the carpet.

"Hi, Detective Kennedy," she said cheerfully when Cara got off the elevator.

"I'm leaving today, Susie," Cara said.

"I doubt it," the girl commented, which made Cara pause, but Susie was already down at the other side of the hall.

Ellie was spritzing her countertop with an antiseptic-smelling cleanser and looked up, all smiles, at Cara's bloodshot eyes.

"See any whales today?" Cara asked, almost gruffly.

"Too much snow," she said.

Outside, it was still a furious snow globe, so she was right about that.

Then she added with irony, "Hope you had a restful night. Now I suppose you'll be wanting to extend your stay?"

"No, I was planning to check out." Cara was testy without her morning coffee.

"Guess you haven't heard, then. The tunnel's closed from the avalanche. It'll be a while before they can reopen."

Cara was stunned into speechlessness for a moment before she found her voice again. "There was an avalanche? How long is it going to be before they clear it?"

"Don't know exactly. A few days? A week? But last time this happened, it took about a month."

"A month?" Thoughts both rational and irrational flooded Cara's mind. The most troublesome was that she had enough pills to last only fifteen more days. Feelings of claustrophobia suddenly started to take over, and she let out a soft gasp.

Ellie smiled. "On the bright side, your room's available through winter."

CHAPTER SEVEN

LONNIE

LONNIE MADE HER WAY HURRIEDLY DOWN THE HALLWAY, with her rubber boots squeaking on the polished floor. *Squick. Squack. Squick. Squack.* She looked through the glass doors and saw snow flying around like clothes in a washing machine. *There's a storm outside. Blast. Gale. Blizzard. Gust. Squall. There's a storm outside.*

She stormed down the hallway and burst through the door. Chief sat at his desk, thinking or meditating, or maybe he was napping. He opened his eyes.

"What is it, Lonnie?" Chief asked.

"How long is that lady going to stay?"

Chief took his feet off the desk. "I suppose until the tunnel re-opens."

"I don't like it. I don't like it. She needs to be gone. I know she's talking about me. Watching me. People are always watching me." Lonnie wasn't sure sometimes whether she was actually saying her words out loud or in her mind.

"Now, Lonnie, Ms. Kennedy's investigating those body parts, so you stay out of her hair, understand?"

"She won't take me away, will she? I'm not going. I won't go back." Lonnie was adamant. She wasn't going back to the Institute. That's where she got backhanded. *They found a hand on the beach.* "They found a hand on the beach," Lonnie said out loud.

Chief looked at her, worried. He rubbed his forehead with his palm—something he always did when he was troubled. "Now, Lonnie, the way I see things, without a whole body, there's not even a homicide. When the tunnel reopens, things'll all go back to normal. You'll see. Now, you just keep your trap shut. Don't talk to her. Don't ask her any questions. Don't answer any questions. You don't want to end up back at the Institute, do you?"

Watch what you say. Watch what you do. People were always watching her. "I don't like it. I don't like it," Lonnie said, shaking her head while looking at the floor.

"Well, if you don't like it, you do as I tell you. Understand?"

Loathing. Displeasure. Irritation. Vexation. Aversion. Antagonism. All the words Lonnie felt were building inside her, ready to erupt.

"Where's Denny?" Chief asked, suddenly changing the subject. "Remember how he escaped last time?"

"He's in the barn."

"Why don't you make sure he's okay?" Chief got up and led Lonnie toward the door. "You don't want the wolves to get to him."

Lonnie nodded. She had to take care of Denny. "The wolves are coming." Lonnie needed to make sure the doors to the pen were locked. *Closed. Sealed. Cinched. Fastened. The wolves are coming.* "Awoooo!" She let out a howl.

CHAPTER EIGHT

CARA

J.B. TOOK CARA THROUGH A PEDESTRIAN TUNNEL, LEADING the way to the Salty Pub. Spiral shadows cast by yellow-tinged lights on the concrete walls made a dizzy illusion, and it felt as though she were walking into the center of a hypnotic swirl. It did nothing to diminish her claustrophobia. The deeper they burrowed in, the more difficult it became to breathe, and she felt suddenly hot beneath her parka despite the chilling temperatures. She reached to unzip her jacket and almost lost her balance, so she stalled in her tracks. She had to tamp down the overwhelming panic and feelings of being on the precipice of death before they overwhelmed her.

J.B. turned back toward her and was surprised by her ashen look. "Are you all right?" he asked.

Cara tried to shake it off and took a deep breath. "I'm fine. I just haven't eaten a proper meal in a while," she said. The last part was true enough.

AFTER SHE HAD shown J.B. the match between the print and the logged evidence, suggesting that the victim had probably been alive at Hidden Cove in the last few days, he seemed eager to assist in the investigation and promised to get his hands on Ellie's registry. They decided to keep the information to themselves for now. No need to cause unnecessary panic about a possible murderer under their roof while the tunnel was closed. J.B. wasn't as convinced as Cara that a killer could be found among the full-time residents of Point Mettier. They were a hodgepodge of strange and secretive people, but murderers?

The general goods store, not surprisingly, was a Moroccan desert in terms of anything appetizing for a meal, so when J.B. offered to take her to "sample the fine dining in the area," Cara didn't hesitate to say yes. There were only two restaurants open this time of year— the Salty Pub and Star Asian Food. Cara had opted for the pub. Outside, it was still a winter wash, so J.B. suggested the tunnel. Was it too late to back out?

After no plausible excuse had come quickly enough, Cara finally steeled herself through the underground passage. Her thoughts of certain doom were temporarily distracted by the appearance of a middle-aged woman with a sensible blond bob traveling in the opposite direction with a brown, grease-spotted take-out bag of food.

"This is Debra Blackmon. She's one of the schoolteachers." J.B. introduced them. "Debra, this is Detective Kennedy. She got stuck here on account of the avalanche."

"Sorry to hear that," Debra responded. "Hope the tunnel reopens soon," she said, then cinched her coat tightly around her and scuttled off without another word. Cara wasn't exactly sure whether her remarks were for Cara's sake or the town's.

Cara was all too glad when the tunnel finally broke near the waterfront area and they emerged at the entrance to the bar. To her dismay, the inside of the pub felt small and closed off, but at least there were windows and the ceiling was high. The bar had a smattering of people and red bar stools, and a counter that had been fitted with padded bumpers, probably as an insurance measure after buzzed patrons had fallen and hit their heads on its wooden edge. There was a big-screen television hung up in a corner, but at present it was turned off—no doubt lacking any usable signal in the midst of this storm.

The alternative for entertainment was a petite lounge singer on an upraised stage, whom Cara immediately recognized as the Japanese woman on the cover of the record album. She looked even older in person but wore the same sparkly dress and feather boa. The song had the same refrain of "old-time jazz," only now it was peppered with high-pitched squeaks from the mic's feedback. No one seemed to be paying much attention to her, despite how small the place was.

J.B. motioned Cara toward the counter, where she nearly bumper-carred into a Native toting a glass of whiskey. She recognized him from the tollbooth.

"Jim, this is Cara," J.B. said to the man.

Jim eyed her disaffectedly and didn't bother to offer his hand.

"She's handling the investigation on those body parts that washed up in Hidden Cove," J.B. continued. "Cara, this is Jim Arreak. He's the—"

"Tollbooth operator." She finished the sentence.

"Oh right. I guess you would have already met."

"Not formally," she said.

"Guess you'll be stuck here for a while," Jim said matter-of-factly. He still sported the same timeworn Seahawks baseball cap.

"So I've been told."

"I recommend you leave first chance you get." Jim had a serious expression on his face; the intensity of his dark eyes was off-putting.

"Why's that?"

"'Cause of what's coming."

Cara didn't know whether to take that as a threat or not. Jim didn't seem hostile but wasn't exactly friendly either. "The storm, you mean?"

"No. Storm's already here." Jim didn't elaborate, and with that, he moved off.

J.B. laughed nervously. "Jim likes to scare people. I think he believes it's an unofficial part of his job description to keep visitors from staying too long."

"This town seems to be full of friendly people." The irony of her remark was not lost.

"You'll get used to it. People here like to keep things a certain way. They don't warm too easily to strangers. When I first got here, it was like hitting a concrete wall over and over, and I've been chiseling away at it ever since."

J.B. moved to the bar, and a multi-pierced and multi-tattooed bartender greeted him. "Name your poison."

"Get me a Bud Light and . . ." J.B. turned to Cara with a question mark.

"A Jack and Coke," she said.

The tattooed bartender nodded and busied himself with getting their drinks.

Cara shifted her attention back toward the sad Japanese woman on the stage, who strutted and gyrated, trying to be sexy somehow, despite her age and faded makeup.

"I saw her album in the hotel room."

J.B. followed Cara's line of sight. "Yeah, that's Mariko. She came from Japan and used to be a star. Or at least that's what she tells us. She gave free copies of her album to Ellie's inn . . . for self-promotion, I guess. The Japanese tourists seem to get a kick out of it. Anyway, there aren't a lot of entertainers who decide to stay here."

Cara wondered what it was that compelled Mariko to stay. Was it that she could always be the biggest star in town, even if it was a paltry-size town?

After J.B. insisted on paying for the drinks and ordered fish and chips for their table, they headed over toward one of the booths. The other patrons, in various states of sobriety, took notice, but only Mariko seemed glad to have the extra audience.

Chief Sipley sauntered over to their table with a beer in hand, and it clearly wasn't his first. "Well, aren't you the cute couple?" he taunted. "I was beginning to think J.B. here was batting for the other team until you came along. But I guess it just took a woman who was pretty enough to get him out of his cold, lonely apartment."

J.B. looked embarrassed. Cara roiled inside at Sipley's jabs, even if he was intoxicated.

"I know we haven't got the best pickings here in Point Mettier," Sipley went on, "but after a few of these"—Chief Sipley raised his glass—"everybody starts looking good." He laughed a little too loudly and downed his beer, then made his way toward a robust woman who joined him in unprompted laughter.

J.B. was now as red as a beet and cowed into silence, so they watched Mariko working the stage.

She had moved on to another jazzy song, trying to engage the apathetic audience. "Everybody, clap your *handsu!*" she shouted into the mic. She threw her hands in the air and let out an emphatic "Woo!"

After a long beat, Cara broke the silence at their table. "So, what brought you here to Point Mettier?"

J.B. took a large swig from his bottle. It was a simple enough question but seemed difficult for him to answer. "Well, I told you I was hoping to move up to detective rank and I figured there wasn't going to be much competition in a city like this."

Cara looked at him and noticed for the first time that his eyes were green, with an almost orange sunburst around the iris. He avoided her eyes, looked down into his bottle.

"C'mon, J.B., I'm a detective," she said. "You know I'm not buying that one."

He sighed. "All right. I've never even told Chief this story."

Cara was even more curious now.

"I had just gotten out of a relationship. You know how it goes . . . Thought I found the one, thought we were going to spend our lives together. Bought a ring and everything. Then on the day I decided I was going to propose, I pull up into the driveway . . . and I see someone else's car . . ."

Cara winced internally.

"The thing is, I recognized the car right away. So I walk into the apartment, and sure 'nough, there they were, my girlfriend and my station partner."

"Jesus. I'm sorry," Cara said with honest empathy. She wanted to pat his hand in sympathy. Tell him she understood. Maybe it was the alcohol drowning her defenses.

"How did I not see it? All the time, right there under my nose. My own partner." J.B. took another swill, full of bitterness. "After that, I just wanted to get somewhere far away. Didn't even want to talk to anybody for a while. When I saw there was a post here, I decided it was as good a place as any."

They wallowed for a moment, and Mariko finished her set, leaving a void of silence. Cara almost felt like opening up to J.B. then. She wanted to confess that she'd had suspicions about Aaron before he and Dylan disappeared in the woods. By then, they had been married for six years. She wanted to tell J.B. that she wasn't actually there in Point Mettier on official police business. The lie gnawed at her, made her near-empty stomach churn more than the alcohol, but then a gray-haired waitress sucking a toothpick plopped a greasy platter of breaded cod and fat wedge-shaped fries on the table, and Cara remained silent. *The Point Mettier Tunnel will open tomorrow, and then I'll be gone,* she convinced herself.

CHAPTER NINE

AMY

AMY STOOD INSIDE THE BLACKMONS' APARTMENT, WAITING for Spence to appear. The room smelled like a combination of cinnamon and soap, and a dishwasher chugged laboriously in the background. Amy was dressed in a white blouse and a blue denim skirt, which was outside her norm of jeans and a T-shirt.

Spence's brother, Troy, sat in front of the TV console, deep in his video game, shooting up Nazis in a virtual World War II arena.

Amy had tried to engage him at first. "Hey, Troy," she had said after walking in.

"Hey," he had responded, but he hadn't bothered to turn back to look at her, too engrossed in commanding staccato popcorn bullets with his virtual gun. Troy and Amy had probably never exchanged more than five words at a time. Amy wasn't sure if he was really shy or maybe he had social anxiety, and she didn't think it was her business to ask.

"He'll be out in a sec," Mrs. Blackmon said, emerging from the hallway leading to the bedrooms. Spence's mom was all right, as far as teachers went. Ma probably would have liked her to be stricter.

Spence finally appeared in cargo pants and a T-shirt. Mrs. Blackmon scowled at him. "You aren't dressed."

Spence looked down at his clothes. "Yeah, I am."

Mrs. Blackmon simply sighed and let it go. It wasn't as if anyone besides Mariko really cared what anyone was wearing, and Mariko always made everyone else feel underdressed, no matter the occasion.

Amy tried to engage Troy again. "Troy, aren't you coming?" Troy didn't seem to hear her.

"Nah, not this time," Spence replied for him. "C'mon." He put his arm around Amy's shoulders.

If Ma had seen Spence putting his arm around Amy like that, she would have killed them both, but Mrs. Blackmon was one of those cool white moms. "Have fun," she said.

THEY WALKED DOWN the hall toward Mariko's unit. Everyone in Point Mettier had to be a little bit off their rocker, but "creepy as all hell" was a better description for Mariko. Mariko insisted that everyone, including the kids, refer to her only by her first name. Amy couldn't actually remember her last name. It had at least three syllables in it, but that detail was lost to her. Every year, all the children and teenagers in Point Mettier were invited to her sad birthday party. To be honest, Amy didn't think anyone would have attended voluntarily, except that Mariko actually *paid* for them to be there. They just had to sit around for an hour or two and eat cake. Amy had figured out years ago that it wasn't really Mariko's birthday, but probably some poor kid's who had died or maybe been miscarried—a daughter, to be specific— and whoever the kid was, she must have been around Amy's age.

Mariko answered the door in a tight-fitting dress and old-timey gloves that went up past her elbows. She wore bright red lipstick and a string of pearls hung around her neck. With her mini-beehive wig, she was trying hard to channel Audrey Hepburn, but it wasn't working.

Mariko was someone who rarely left her apartment without makeup and a wig. Once, Amy had caught her throwing out the trash in her nightgown and pink slippers. Her gray-streaked hair was frizzed out like a bird's nest, and her age spots and other blemishes hadn't been covered in layers of powder yet, so Amy almost didn't recognize her. Seeing Amy's shocked look, Mariko had dashed back to her room like a frightened mouse.

"COME IN, AMY-CHAN! Spensu!" Mariko said at the door. She always added that extra vowel to Spence's name. The apartment was as neat as a pin, with spotless Berber carpeting and waxed wood furniture that gleamed in the dim light. They all had to take their shoes off upon entering the foyer, and there were already piles of footwear at the entrance.

The table was set with rose-patterned Mikasa plates and a home-made birthday cake sat in the center. It was nicely decorated, with strawberries floating like little dimpled red buoys on a sea of frosting. Fifteen candles were half-submerged and ready to be lit. There were also cookies and party favors that were probably purchased from a dollar mart in Anchorage.

Everything looked pretty and almost pleasant, but, of course, this being Point Mettier, there had to be something off-kilter. In Mariko's unit, it was a large glass case along the wall of the living area, filled with those freaky dolls. Porcelain girls wearing Victorian dresses stared out from inside their transparent cage, wearing expressions of permanent surprise. Amy shuddered every time she saw the display.

Not all the kids came to the party, even though there was an open invitation. The newer kids, especially, tended to stay away. That was understandable, since who would really want to spend time at some crazy-lady-who-might-be-a-serial-killer's party? But for the old-timers, like Amy, this was just another day in Point Mettier. So there were twelve settings in all, including Moose Lady Lonnie's. Lonnie wasn't technically a child, but Mariko sometimes treated her like one, baking her cookies and giving her presents like she did with the other kids. In any case, Moose Lady Lonnie seemed to actually enjoy Mariko's parties, so it was all good. She was already sitting at the table and had on an orange beret.

"Pretty cake. Sweet as sugar. Sugar pie. Danish. Tart. Whore," Lonnie said.

All the kids laughed at that and Mariko scowled, but she continued pouring green tea into everyone's cup and then moved on to lighting the candles.

"Okay, everybody, we sing 'Happy Birthday'!"

Mariko led the song, clapping at every beat. Every year, she skipped the "dear" part, so it went, "Happy birthday to you. Happy birthday to you. Happy birthday, happy birthday. Happy birthday to you."

Who exactly they were supposed to be singing to was anybody's guess, and Amy always felt sad about it. Mariko blew out the candles herself. Spence had told Amy he thought the whole thing was morbid. But at least he kept his mouth shut instead of saying anything snarky or mean. Maybe he thought what Amy thought, which was that this was some freaky, demented way of dealing with loss.

Mariko sliced the cake and parceled it out. Amy relished her piece, which was airy and sweet, but not too sugary. Ma never baked, so it was a rare treat for her. Spence glanced at his watch, planning his time of escape. The only thing really keeping him there was the promise of money for weed.

"Okay, time for birthday present!" Mariko exclaimed when they were done eating cake. No one brought presents with them, but Mariko always had one she'd bought herself. Lonnie clapped her hands gleefully at the sight of the neatly wrapped box with a ribbon.

"Lonnie-san, you open?" Mariko handed the box to Moose Lady Lonnie, who gladly obliged.

"Open. Unwrap. Uncover. Unravel. Unmask. Bare. Betray. Expose," Lonnie said, as she took the ribbon off and tore at the paper.

Amy already knew what would be inside. It was the same every year. It was another one of those creepy dolls in Victorian dresses and with ringlets. The first time Mariko gave Lonnie the wrapped package, Amy was afraid that Lonnie would misunderstand and think it was her own birthday party, but after opening the gift, Lonnie fawned, "Pretty doll," and handed it back to Mariko. Now it was almost a ceremonial tradition for Mariko to open up the glass doll prison with a key and for Lonnie to carefully place the latest addition next to the others. Now fifteen dolls stared out at the party guests.

At that point, Spence looked at his watch again. Nearly six. He put his hands on the table and got up. That was the cue for everyone else as well.

Mariko quickly moved to the foyer, getting a stack of red envelopes to pay them their fees for attending. It didn't feel too weird for Amy since it was an Asian tradition to give kids red envelopes filled with money on certain occasions. "Thank you, Mariko," they each said as they filed out. When she got to Joel Camacho, one of the kids from Guam, Mariko dished out two envelopes.

No one said a word because they already knew what the second envelope was for. Joel was being paid to scare the detective from Anchorage by knocking on her door a few times in the middle of the night and then running away—the Point Mettier version of "ding-dong ditch." It was always fun to play tricks on the otters, so it was no big deal, but no one had ever been paid to do it before, so Joel had bragged about it at school.

When it was Spence's turn, Mariko gave him his envelope and put a hand on his shoulder. "Tell Troy to come next year," she said. Amy halfway expected Spence to recoil in horror and tell her to fuck off, but Spence just nodded back at her.

"Yeah, I will," he said.

CHAPTER TEN

CARA

AT THE FIRST FINGER OF SUNLIGHT, CARA BOLTED UPRIGHT from her sleep, believing for a moment that she was at home in her apartment, then realizing that the musty-smelling unit was not hers, just a transitory space she was holed up in until the tunnel reopened.

Seeing a sliver of hope for a sunny day, she decided it was time to get some much-needed fresh air.

She grabbed her parka, fueled up on black coffee from the general store, which turned out to be not so bad, then bundled up to step outside.

The wind still stung like nettles, and snow flurries painted the air in textured patterns, but someone had attempted to shovel the walkway and Cara inhaled deeply, welcoming the fresh burst of oxygen. She didn't have a particular destination but crunched the snow with her boots in the general direction of the pier. She could see beached ships looming in the distance like maritime ghosts, their masts piercing skyward.

About a hundred yards into her walk, her cell phone buzzed. It was J.B.

"Hey, J.B., is the tunnel open?" Cara jumped the gun, hoping for some good news.

"No, Cara, the tunnel's still closed. And . . ." Then there was an interminably long pause.

Cara had to make sure they were still connected and prompted J.B. with a "Hello?"

J.B. came back to life on the other end. ". . . There's something I need to talk to you about."

Cara could tell from his tone that something was amiss. The usual warmth in his voice was gone. Instead, there was a frigid blankness to his voice, like the snow enveloping the landscape.

"I called Anchorage PD about getting a warrant for Ellie's registry," J.B. continued. "I have a buddy out there named Charlie Wilkes, so I figured he'd do me a solid and fast-track the paperwork."

Cara felt her chest tighten and her pulse quicken. She knew what was coming.

"I told Charlie that you were here working the case," J.B. went on. "He said he knew who you were but that you were taken off active duty."

The accusation settled for a moment like a dead-lift weight. Cara's hand started to shake. "I . . . can explain," she began, but she didn't really know how she could justify anything.

"I wish you would," he said, and the cold disappointment in his voice felt like a slap in the face. "And I'm going to have to let Chief Sipley know."

"Wait," Cara pleaded. "I know I was wrong in not telling you from the outset. I'm not officially working for APD on this case. I swear that once I had enough to go on, I was going to forward everything to the right people and let them handle it from there." Silence on the other end. "I just . . . I just didn't want to see them drop the investigation so quickly. And now we have some quantifiable evidence. That's all I wanted. Before you tell Chief Sipley, just give me a chance to talk to you in person." The next few seconds felt like an eternity.

"Okay," J.B. said finally.

"I'll meet you at the office in ten," Cara said, and hung up the phone, feeling like a grade schooler who had just been reprimanded and called into the principal's office. She had fabricated her identity in the past to get information she needed, but with J.B., it felt as if she had been betraying a good friend, despite having known him for less than forty-eight hours. These past two days she had been setting up a minefield of dishonesty, and now she had finally tripped a bomb.

A LITTLE OVER a year ago, Cara's life with Aaron had fallen into a rhythm of familiar contentment. Cara had made detective rank and Aaron was a senior officer at his biotech company. They had purchased a two-story, four-bedroom house with plenty of room to grow their family. They had video-documented hours of every stage of their boy Dylan's life—walking, talking, giggling—as if they were all little impossibilities. There were nights of attentive lovemaking followed by quiet mornings when Cara caressed the bristle of Aaron's chin stubble while he drew lazy circles on her back. They discussed their thoughts, their fears, their innermost secrets.

Cara didn't know exactly when the seeds of discord were sown and began germinating fears and nurturing doubts. There was a spike in Aaron's late-night hours and the overnight business trips grew more frequent. It was the price that had to be paid for Aaron's promotion, she reasoned to herself while staring up at their bedroom ceiling alone one morning. Back when they had first moved in, they had scraped off the original popcorn and covered it with a smooth plaster. They were so full of verve and hope in their new house. Now she could see a hairline crack creeping its way down the middle of the finish.

It was while she was having to run an errand to the grocery store after work, when Dylan was having a particularly bad day, that her resentment really overflowed. Dylan had been crying in earsplitting screams while she bundled him into his down jacket, winter bomber hat, and muffler, and then tried to strap him into the booster seat. It was all of forty minutes before they were even on their way. He cried and kicked the entire way to the store, and once there, he screamed as if he were slowly being murdered, and yet she was the one receiving the knife glares of disapproval. And all the while, she kept asking herself, *Where is Aaron? Why isn't he here to help me with this?* It was so maddening, she had forgotten to pick up the milk she had gone to the store to buy in the first place.

Instances of conceivable betrayal and the possibility of Aaron's unfaithfulness began sending Cara down a well of despair. It consumed her waking thoughts, even more than the murder case she had been investigating—a case in which teenagers were catfished into murdering someone for the simple but false promise of money. The crime committed by these heartless teenagers was evil and unfathomable, but not personal to her.

Cara knew she was crossing the line when Aaron received an after-hours phone call one night, and after he said he had to leave, she made the decision to follow him. Cara grabbed her keys, tucked Dylan into the back seat, and prayed he wouldn't wake from his sleep.

She had tailed people more than once in the line of duty, but this time, she felt like she was the one perpetrating a crime. She stayed far enough behind so that she wasn't in the line of sight of Aaron's rearview mirror but was close enough to keep a bead on him. Onto the main drag of O'Malley Road. Past the Seward Highway and merging onto Minnesota Drive. Up to the northeast edge of town, not too far from Elmendorf Air Force Base. They finally stopped in front of a nondescript three-story industrial space, Almagor. It was the biotech company where Aaron worked.

Cara had switched off her lights and rolled into the parking lot, ready to make a U-turn, feeling embarrassed and guilty, when another car pulled up to the entrance. A woman was driving the gray Ford compact. Cara couldn't see her features in the dark of night, but she looked young, possibly in her early twenties, with long, lustrous hair. For a moment Cara forgot how to breathe and she felt like she was tailspinning again into a bottomless well. That's when Aaron glanced toward the parking lot and spotted Cara's SUV, and she knew he had immediately recognized her Chevy Suburban.

Later that night, she and Aaron engaged in a skirmish of hurt, launching verbal grenades and unfounded accusations.

"Who is she? Why were you meeting her?"

"She's a custodian, for God's sake! She was there for after-hours cleaning. I was just saying hi, making small talk. I don't even know what her last name is. If you want to check with our cleaning service, you can ask about Jennifer."

He passed her his phone with the number for "Anchorage Pro Cleaners" on it. Cara followed through with the call. Though it was quite late, someone picked up and corroborated that there was a Jennifer on the cleaning crew for Almagor Tech.

Cara began to doubt herself. Was she overreacting? Had her role as detective infiltrated her personal life so that she was looking for clues to a crime when there was none committed? After all, there was no kiss between two lovers in the parking lot. Not even a hug. But then again, Aaron had spotted her before there was time for any kind of amorous exchange.

"If you can't trust me, this marriage is over," Aaron said.

IT WASN'T LONG after this that they decided to take some much-needed time off work. Aaron told her that he sensed the amount of overtime he was working was causing a rift in their marriage. A cleansing with nature could give them a fresh start. It was a spur-of-the-moment decision, without much time to plan the logistics, and Cara's heart leapt at the chance to press the reset button. In Talkeetna, on the road to Denali National Park, she found a quaint two-bedroom cabin that promised sweeping mountain views and had a last-minute cancellation. So they packed their boots, their hiking gear, and enough food and supplies for a week, then headed out.

Denali National Park never grew old for Cara. Six million acres

and the highest mountain in North America. Aaron preferred staying in Talkeetna, where there was better fishing and freedom to
wander. On the drive, it was as though the cloud hanging over them
was already lifting. Aaron sang road songs for Dylan.

If you're happy and you know it, clap your hands.
If you're happy and you know it, clap your hands.

Cara and Dylan clapped along at the right moments, accompa-
nied by bursts of giggles.

Cara finally felt content and at peace, away from the murder
cases and the gray pall that she felt while in Anchorage. They spent
the first day on breathtaking hikes, where every vista was postcard
perfect. It was early in September, not the optimal viewing time for
the aurora, but still, thanks to a coronal hole, neon green lights floated
across the night like Christmas ribbons gifting the star-filled sky. It
was moments like these that reaffirmed Cara's love for Alaska and
all its cathartic beauty.

On the third morning, Dylan wanted to look for snowshoe hares,
so Aaron traipsed out with him early, carrying his camera gear and
tripod, while Cara opted to sleep in. She withheld her instinct to
worry when they didn't return for lunch. She had already tried to call
Aaron's cell but wasn't surprised when the call went straight to his
mailbox. Dead spots in the wilderness area were to be expected. She
left a message anyway and sent him a text for good measure. Then she
began preparing grilled cheese sandwiches and hot tomato soup for
them, expecting them to walk through the door at any moment.

At midafternoon Cara went to the check-in area for the lodge.
Aaron had taken the SUV, so she had no means of transportation. She

explained to the lone woman at reception that she was worried that her husband and son might be lost hiking and she didn't want them stranded out there overnight. The woman couldn't leave the desk, but she called a friend of hers, a quiet, grizzled man with a red plaid shirt and hunting cap, who volunteered to drive Cara up and down the roads so that Cara could scan for signs of the car. Perhaps Aaron had run into car trouble, but they saw no sign of the SUV.

The local police were initially unhelpful upon hearing that the pair had been missing for only an afternoon and told her to call back if they still hadn't returned by the following morning. But the woman at the lodge put calls in to all the local businesses and even texted them an image Cara had on her phone of her husband and son. She assured Cara that Aaron and Dylan would be found soon. Cara was grateful for her sympathy but was quickly devolving mentally and sobbed her way through daybreak. The next morning, the police took the case more seriously and alerted Denali Park rangers as well in case Aaron had somehow driven up there.

An intensive search finally began. Little did Cara know that the search would end up spanning almost a year.

CHAPTER ELEVEN

LONNIE

LONNIE HAD TO FEED DENNY EVERY DAY. EVEN ON SUNDAYS, even in winter, even when it was raining, even when there was a snowstorm outside. She didn't mind. It gave her something to do besides listen to the voices inside her head. There were always voices.

She put on her blue beret, her gloves, her boots, and her big, warm jacket. Down the hall, down the elevator, down another hall, through the tunnel that went to the school, and out the back door.

There was someone else walking in the snow, coming closer, getting larger. It was the police lady. She was watching her. She had eyes on her. *An eye for an eye.*

Chief told Lonnie not to answer the lady's questions. She needed to keep to herself. *Pay no never mind. Mind your p's and q's. Dot your i's; cross your t's. Don't talk. Keep quiet. Shut your mouth.*

"Shut your mouth!" That's what her mama used to tell her. "Or Jake'll get mad." Jake wasn't Lonnie's real daddy. Her real daddy left when she was still wearing jumpers. But Jake acted like he was her daddy, yelling the whole goddamn day and drinking beer and whiskey. Jake always smelled like fish because he worked on a boat. It was better when he was gone all day. Then Mama could read her nursery rhymes and tell her stories. Nursery rhyme time was Lonnie's favorite. Just her and Mama reading stories about animals and people. Jake went out catching cod, catching halibut, catching pollack, catching herring. Jake always talked about what he was catching. *Catch a cold. Catch a thief. There's a catch.*

"If I catch you talking to another guy, I'm gonna fuckin' kill you," Jake said to Mama.

When Jake started yelling and thumping, the whole house shook. Lonnie hid in the closet until it was all over. She heard Mama screaming outside, but she was too scared to look. She could hear the noise. *Racket. Discord. Wailing. Sobbing. Crying. Bang. Thud. Quiet.*

When Lonnie came out, she saw Mama's head cracked open and the blood spilling a line on the floor. Mama was dead.

Jake went to jail after that and Lonnie got sent to the Institute.

THE POLICE LADY saw Lonnie and started walking toward her. What if she started asking questions? "Have to check on Denny," Lonnie said aloud when the police lady was close enough. "Don't wanna talk to you."

"Why not?" The police lady stopped and looked at her. She was always watching her.

"Because you'll ask me questions."

"Is there something wrong with asking you questions?" Now she was even closer.

"You're already asking me questions. But I'm not going to answer. I'm keeping quiet. Silent. Speechless. Mum. Won't tell anyone my secret."

"You have a secret?"

"You're asking me a question again." Lonnie stared at the ground.

"Well, I won't ask any more questions if you'll just tell me."

"There's nothing to tell." Lonnie started feeling confused.

"Then you should have nothing to worry about if I ask you questions."

"I'm not telling you anything!" Lonnie adjusted her blue beret in frustration.

"Telling me what?"

The police lady was making Lonnie's mind spin with all the questions. Chief was going to be upset. "I won't tell you where he's buried!" *Entombed. Obscured. Covered. Hidden. Secrets. Don't tell anyone our secrets.*

The police lady was so close to her now, looking at her face. Watching her. Just like the cameras at the Institute. They were always watching her.

"Where who's buried?"

Lonnie covered her ears so she wouldn't hear the questions anymore. Her mouth was dry. She wanted to see Denny. "I'm not telling you. I'm not telling you!" Lonnie tried not to look toward the barn. But she did. The police lady noticed.

"Is there someone buried in the barn?"

"No! No! No! There's nothing in the barn. Just Denny. The wolves are coming. Don't want the wolves to get him." *Keep your mouth shut. What a big mouth you have. The better to eat you with!*

The police lady started running toward the barn. So Lonnie went after her.

Then the lady started walking up and down the barn, looking at the ground. She looked at the bales of hay. "Hey! You can't go there, lady!" Chief would send her back to the Institute.

Police Lady kept searching. *Cold. Cold. Warmer. Warmer. Hot!* In the paddock area where she took Denny when she cleaned his stall, and where she walked Denny in a circle when it was too cold to go to the woods.

Lonnie started pacing. The police lady looked at her, watched her. Then she took a shovel and started digging.

"Hey!" Lonnie said again in a panic. "Stop that!"

Police Lady wasn't listening to her. She put her back into it and kept at it, moving the snow. It sounded like *shuss splack, shuss splack.*

"You can't do that!" Lonnie insisted. "You need to leave, lady!"

But she wasn't listening. She was digging faster.

Police Lady found a mound beneath the snow. Lonnie let out a low whimper. She closed her eyes and put her hands on her head. "Go! Disappear. Leave. Vanish. Exit. Depart." The police lady kept shoveling. *Shuss splack, shuss splack.* And then it stopped.

Lonnie hoped she would be gone, but when she opened her eyes again, Police Lady was still there, on her hands and knees, scraping away the earth with her hands. The hair, dark, black, wet, was showing through. Police Lady let out a sound like "oh" but with air.

Lonnie saw the shovel on the ground next to her. She picked it up. It was heavy. She used it all the time to clean out Denny's shit.

She started to lift it. Chief said not to talk to her. Maybe she should hit her in the head like Jake did with Mama.

"What in God Almighty is going on here?"

Lonnie had the shovel lifted in the air and Police Lady was still scraping. J.B. looked at Lonnie like she was the devil. She put the shovel down. Then J.B. saw the head that was floating halfway out of the dirt and his jaw dropped.

CHAPTER TWELVE

CARA

CHIEF SIPLEY STILL HADN'T APPEARED AT THE OFFICE, AND Cara was almost convinced he came to the office only for show. J.B. seemed to be mostly a one-man operation.

Back at the barn, after recovering from his initial shock, J.B. had deftly slipped cuffs on Lonnie and recited the Miranda rights, despite her continued dog-like whimpering.

He didn't ask questions and said nothing when Cara told him it would probably be best to exhume the specimen—and by "specimen," she meant "head"—instead of waiting for the tunnel to be cleared for Anchorage PD, especially since the next front was about to blow in. But first, she needed to gather her evidence kit and her camera to chronicle the crime scene. "If I'm acting in my capacity as a trained private investigator, the evidence is still admissible," she reassured him. For better or worse, Alaska had no state licensing require-

ments to declare oneself a PI other than a regular business license—
something she had easily obtained when she was put on disability.

"Why did you kill him?" Cara asked Lonnie.

Lonnie blinked at her. "We didn't kill him," she said, before purs-
ing her lips. "I'm not talking to you."

"*We?* Who's we? Who was with you?"

Lonnie began to sing loudly. "*La la la la la la.*"

Cara knew it was useless after that. She looked at J.B.

"Could've meant Denny. You never know with Lonnie," J.B. said
after a beat.

J.B. PLACED LONNIE in the single-bunk cell adjoining the police office. It was a gunmetal-painted room with a toilet and washbasin
that smelled of acrid antiseptic layered over drunken urine and vomit.
Lonnie had stopped singing and she went back to whimpering when
they left her.

"Is she going to be all right in there?" Cara had to ask once they
were back in the main office. Despite being nearly skull bashed by
her, she was concerned about Lonnie's mental state.

"She'll have to be." J.B. sighed. Then he turned toward Cara and
eyed her with uncomfortable, palpable gravity. "I'm going to have to
call Chief Sipley now. So give me the ten-minute version of your
story. Why are you here? And why were you taken off duty in Anchorage?"

Cara inhaled sharply. She knew she owed J.B. some semblance of
the truth. "I was interested in this case because my husband and son
went missing after they went hiking in the woods. We did a massive
search, but it was as if they had just vanished. A few months ago,

they were finally found. I mean, their remains were found . . . spread out in pieces . . . almost a year after they had disappeared."

It took a moment for J.B. to process. His jaw dropped. He closed it, then opened it again as if to speak, then shut it once more.

"There haven't been any leads. I came here because I just wanted to know if there was a connection."

LOCAL VOLUNTEERS HAD searched the main roads and the most popular trails of both Talkeetna and Denali around the clock for the first few days. Then they started scouring the off-trail hikes, but with land that was nearly the size of Massachusetts, they could cover only a small fraction of a small fraction. On the fourth day, there was a ray of hope when they found the SUV. It was on a gravel road in Talkeetna that was seldom used, even by locals. What struck Cara as odd was the fact that Aaron's belongings were still in the vehicle. His camera gear still lay tucked on the floor in the back. *Why would he leave the Chevy with the keys still in the ignition and his driver's license in the front? Why did he decide not to take the camera on the hike? Why had they stopped on such a remote road?* There were so many more questions than answers.

Cara used all her resources with APD to get K-9 teams and helicopters involved in the search. They began interviewing possible witnesses. Groups of volunteers were shuttled in—some were fellow officers from Anchorage—and they began scouring the immediate vicinity around the SUV. She knew she was receiving special treatment, given the hopelessness of finding anyone who goes missing in the unforgiving Alaska wilderness. Buoyed by thermoses of cocoa and a general sense of good-willed camaraderie, the searchers set out in a gridded pattern like the beads of a giant abacus in mid-calculation. Experienced hikers took to the more popular mountain trails, a chopper scoured the area from the sky, and the dog teams tried to pick up a scent from the clothes Cara provided them.

After a week, the search had turned up nothing save for two cell phones, three single shoes of different sizes, a partially unraveled wool scarf, a red ski cap, and a pair of broken headphones. None of which belonged to Aaron or Dylan. By the end of the second week, the volunteers thinned to a few locals and a few German hiking enthusiasts. After three weeks, the search was declared officially over, and Cara had exhausted all the strings she could pull.

Still, Cara pressed on, trying to get help from volunteer missing person organizations, but with two thousand people going missing a year in Alaska and the harsh winter setting in, it was hard to keep anyone interested.

Cara returned to work, thinking it would help to focus on something other than the disappearance of her family. Her fellow officers went out of their way to be supportive, but she knew that they were starting to avoid her like she was a victim of an Ebola plague. Being around her was like traipsing around a snake pit of taboo words and topics. No one knew what to say around her anymore.

It was nearly a year after Aaron and Dylan went missing when lightning sparked a fire that ripped through 136 acres of forest around Talkeetna, the blaze gorging on spruce trees, alders, sedges, and the burrows of the elusive snowshoe hares that Aaron and Dylan had set out to search for.

Firefighters discovered a skull, and then a pelvis, and then a leg bone. By the end of the day, they had enough pieces of a human jigsaw puzzle to declare them the remains of one adult male and a boy matching Dylan's age. The bones had badly disintegrated in the fire and their pieces had been spread out over a fifty-yard area, mostly down in a ravine off a trail.

Cara was called in to "identify" the bodies, but there was nothing there resembling the human beings she had loved, nurtured, cared for, and revolved her life around. It was an emotional roller coaster of loss and then doubt when they showed her the objects that were recovered near the site—a hunting knife, metal buttons, the remains of an iPhone. "It's not them," she insisted. "None of these belong to Aaron or Dylan. Aaron had a Samsung."

She knew the caseworker, a soft-spoken woman named Louisa, whom she had worked with many times before, but this was the first time Cara was on the other end of her consultation. Louisa gave her a look she recognized as the "poor woman in denial" look.

"Of course, we didn't expect all the items to belong to them, given that many people pass through the area, and some of the items might not be recognizable due to the damage in the fire," she said.

For a moment, Cara wanted to slap Louisa for treating her like a clueless victim, but she simply repeated, "It's not them. I want a DNA test."

Then came the excruciating wait after she had sent in hair samples picked off Aaron's and Dylan's clothes. On a gray Tuesday, Louisa called to tell her that the DNA samples were a match.

Cara fell into a catatonic state after that. She hadn't prepared herself for this possibility. Up until then, she felt that as long as there was no proof that they were dead, they were still alive. And now that there was proof, there still wasn't closure. Instead, there were questions. So many questions. With the state of the remains, it wasn't possible to determine the cause of death. Had they gotten lost and then died of hypothermia? Had one of them tripped and fallen down an embankment? Poison berries? A combination of events?

And why were the bones scattered? A fire didn't do that. "Scaveng-ing animals" was the explanation from the firemen who discovered the remains. *Were there wolves? Or was there another human involved?*

Cara made herself persona non grata at the station, prodding for further investigations and butting in to other cases that involved miss-ing persons or dismembered bodies. She left messages with PD units throughout the state until they stopped calling her back altogether.

The only person left who continued to engage her was a mousy administrative assistant named Wanda who spoke an octave higher than anyone else and sported a retro eighties-style feathered cut. She would tear up with every mention of Dylan. Wanda had a child the same age as Dylan who had attended the same preschool, so her em-pathy ran deep. "I'm here if there's anything you need," she would say, though there was nothing, really, that Wanda could provide be-yond tea and sympathy. Still, Cara appreciated the gestures.

In the end, the station chief called Cara into his office and told her she needed to see Dr. Fisher—a psychologist they used to assess of-ficers after a trauma.

"I WAS LET go from active duty because afterward, I failed a psych eval-uation," Cara said flatly to J.B. "The shrink I was assigned to said I was suffering from PTSD and it was hampering my abilities as an investiga-tor. I was taking a cocktail of meds to deal with things, but that wasn't exactly considered a plus for the job. So I'm on disability right now."

"Oh," J.B. finally managed to squeak out. He was grabbing for words when Chief Sipley entered, and both Cara and J.B. were quiet.

"Who died?" he asked, and although it was meant as a joke, it seemed a wholly appropriate question.

CHAPTER THIRTEEN

AMY

WHEN IT CAME DOWN TO IT, AMY REALLY KNEW VERY LITTLE about the details of Ma or her past. Amy had been told that she grew up in the boondocks of China—in a place called Liaoyang, where Amy was born. On a satellite map, it's a tiny, nothing city in the shape of a half-eaten doughnut somewhere between Beijing and North Korea. The highlights of its unremarkable wiki entry were a university with some kind of foreign studies program and a sports arena for basketball and volleyball games. And yet, this yawn of a town still sounded ten times more interesting than Point Mettier. There were no university sports facilities within miles of the Dave-Co. Instead, they had a sad indoor playground covered in sawdust with a squeaky swing set, from where, as a kid, she had watched snow flurries through glass-paned windows. So Amy was at a loss as to what made Ma move them *here*. There were Chinese communities in exciting places like New York and San Francisco and Los Angeles. She doubted that most Chinese mainlanders had ever even heard of Point Mettier, Alaska.

Ma had told her that her father had died in a factory accident right after she was born, but so many details about him were lacking that Amy had long ago decided that Ma had gotten knocked up and then run away from China (where things like that actually mattered). Ma was a single mom raising a bastard child, so she had to come all the way to some tucked away corner of America in order to escape being the Hester Prynne of Liaoyang. Who knew? Maybe her father was a *guizi*—a foreign devil.

That was Amy's running theory. And maybe that's why Ma hated her. Okay, "hate" was a strong word, but there was a strong probability that Ma disliked her. Ever since Amy could remember, they had been at war with each other, using hurled insults, frigid stares, and, occasionally, actual physical objects thrown across the room at each other in acts of frustration.

When Ma said her name, it was usually in the tone of a curse word. "Amy! Clean your room!" "Amy! You forget to take out trash!" which might as well be "Shit! You forgot to take out the trash!" Amy responded in kind. "Ma! I'm doing my homework" in the tone of "Fuck, Ma!" Needless to say, it was never easy to have a serious conversation with Ma.

The truth grenade finally detonated when Mr. Healy's extra credit assignment revealed what Ma was really hiding. Mr. Healy was Amy's math and science teacher. He was as bald as a cue ball and always wore patterned sweaters that looked like they were knitted by somebody's grandma. With his drugstore reading glasses perched halfway down his nose, Mr. Healy had led the class with a cooking science demonstration, teaching them how to extract DNA from green peas by using a blender and making a putrid-looking juice mixture with detergent and alcohol. At the end, what magically materialized was pretty anticlimactic. Amy had been expecting something along the lines of those colorful double helix things you always see in science videos, but ultimately, the building blocks of life looked just like loogies.

For optional extra credit, Mr. Healy ordered a bunch of those DNA testing kits that people could use to find out about their own ancestry and look at their inherited genetic traits, like whether they'd end up bald like Mr. Healy or have a unibrow, and other stuff that's coded in human cells. When they got their results back, they were supposed to write a report about their findings.

At first, Amy was just as excited, for once, about homework as the rest of the entire class of eight was, and realistically, it was hard not to opt in to something that most of the class was going to do anyway. Most of the class, that is, except for Spence, who was Mr. Too Cool for School. Marco Salonga had even suggested that they video record their results live for his YouTube channel. Marco had 162 subscribers on his channel. A lot of them were from the Dave-Co, or members of his very large extended family, but there were fifty or so random strangers. Spence's response was, "I don't want to be part of your self-esteem-destroying, FOMO, echo-chamber, dystopic, herd-mentality social media experiment." Students had to get their parents to sign off on the DNA testing, and with Ma, that was easy because she never read anything and all Amy had to say was, "This is for school," and Ma would obediently scribble her consent.

Amy completely expected to find out she was 100 percent Chinese, but then there was still that off chance that her father was a foreigner who wound his way to the nether regions of China and knocked Ma up. Amy always thought she looked a little paler than a typical Chinese, but maybe it was for lack of sunlight. Regardless, no one in Point Mettier would care really if she were half something other than Chinese, so she hocked her spittle into the tube, placed it in the plastic biohazard baggie, and shipped it off.

The results finally came in to her email inbox a little before the time that the body parts washed up. Seeing the email in her inbox, Amy felt a flutter of excitement in her stomach. She braced herself, and maybe even hoped that her father wasn't Chinese. She took a deep breath and clicked to open the results. Color-coded tables and pie charts popped up, but the mostly monotone bars matched the hues of her disappointment in seeing that she was 99.4 percent East Asian. All the anticipatory jitters were dashed. *Who would have figured?*

But when Amy drilled down to the breakdown box, her heart nearly stopped. *Oh my God, oh my God, oh my God!*

Amy stared at the numbers that declared her to be 85 percent *Korean*. The cornucopia of "other" Asianness in her genes showed she was even more Japanese than Chinese.

Her entire life she had believed she was Chinese, had watched Chinese movies on streaming media, had spoken with Ma in Chinese, and had even tried to learn to read and write Mandarin through an app. She and her mom ran a Chinese restaurant, for God's sake, and now these numbers were telling her she was less than 10 percent Chinese? It roiled her inside. It seemed like everybody in this fucked-up one-building nutcase town was lying about something, and Amy had been living the biggest lie of all. It was one thing to lie about who her dad was, but all along Ma had been lying to Amy about herself as well?

"What the fuck?" Amy yelled, marching from her bedroom to the living room. She didn't care that she was swearing or that Ma was in the kitchen preparing food while watching her favorite TV show—the one where people find old, used, ugly crap in their basement and think that some geezer is going to pay a boatload of money for it (and that's how you know old people are crazy). Ma liked the show because it was simple to understand and because she liked the idea that people can seemingly make money by doing nothing in America.

Ma, in her usual communist-beige pants and shapeless blouse, which looked more like pajamas than real clothes, was caught off guard by Amy's sudden outburst. Instead of shushing her, she stopped chopping onions and stared at Amy with a kind of mouth-half-open perplexity. So Amy continued.

"We're not Chinese, are we?"

"Who tell you this?"

"The DNA test told me. We're doing it for science class. We're Korean. Not Chinese."

Ma put her knife down, in almost slow motion, which was kind of creepy in the moment. "Did you tell anyone?"

"No!" Amy shouted, wondering how this could be the first thing out of Ma's mouth.

"We are Chinese," Ma said with deliberation. "We are Chinese. Not Korean. You cannot say to anyone. Understand?" Her eyes were wide and her labored breathing made her sound like she was trying not to go ballistic.

"Why the hell are we pretending to be Chinese instead of Korean?"

"Because we are not South Korean. We are from North Korea."

North Korea? Crazy-dictator-who-has-no-problems-executing-his-own-uncle-by-firing-squad-led North Korea? Holy shit! Amy started shaking. The impossible notion of being from North Korea had never once entered her mind.

"We not here legal. If someone find out, we get deported. Understand? Then we have no place to go. No place. We cannot go back because we will die. Your dad, he die so you and I can escape."

If it weren't for the scientific proof sitting in her inbox, the words coming out of her mother's mouth would have seemed like some crazy and cruel joke she was playing, but Amy knew it was not. Amy started crying; whether they were tears of shock or fear or ultimate understanding, she wasn't sure. Suddenly things started to make sense. Why there was nothing about their past. No photo albums, no home videos, no documents, nothing that would connect them to where they had come from.

Then, for the first time in ages, Ma pulled Amy in for a hug. She smelled of onions and soy sauce and her grip was strong like a vise, but tears were pouring out of her in heaving sobs. "He died for you. I came here for you. Everything for you," she said.

CHAPTER FOURTEEN

LONNIE

LONNIE PACED THE LENGTH OF THE TINY CELL. *BARS, BUNK bed, toilet. Toilet, bunk bed, bars. Bars, bunk bed, toilet. Toilet, bunk bed, bars.* "Who's gonna take care of Denny?" she whimpered to herself. "Gotta take care of Denny."

Beyond the door, she could hear J.B. and the police lady talking in the other room, buzzing like busy bumblebees. They were probably talking about her. They were always talking about her. After a while, the busy buzzing stopped and Chief opened the door to the cell area. He looked at her, scowling.

"Lonnie?" he asked.

Lonnie didn't know why it was a question. "Gotta take care of Denny."

"I'll take care of Denny. You don't worry about him," Chief said.

Lonnie finally sat down on the lower bunk bed and put her hands on her head. Her head ached. *Head for the hills. Make some headway. She headed away. They were ahead.* "They found the head. They found the head." She said it aloud.

"Now, where in the Sam Hill did you find that head, anyway, Lonnie?" Chief asked. "And why didn't you tell me about it?"

Lonnie repeated what Chief had told her. "Don't talk. Don't ask any questions. Don't answer any questions. Just keep your trap shut."

"I didn't mean me, Lonnie. You should always talk to me," Chief said. He looked frustrated, like the way Mama used to look at her sometimes.

"I found it on the beach," Lonnie said. "It was a bad thing. Evil. Vile. Wretched. Rotten. Horrid. Better to be buried." Lonnie resumed whimpering.

"Don't you worry about anything. They can't talk to you, they can't ask you questions unless you have a lawyer, and they can't get a lawyer with the tunnel closed."

"I'm hungry," Lonnie said. Her stomach growled. Past lunchtime. "Can I get my fried rice? Star Asian Food."

"Don't worry. I'll get you your fried rice. Now, remember, don't you go answering any questions that police lady or J.B. asks, okay?"

"Don't answer any questions. Just keep your trap shut."

"That's right, Lonnie."

"Is she gonna send me back to the Institute?"

"No, Lonnie, that's not gonna happen."

AT THE INSTITUTE, the lights were always blinking and blaring. Yelling. Running. Doors slamming. The white-haired man with the long, dirty beard was always talking inside the room with the metal door. "There's a hole in the floor!" He said the same goddamn thing all day. "The people down there are waiting to get you. Judge, jury, and executioner." He could talk, gab, rant, speak, chatter, prattle, yap, all day.

Sometimes the nurses did the yelling, or the guards, running down the hallway like mad chickens.

Mondays were arts and crafts. Wednesdays were movies. Fridays were supposed to be dancing and listening to music, but nobody really listened. Everybody was crying or yelling or talking. Lonnie liked Saturdays best because sometimes Paws 'N Love came and Lonnie could pet the dogs and the cats and the bunnies. She liked to pet their soft fur, like touching clouds. Nurse Myers told her, "If you keep trying to hide the bunnies, you're not going to be allowed to participate anymore."

Most of the time, at the Institute, they just stayed in their rooms. Cold and white. The walls, the floors, the coats, their masks, the bed, the sheets. Cold and boring as hell. Lonnie read a lot of books there. Stories and fairy tales. They had a Bible and a dictionary in every room. Lonnie preferred the dictionary. Not everybody at the Institute could read, but Lonnie knew how, and it kept her mind focused on the stories instead of the yelling or the thoughts in her head. But they were watching. They were always watching.

Lonnie couldn't remember how long she'd been there at the Institute. Christmas and then Easter, Thanksgiving, another Christmas. Crafts, games, music. Crafts. Games. Music. Pets. Christmas. Easter. Thanksgiving. Christmas. Easter.

But one day, the nurse came and grabbed her like it was time for her pills and said, "Pack up your things. Your daddy's come to get you."

"My daddy?" Lonnie sat down and started whimpering because she thought Jake was in prison, and the Institute was better than being with Jake. "I'm not going with Jake," she yelled, and when the nurse tried to hold her, Lonnie spit on her.

The nurse looked like she was going to slap her with her cold hands, but there were cameras watching. Always watching.

"No, Lonnie," she said. "Not Jake. Your real daddy."

"My real daddy?" Lonnie couldn't remember her real daddy. "Who's my real daddy?"

"Mr. Sipley. He's a police chief. He's going to take you home with him."

That's how Lonnie ended up in Point Mettier. Chief gave her her own place and pretty much left her alone, but Lonnie knew Chief was always looking after her.

"FRIED RICE," LONNIE said. "Can I have my fried rice?"

CHAPTER FIFTEEN

CARA

"THANKS FOR COVERING," CARA SAID, ONCE SHE'D RETRIEVED her camera and her black-boxed evidence kit and she and J.B. were headed back toward Lonnie's barn.

When Chief Sipley had arrived at the police office, J.B. had given him an update. "Detective Kennedy and I are going back to the barn to bag the head. Then I'll call Anchorage PD." With the word "detective," J.B. had given her a get-out-of-jail-free pass.

Cara finally faced the music and said, "I'm sorry I lied to you." "Sorry" was not her strong suit, but she swallowed her pride, knowing J.B. deserved this much.

J.B. turned silent for a moment. "I get it. I know why you did it. I guess if I were in the same situation, I'd probably be looking for answers too. I mean, it doesn't make it right, but I get it. And . . . I'm sorry about what happened to your family," he added, looking down at the trodden snow.

Cara felt a sense of relief. Maybe because she felt it was imperative to have *someone* on her side in this town where people were as icy as the weather.

"But do you really think there's some kind of connection to this case?"

"Not if Lonnie killed this man," Cara admitted. "Maybe she killed him by accident, but this doesn't wash with the MO of a serial killer who might have lurked in Talkeetna a year ago."

J.B. nodded. "I've only been here for a year, but I've never seen Lonnie leave Point Mettier, so it'd be hard to imagine her going out to Talkeetna, or anywhere else, for that matter."

Cara sighed, beginning to doubt herself and her quest. Animals. Maybe that's all it was, and why was she wasting her time lying to people on the basis of a theory that couldn't hold water? It had cost her her position and now maybe it was costing her her sanity. Still, there were lingering questions about Lonnie. Did she really have the fortitude to chop a body into pieces and throw them out to sea? And why would she then keep just the head? "Who takes care of her?" she asked.

"I guess we all do in a way. Everyone chips in to pick up things for her on our shopping outings. There's a lady, Mrs. Sutter, who's only here during tourist season. She has a shop on the pier and pays Lonnie to let customers take photos with Denny. It attracts a lot of business. The money goes to a 'Lonnie Fund.' I think Chief Sipley's in charge of it."

They reached the green-roofed, one-stall barn, where Denny pawed the ground restlessly with a snort and shook his antlers at them, as if sensing that they were Lonnie's adversaries.

Cara looked at J.B. "You wanna search the premises while I bag the head?" It was more of a directive than a suggestion. "Anything that might look like a weapon. A shovel, a blunt object . . . Keep your gloves on and holler if you see something."

J.B. nodded.

Cara began by snapping a series of photos of the grave site. Then she carefully extracted the entire bluish gray head. Apart from its discoloration, it was remarkably well preserved in the frigid weather. The cranium was large and had belonged to a male, possibly in his forties, probably Caucasian, and with a tattoo of crossed arrows pointing in different directions visible on his left cheek.

Toward the top of the skull there was a hole, which Cara had assumed was the result of blunt-force impact, but now she could see that it was the exit wound of a gunshot. The lower cheek and jaw were splintered open where the bullet had entered before exiting out the back of the cranium. The entry wound had left part of the jaw exposed and the victim's teeth partially visible, making it look as though he were frozen in some kind of macabre, lopsided smile.

She couldn't be absolutely sure that the head and body parts all belonged to the same man until there was a medical examiner's report, but given the level of decomposition, which would be consistent with the timing of the footprint, Cara's guess was that they all belonged to the same man. Unless it was proven otherwise, that was the assumption she had to make.

"It's just hard to fathom that Lonnie could have been so . . . ruthless," J.B. opined.

"We're not ruling out the possibility of an accomplice," Cara offered. "Or that Lonnie's covering up for someone else. But one thing

I know now is that the victim was shot, and that makes this a homicide."

Once they were satisfied that they had given the barn a thorough scouring yet had found nothing more, they headed back to the office.

CHIEF SIPLEY HAD lost his usual jovial demeanor and sat at his desk with a constipated expression, flipping through forms. Cara wasn't sure if he was actually working or just giving the impression that he was.

She cleared some space off one of the gray metal desks and carefully unwrapped the plastic from the grinning head for both Chief Sipley and J.B. to examine. "Look familiar?" Cara asked. J.B. forced himself to study the head up close, and the color quickly drained from his face.

"He's not a Point Mettier resident," Chief said with conviction.

"But there's something about him that seems vaguely familiar. Like maybe he was among the crowd of tourists visiting," J.B. offered, while giving a wincing glance at the John Doe.

"Well, clearly, he's been shot, and Lonnie doesn't own a rifle or a pistol," Sipley said. "We made sure of that. So you've got the wrong person sitting in the bullpen."

"Did she have access to a gun? How many people here have rifles?"

J.B. balked at her question. In Alaska, asking that question was like asking how many people have winter coats.

"Has anyone's weapon gone missing or unit been broken into?" Cara continued when no answer was forthcoming.

"Nothing's been reported, but we can put out a bulletin," J.B. said.

"How about surveillance cameras? Anything we can take a look at?"

"The way people see it here, cameras are an infringement on people's right to privacy," Sipley said. "So, in other words, no."

"Could I also get a list of all the residents who live here and the store owners, including the ones that have left for the season?"

"I can put that together," J.B. volunteered.

"Boy, she's got you whipped," Sipley remarked to J.B. Then he added, "Do you have to keep that gruesome Halloween prop on the desk like that? That pumpkin head's gonna give me nightmares."

"Is there a freezer we can requisition?" Cara asked.

"We could ask Chuck Marino. But we have a mini fridge right here," J.B. offered, to Sipley's dismay.

"Chuck Marino?" Cara asked.

"You've met him. He owns the general goods store."

"Ah." Cara was a regular patron now of the long-bearded man's shop.

Chief Sipley grumbled, "There's a crime scene going on in that fridge right now, what with leftovers of God knows what from who knows when. We could probably donate some specimens to Mr. Healy's science experiments."

"I mean, just temporarily, until we can sort out a freezer space. I'll get it cleaned out first, if you just hang on a second," J.B. said, looking guilty and embarrassed, even if Chief Sipley was just as responsible for the remnants in the fridge.

"Take your time. He's not going anywhere," Cara said, nodding toward the grinning head.

CHAPTER SIXTEEN

AMY

AMY ROLLED HER BLUE FOLD-UP WAGON FULL OF TAKE-OUT orders down the hall, its rubber wheels squeaking on the vinyl floor like chatty mice. During the off-season, when the weather was bad Ma would just run a limited version of an order-out service from her kitchen at the Dave-Co, since no one was going outside to trudge to a not-so-great-even-for-white-people Chinese restaurant, not even through a tunnel.

Not much had changed on the surface since the earthquake revelation that had shifted Amy's entire world.

"What am I supposed to do, Ma? Am I supposed to just keep pretending I'm Chinese?"

"We are Chinese on passport. We are Chinese on all papers. We have to be Chinese," Ma had said stalwartly. "Cannot tell anyone. Make promise."

Amy had come up with some lame excuse for Mr. Healy about Ma accidentally throwing out her saliva sample before she had a chance to mail it out. He offered to write the company to get her a new kit, but Amy told him she was going to opt out of the extra credit assignment because Ma thought it was unsanitary and unnecessary. Mr. Healy nodded in understanding because it was a completely believable reaction from Ma.

After grilling Ma for info, Amy learned that she and Amy's father had both worked at a food-processing factory in northern China, where they had learned to speak fluent Chinese. Tens of thousands of North Koreans worked in China in restaurants and factories, all supervised, of course, by North Korean state groups. It was a huge money-generating operation for the regime. The laborers worked eight hours a day but saw only 10 percent of their wages, while the crooked North Korean government took the rest of it. Her parents' Chinese employers allowed them to work overtime without reporting their hours, and that's how her parents had saved the money to pay smugglers to take them on a grueling journey that crossed thousands of miles through China and several Southeast Asian countries. Ma wouldn't say how her dad had died, and Amy could see that it was too painful to talk about, so she didn't pry. After Amy's father died, Ma made the decision to get them to America, and to this remote location, far from the grip of Immigration.

For a while, Amy felt as if she were living with a proverbial axe hanging over her head, ready to fall as soon as she let slip that she wasn't actually Chinese. But it wasn't like she could actually speak Korean, or even remotely knew how to act like she was Korean, and after a while, everything seemed to go back to normal. In fact, if anything, it brought her and Ma closer. Amy finally knew what sort of Gulag-flavored sacrifice her parents must have made to get her somewhere that, if not ideal, was probably far better than whatever life they would have had under a maniacal dictator's rule, by which hundreds of thousands died of starvation every year. Ma went from zero to hero in an instant.

After Amy stumbled on the body parts, Ma's fears were renewed because that meant police would be sniffing around, and she equated the police with Immigration. "Don't worry," Amy told Ma. "Since I'm the one who found the body parts, they won't want to look at me as anything but a witness," she said. That seemed to be true after Officer Neworth from Anchorage PD took her testimony. It sounded to Amy like it was going to be another of the macabre cold-case incidents of body parts washing up in Alaska and the Pacific Northwest that no one believed had to do with any kind of crime. But then the detective lady had arrived.

Still, all they could do was go about doing what they had always been doing since Amy could remember, and today that meant delivering take-out orders.

FIRST STOP WAS a box of kung pao chicken and chow mein noodles for Mrs. Ellie Wright. She lived in the suite adjoining the check-in office for the Cozy Condo Inn.

Even before she knocked on the door, Mrs. Wright's yappy terrier, Vlad, started barking and growling like he was on some kind of dog crack. Mrs. Wright opened the door. She had a cigarette in one hand and a remote in the other. "Come on in, Amy. I gotta go look for my wallet," she said in her deep, parched-like-an-alligator voice.

"You can pay Ma later, if you want," Amy said, standing at the door, waving the smoke away and trying to ward off Vlad, who danced around her, baring his teeth like a crazed piranha.

"No, no. It'll just take a minute." She wagged her finger at her dog. "Shush, Vlad. Behave!" That did nothing to quiet Vlad. "Sit down on the couch, honey. Vlad'll shut up when we're both sitting."

Amy came in with a bit of reluctance, leaving the wagon outside, because if Vlad messed with the food, there'd be hell to pay. She shut the door and put Mrs. Wright's order on the kitchen counter, then sat on a brown faux leather couch with armrests that were pocked with cigarette burn holes and Vlad's bite marks. Just like Mrs. Wright had said, when Amy sat down, Vlad stopped barking and jumped up on the couch instead, quietly staring at her.

On the coffee table was a bottle of gin and a half-empty glass along with an ashtray. On the TV, the brainwashing news media that was destroying America blared out their hate-for-profit vitriol. Amy wouldn't have been surprised if Mrs. Wright was one of those news zombies who kept their TVs on from morning to night and believed every conspiracy theory that was doled out by a ranting opinion host. Those self-righteous, misogynistic, white-male-power xenophobes probably thought that Alaska Natives were the immigrants instead of themselves or their own ancestors. But whatever. Everybody was going to die from climate change in the end, no matter their color or party.

"Can't stay long. I have another delivery," Amy called out.

"Just found my wallet," Mrs. Wright yelled back.

On the wall was a framed cross-stitch that read SARCASM, JUST ANOTHER FREE SERVICE I OFFER. Next to that was a display of rifles on racks. Amy didn't know as much about guns as the other kids because Ma wouldn't allow anything like that, but even Amy could recognize that one of the guns hanging on the wall was a semiautomatic weapon.

Amy had heard the rumor that Mrs. Wright used to be a bank robber. Amy pictured Mrs. Wright, or whatever her name really was, with some crazy wig and sunglasses, waving that same semiautomatic weapon hanging on the wall, telling everyone in the bank to "hit the floor and put your hands on your head." Despite Mrs. Wright's being as old as she was, Amy didn't think it was a stretch for her. She could be as scary as hell sometimes.

Mrs. Wright finally returned with some bills and told Amy she could keep the change.

"Thanks," Amy said to her as she took her cash.

"Do you know what's going on at the police station?" Mrs. Wright asked.

"No, why?"

"I just thought I saw some commotion outside with Lonnie and that Anchorage lady and J.B."

"I don't know, but I have to make a delivery there."

"Well, you let me know what you find out," she said, and put another twenty in Amy's palm.

AMY HEADED DOWN the elevator to the first floor with the wagon in tow. Chief Sipley had started out by ordering "Lonnie's usual," then paused before he said, "It's gonna be a long day. What else you got?"

Amy told Chief Sipley that the only other items on the menu that day were kung pao chicken, chow mein, and egg rolls, so he ordered a couple of each. That's how Amy knew Mrs. Wright was right in assuming something big was going down at the police station involving Moose Lady Lonnie.

Amy knocked on the door at the end of the hall, softly at first, then louder, but no one answered. After waiting a beat, she twisted the knob and pulled in the cart.

What she saw was something straight out of a horror flick.

A severed head, with a hole in it and pieces of skin missing around the mouth, exposing fatty innards and flesh. It looked to her like some kind of bloated zombie, smiling in a sinister way at her. She had seen gruesome things like this on TV in war movies and gory thrillers, but all the prosthetics and movie magic could not have prepared her for the real carnage lying in front of her. Amy's stomach lurched. She dropped the handle of the wagon and made it to the nearest trash can before her lunch rocketed up through her esophagus.

"Holy shit!" Chief Sipley exclaimed, slapping his forehead. "I forgot completely about the food."

Detective Lady, who was wearing gloves, made a quick motion to cover the head with a plastic bag. J.B. was busy at the mini fridge with a garbage bag, dumping out what must have been moldy old food and ancient condiments. Detective Lady carefully carried the wrapped-up head to the mini fridge and placed it in a cleared-out space next to a jar of mayonnaise and a bottle of mustard. But Amy could never unsee what she had just seen. A hand, a foot, and now this? She knew she was probably scarred for life.

J.B. poured some water from the cooler into a paper cup and handed it to her. "You okay, Amy?"

No. Amy wasn't okay. She wasn't okay at all. It wasn't just the vividly horrific carnage that she would never be able to erase from her mind; it was also the fact that Amy had actually seen this man whose head was now in a mini fridge. She'd seen him when he was a living, breathing being, before he was reduced to shark chum. In fact, just a couple of weeks ago, she had made a food delivery to the very room he was renting at the Cozy Condo Inn.

CHAPTER SEVENTEEN

CARA

CARA ASKED AMY TO EXPLAIN IN DETAIL WHAT SHE REMEM-
bered about the man and the delivery she had made. Cara had passed
Amy in the halls once or twice, but each time, the petite Asian teenager with raven hair had avoided meeting her eyes, so this was the
first time they were actually exchanging words.

Amy recalled that the man with the arrow tattoo was staying in one
of the south-facing rooms and had ordered something standard, like
fried rice and orange chicken. She couldn't remember exactly. She had
knocked on his door and the heavyset man with dark hair had taken
the delivery without a word and shut the door. It wasn't much to go on.

"Do you have the name the order was under?" Cara asked.

"I don't remember," Amy said. "And we just take down room
numbers for Dave-Co orders."

"Thank you, Amy," J.B. said, and Amy was free to go, but Cara couldn't shake the sense that Amy seemed nervous and either was hiding something or knew more than she was saying. She still wouldn't meet Cara's eyes, and her leg tremored uncontrollably, but then again, it wasn't every day that someone witnessed a severed head.

CARA WAS NOT by any means an expert on Chinese food, but compared to the establishments in Anchorage, Star Asian Food might as well have been called *One Star* Asian Food. The chow mein was dry and tasteless, while the kung pao chicken was covered in a gooey, undefinable sauce. The fried rice was the most palatable item, probably because its saltiness overpowered everything else. If Lonnie was eating this every day, Cara had serious concerns about her health.

Cara made another attempt to talk with her, but her uncooperative refrain was, "I'm not talking to you. Not a word." It didn't help that Chief Sipley made a case for her after clearing a space among the take-out boxes on the metal desk and parking himself on top of it.

"Look, Detective," he began, "Lonnie's not a killer any more than J.B. here is a child molester." J.B. flashed a look at Sipley, both bewildered and shocked to be drawn into the conversation in such a nefarious comparison. "There's no dang reason why anyone would throw parts of a body out to sea but then decide to bury just the head," he continued, and Cara had to admit he had a point. "She probably just came upon it by accident and then decided to put it in a hole in the ground because it was an abomination to her."

"We're talking about someone who just tried to whack a hole in my cranium," Cara countered.

"You might have noticed, but Lonnie doesn't always act in a way that's logical," Chief Sipley said. "She was just upset that you were invading her space."

Cara felt that Lonnie might be a little more logical than Chief Sipley made her out to be, but she kept quiet.

Chief Sipley leaned forward an inch, taking a Rodin's *The Thinker* posture. "With her fragile psyche, she ought to be held in a hospital instead of a jail cell." As if on cue, a dismal moan came from the cell where Lonnie was being held.

"But there isn't a hospital here," J.B. interjected.

"Which is why we should let her go back to her apartment. I mean, what is she going to do? Drive off when the tunnel's closed? Into the middle of a snowstorm?" It seemed as if this was the conclusion Sipley had been steering the conversation to from the outset. "And I'm telling you, if I have to take care of that damn moose every day, I might just be inclined to set him free instead."

Cara was silent for a moment, weighing thoughts in her mind, then surprised both Sipley and J.B. when she admitted, "I don't believe we have enough evidence to charge for a murder yet." It was true enough.

"What about her attempted assault?" J.B. asked.

"I'm not pressing charges," Cara said. Lonnie was a dead end to her right now, and as Sipley implied, the Davidson Condos was like one giant prison anyway. But most of all, Cara didn't know if someone like Lonnie could survive being holed up in a jail cell. "I'm more interested in finding out who the victim is before we can look at suspects and motives. We need to get ahold of that registry from Ellie Wright."

"Well now, that's some sensible thinking," Sipley said, as if he were a schoolteacher applauding one of his students. He got up from the desk, taking the leftover boxes, and went to the mini fridge, forgetting about the head. He gave a little "Ah!" exclamation. "Goddamn it!" he said. "That piece of ghoulery is going to give me nightmares. Can we find a freezer space for it sooner than later?"

"It's probably a good idea to prevent decomposition," Cara concurred.

"I'll go talk to Chuck. I mean, he's got that freezer for selling meat. Though I know he won't like the idea," J.B. offered.

"He sells meat?" Cara brightened. The thought of living on Star Asian Food or bar food for the duration of her holed-up-like-a-rabbit stay did not appeal to her.

"Oh yeah. I mean, it's only for residents, but given your circumstances, I'm sure he can make an exception. I guess I should have thought of that earlier."

Sipley gave J.B. a look as if he wasn't supposed to have spilled a members-only secret.

CARA AND J.B. followed Chuck Marino to the bowels of the building. J.B. had found a cooler to put the head in, concealing the atrocity. Cara wasn't sure if Chuck knew exactly what was inside, but he agreed to rent some space out to the police department.

Cara's heart began to pound in double time as they descended the stairs to the basement level. It felt like the weight of the building was pressing down on her here, where the air was thick, with a metallic aftertaste. But at least, when they got to the bottom, it opened into a vast, pillared room instead of chopped-up, closed spaces. The dark concrete section they were led to looked like an apartment's laundry room, except instead of washing machines, rows of deep freezers were padlocked, and their power cables dangled from the ceiling like electric umbilical cords in a mad science experiment. When Cara stared at the odd view, Chuck explained that the basement sometimes flooded, so it was deemed safer to have the outlets on the ceiling instead of the floor.

Two of the freezers belonged to Chuck—one for meat and the other for fruits and vegetables. He unlocked one of the white, coffin-like chests, and Cara half expected to see a dead body already in it. But instead, there was a cornucopia of meat cuts, bacon, and sausage. He opened the second freezer for Cara to shop through as well. She was almost giddy to see frozen vegetables, fruits, and even bread. During the high season, a number of people worked in Point Mettier, renting out Ellie's rooms at special monthly rates, so thankfully each unit was equipped with a functioning kitchen and some basic cooking utensils.

"You'd be amazed at what you can keep in the freezer," the normally stiff-as-stone clerk told her. "Do you know that frozen fruit tastes better and has more vitamins than fresh fruit? That's because they're picked when they're ripe, while the ones at the grocery stands are picked when they're green," he said.

"Is that right?" she responded, already perusing the bonanza of food and placing items in a plastic bag Chuck had brought down with him.

"As you can see, we're ready here for the apocalypse," he said with boastful pride, and Cara sensed that Chuck almost wanted it to happen so he could prove it true.

J.B., meanwhile, quietly stacked some of the meat to one side and carefully placed the cooler box that was duct-taped and labeled with a Sharpie as POLICE PROPERTY next to some frozen venison and pork cuts.

Suddenly, a sound like a hinge creaking interrupted them from the dark deeper recesses of the basement, and Cara saw a shadowy figure out of the corner of her eye that sent a chill up her spine.

"Hey!" Chuck beamed his flashlight toward the sound.

A voice finally returned the call. "It's just me."

"Spence." J.B. acknowledged the wide-eyed teen emerging from the far corner of the basement. "What are you doing down here?"

He was a handsome teenager, with sandy hair, pale eyes, and a self-assured swagger. Cara recognized him as someone she had passed in the hall. When she had first seen him, Cara had felt a momentary pang, wondering what Dylan might have looked like if he had lived to be that age. Would he have had the same swagger? Worn the same kind of jeans? Would he have styled his hair with the same slicked-back look? She was still triggered by these things—the same color eyes or the same color hair as her boy's. Sometimes, it was all she could do to keep herself from rolling into a ball and crying.

"I was just getting something out of our storage locker," Spence said, then crossed toward the lockers lined up on the far wall like crypts in a mausoleum. No one believed Spence's on-the-fly excuse, but no one said anything in response. But later, as they made their way back up the stairs, with J.B. relieved of his cooler and Cara carrying her bounty of food, Chuck commented, "I guess there's only so many places here for a kid to smoke a doobie."

CHAPTER EIGHTEEN

LONNIE

LONNIE HAD ON A GRAY SKI CAP TODAY. SHE LOOKED LEFT and right and left again, making sure that the cop lady wasn't outside. She headed toward the stable. *Stable and steady. Balanced. Calm. Safe. Solid. Sound. She heard a sound.*

It was Denny, making a *whoosh* noise, like he was letting out a great big breath—a big moose sigh, blowing all the straw beneath him.

Lonnie had brought raspberries. She had thawed them from the frozen bag she bought from Chuck. Four dollars a bag. She had put them in a plastic Tupperware. She liked the sound the Tupperware made. *Click clack. Click clack* and it was locked. *Secure. Closed. Cinched.*

Denny ate the raspberries and licked her hand with his big wet tongue. When he finished eating all the raspberries, Denny made another *whoosh* sound, exhaling warm moose breath that tickled.

Lonnie was glad she was out of jail so she could take care of Denny like she had every day since she'd found him. Even when there was a full gale storm outside, Lonnie leaned into the wind and pushed her way for the short distance to the barn. There were only a few times Lonnie could remember when she was real sick, and then Chief had to go out for her. *Gotta take care of Denny.*

Lonnie had to clean out the old straw. Shovel the shit. Stick it in the wheelbarrow. Rake in the new straw. Make everything clean. She didn't mind. She liked working and not hearing voices in her head. Lonnie put the bridle she had made for Denny on him and coaxed him out of the stall so that she could walk him around the paddock. "Come on, Denny, Denny, Denny," she said, singing it like a song. "Come on, honey bunny." *Bunny rabbit. Jackrabbit. Jack be nimble. Jack be quick. Jack fell down and broke his crown.*

Denny followed her out to the paddock, and when she saw the hole in the ground, she stopped in her tracks. It was the hole where the bad man's head had been. His hair was dark and black and wet. The bad man's head had a hole in it. *There's a goddamn hole in the floor.*

Shuss splack, shuss splack. That's the sound the police lady's shovel made.

She heard a sound. *Noise. Racket. Din. Chatter. Shout. Screaming. Yelling.*

Lonnie closed her eyes. She had heard a sound. She had heard a sound outside the barn. Screaming and yelling, just like at the Institute.

There were the voices. "I'll cut you up!" the voice shouted outside. "I'll cut you to pieces!"

Screaming and screeching.

The kittiwakes were screaming. Descending. Pecking at some-

CHAPTER NINETEEN

CARA

J.B. HAD MANAGED, BY SOME SMALL MIRACLE, TO GET AHOLD of Ellie Wright's registry. His contact in Anchorage had come through with a warrant after J.B. told him about the new evidence—namely, the head sitting in Chuck's freezer. He explained that he was officially leading the investigation, while Cara was only lending her evidence-collecting expertise. A white lie.

J.B. delved into the registry printouts with the gusto of an eager hound on a fox hunt. He split with Sipley a list of the names and phone numbers of people who had stayed at the inn during the range of dates they were looking at, and they began making calls. He would make a good detective, Cara thought. His enthusiasm reminded her of herself when she was starting out—when she was still ambitious, still optimistic, and still undaunted by the many horrors of humanity that she had come to witness on the job.

Meanwhile, Cara quietly began searching database records that she still had access to, to see what she could ferret out about the Point Mettier residents on her list. Luckily, her access to police files had not been completely wiped, since technically she was still an employee. She started with the people she thought Lonnie was closest to and the neighbors around Lonnie's unit. What she found, she decided to keep to herself for a while.

Several hours and numerous calls later, J.B. said excitedly, "I think I've got something here." Cara and Chief hovered over his desk as he showed them a name he had circled. "Everyone I've called on the list so far's been accounted for, but according to Ellie's ledger, this man paid all cash up front for the three days he stayed here. Who does that? And when I called the number he wrote down, it wasn't in service. I have a hunch that this is our man."

The name on the sign-up sheet was *Charles Dodger.*

"Sounds like an alias," Cara said.

"I looked up the address he had down, and it's bogus, too," J.B. added. "Seems like everything he wrote down was a lie."

"I'll talk to Ellie," Sipley offered, but Cara wasn't about to let him go without her.

"I'll bring my evidence kit," she said. "We ought to swab the room he was staying in."

ELLIE WRIGHT OPENED up the room that J.B. had associated with the mystery guest—Room 42. She hemmed and hawed as if it took a lot of physical effort to turn a key in a lock.

Once inside, Cara surveyed the space, which looked much like her own suite, except instead of the harbor, it faced the mountains, which at the moment were a hazy blur of spruce trees through sheets of falling snow. The room had the same layout as hers—the same dark grandma furniture, a functioning kitchen, and roughed-up beige carpet with a smoke-filled dinge.

As Cara unpacked her fingerprint kit, Sipley began asking Ellie questions. "Can you tell us what you remember about Charles Dodger?"

"Well, to be honest, I don't remember most of my customers. People check in and check out, and after so many years, they kind of just blend together. And my memory's not what it used to be. I usually only remember the fussy ones. Like I'll remember Ms. Kennedy, of course. But Mr. Dodger must've been a quiet one."

Cara ignored the stab at her as she put on her gloves and headed toward a light switch to dust for prints.

"So he checked in and checked out without a problem?" Sipley continued.

Ellie looked down at the piece of paper Sipley had handed to her—a copy of the printout of Charles Dodger's hotel records. "Well, there's his signature, so it sure appears so. Three nights from October twenty-fifth."

"Has anyone checked into the room since then?"

"No. End of season. People prefer the rooms facing the harbor anyway."

"Well, thanks for cooperating, Ellie. We'll just scour the room. See if Mr. Dodger left anything behind. Shouldn't take too long." Sipley donned his latex gloves, went off to the bedroom, and checked the closets and rifled through drawers.

Cara took the opportunity to grill Ellie herself while she lifted a few prints and labeled them on backing cards—four-by-six index cards used for cataloging the unintentional mementos left by criminals or victims. "Are you certain you don't know Charles Dodger or ever met him before in your life?"

"Of course I'm sure." Ellie shot her a look full of venom. "You think I'm lying?"

Cara paused for a moment to look Ellie in the eye, wanting to gauge the reaction to the information she had recently dug up. "I looked up your files. I know you've spent time in jail. For a number of bank robberies, and abetting an armed robbery at a jewelry store."

Ellie stiffened. "That was a long time ago. I served my time. Chief will tell you that I've been a model citizen in Point Mettier. And what does that have to do with anything? If you're accusing me of anything, I have a right to an attorney."

"I'm just wondering what happened to your husband. Shane Mac-Cullum, I believe his name was?"

"We've been divorced for twenty years. I don't know what he has to do with anything."

"He was your partner in crime. You two were a regular Bonnie and Clyde. But then he took the rap after you gave testimony against him to get a lighter sentence."

Ellie looked as though she was ready to stab Cara in the eye with an ice pick. "Where is this all going?"

"You put out a restraining order on him after he got out of jail. When was the last time you saw your ex-husband?"

Ellie laughed loudly. "If you're trying to insinuate that Charles Dodger was my husband and I killed him, you're insane! If you haven't checked your math, that man was far too young to be my husband."

Cara smiled wryly. "I thought you said you didn't remember any-thing about him. Clearly you do remember what he looked like."

Ellie stopped laughing and was speechless for a moment.

"I sent Ellie a photo in advance, seeing as she was going to be a cooperating witness and not a suspect," Sipley said, lumbering back from the bedroom.

Cara shot Sipley a sour look. Clearly, he was trying to foil her in-vestigation at every step of the way. She stopped her line of question-ing and went back to lifting prints off the door handles, the windows, and the bathroom fixtures. Some of the prints looked usable, others, not so much. She carefully labeled and sorted everything, usable or not. Sipley searched through the living area and kitchen before planting himself on the faux leather sofa and making small talk with Ellie. He talked about holiday plans. Deep-frying a turkey. Would Ellie like to join him? But no, Ellie was going to fly out to visit a dis-tant relative in Texas. All the while, Cara simmered while she fin-ished up her work.

When they finally got back to the office, J.B. looked up from his computer and asked, "How did it go?"

"Didn't learn anything new, but Detective Kennedy here added a bunch of prints to her evidence collection. I think she's ready to start a gallery."

Cara put her evidence kit down with a heavy thump on the metal desk that had become her designated space, then spun toward Sipley. "Chief Sipley, I know you did not send Ellie a photo of the victim. All the evidence photos are in my laptop."

"Did I say photo? I meant info," Chief said, nonplussed, and set-tled down into his chair with his feet up on the desk.

"You need to recuse yourself from this case."

"Excuse me?" Sipley said peevishly.

"You heard me. You need to recuse yourself because of your relationship to a suspect." Cara could hear her voice rising.

Sipley was suddenly attentive and put his feet back on the floor. "We have a suspect?"

J.B. followed their exchange, watching their volleys like a chair umpire at a tennis match.

"Lonnie Mercer is your daughter by birth."

J.B.'s mouth dropped. Sipley looked livid but kept quiet, so Cara continued.

"It wasn't too difficult checking records with psychiatric facilities in the state to find all of Lonnie's info. You know I could have you charged with misconduct for lying to a police officer."

Chief Sipley's mouth curled. "Likewise, Ms. Kennedy. I could have you charged as well for lying about being an officer on the case."

Cara was stunned into silence for a moment, and she could feel her cheeks grow hot.

"I do my homework too, Ms. Kennedy."

"Well, technically, she's still an officer. Just on disability," J.B. offered.

"I'm here as a private investigator."

"Hired by whom?"

"I'm working pro bono."

"Bullshit! I know about your husband and kid, Ms. Kennedy."

Cara felt as if she were being run over by a semi. Chief Sipley had feigned disinterest, but all the while he had been investigating her. *Or had someone told him?* Cara glanced over toward J.B.

"Don't worry, I haven't told Anchorage you're on the prowl here," Sipley said. "Seems like we both hold the aces."

"I'm not interested in coercion. I'm just interested in the truth, Chief Sipley. Are you covering for Lonnie or Ellie, or is one of them covering for you?"

"The truth is, Lonnie found that head and decided to bury it. Sure, I don't want to see Lonnie go to jail or back to the mental facility, so I look out for her, but that's all. And Ms. Wright rented a room to a man whose head might or might not be in the freezer downstairs, and that's all she's guilty of."

"So what about you? What are you guilty of?"

Sipley got on his feet like a lumbering bear showing his full height. "The better question is, what evidence do you have? 'Cause we both know you don't have shit. Not even the real name of the victim."

Cara had to admit she did not.

"Hell, I know you don't want me to tell you how to be a detective, but you can't go around pointing fingers when you've got nothing. And I mean zilch."

The reprimand stung, especially in front of J.B. "Regardless, I think it's best if J.B. takes the lead and you step down. Anchorage has already approved his taking the helm on the case until the tunnel reopens."

J.B. looked slightly guilty when Sipley darted a look at him.

"And don't forget, Chief Sipley. I dropped charges of attempted assault by Lonnie, but I can still resurrect them."

"Touché, Ms. Kennedy, but I know you have . . . issues concerning your mental health, so you know as well as I do that whatever testimony or expertise you think you may be bringing to the case can all fall under scrutiny."

They exchanged fiery glares, filling the room with unsettled tension, before Sipley finally stormed out of the office.

J.B. looked at Cara. "Well, those were some major fireworks, and I'm beginning to wonder if there's anyone here who isn't lying about something."

Cara looked at J.B., examining him with similar thoughts, but said nothing.

CHAPTER TWENTY

AMY

AFTER AMY WAS EXCUSED FROM THE "WHITE ROOM OF QUES-
tioning" at the police station, she went home but didn't tell Ma about
what happened. She knew Ma would go nonlinear about her talking
to police yet again. Amy made a halfhearted attempt to concentrate
on homework, but nothing could erase the freak show of death she
had just witnessed, so she decided to head to Spence's.

Mrs. Blackmon, who was a much more perceptive human than
Ma, saw straightaway that Amy wasn't herself. The first thing she
said was, "What's wrong, Amy?" Then she waved her into the room
when Amy didn't answer. "Something happen?"

"I was at the police station," Amy said, and after a deep intake of
breath, added, "They found a head."

There was a look of horror on Mrs. Blackmon's face. "A head? You mean a human head?"

"Yes."

"Is it the same victim as those body parts?"

"I . . . don't know," Amy responded, realizing that she had just assumed it was, but now that Mrs. Blackmon mentioned it, there was no way to be sure. "But I think so."

Mrs. Blackmon put on her teacher-counselor voice. "Do you want to talk about it?"

Amy did want to talk about it, but not with Mrs. Blackmon. "No, I . . . I'll be all right. Is Spence around?"

"He's in his room," Mrs. Blackmon said, before adding, "You know you can come to me anytime. I'm always here for you."

"Thanks, Mrs. Blackmon." Amy could still feel Mrs. Blackmon's look of concern as she made her way down the hall.

AMY NAVIGATED AROUND clothes islands, orphaned electric cables, and a twenty-five-pound barbell to get to the bed, where Spence was playing a game or watching porn or whatever on his device. Amy interrupted by throwing her arms around his neck and holding on to him as if he were the last raft from a sinking *Titanic*.

"Hey, what's the matter?" he asked, taking out his earbuds and looking into her eyes. He tried to soothe her, stroking her hair.

Amy repeated what she had told Mrs. Blackmon. She could feel a slight tensing of his muscles. Then he pulled his head back—kind of like the way Mrs. Kirby's cats prowling the hall on the fifth floor would freeze and back away when you reached out a hand, despite their looking all friendly just a minute before.

"No shit! Where'd they find it?"

"In Lonnie's barn."

"Moose Lady Lonnie?" Spence's eyes grew wide. "Are you sure? I mean, she's crazy and all, but I never figured her to be a murderer. Did they arrest her?"

"They had her at the police station."

"Shit! I saw them putting something in one of the basement freezers today. Think it's the head?"

"Probably," Amy answered.

Spence seemed to mull. "Do they know who the vic is?"

"No, but . . ." Amy hesitated for a moment, then looked in Spence's eyes as she said, "I think I saw him before he died."

"You saw him in the flesh?"

Amy nodded. "I think I delivered food to him when he was staying in one of Mrs. Wright's suites."

"Fuck!"

Images of the tattooed head on the metal table, grinning at her, sent chills up her spine. She started feeling queasy again. "I wish I hadn't seen anything at all," she said. "Can we just cuddle?"

Spence enveloped her in his arms and Amy felt comforted by his warmth. Then she finally let the waterworks go. All her pent-up fears and emotions came gushing past her false front of toughness. And then she actually started physically shaking. Whether it was because of anxiety or PTSD or her monthly hormones, she wasn't sure.

"Hey now," Spence said, turning all tender. He put his hand on her cheek and then kissed her tears.

He made a staccato trail of soft pecks before covering her mouth with a hot, breathy kiss. Amy pulled back, extricating herself from his embrace, and he looked at her, confused.

It wasn't like they hadn't done this before.

In fact, it wasn't too long ago that they had finally planned to seal the deal and lose their virginities. Ma had never discussed sex with Amy, and thank God for that, because that would have been an awkward convo. In much of Alaska, sex education was a joke. They were taught abstinence, and nothing about contraception, so naturally, Alaska was number one in chlamydia cases and number two in gonorrhea in the nation. But Amy had vigilantly learned everything she needed to from movies and the Internet.

She and Spence had never actually followed all the way through, though. For one thing, condoms were harder to come by than drugs in Point Mettier. Mr. Marino sold them in his store, of course, but what teen was going to buy condoms where an adult spy was going to blabber to their parents? So either you had to come up with an excuse to go into Anchorage or, since that wasn't always easy, you could do what Spence did, which was to pay one of the older Camacho brothers for a stash of happy hats he already had on hand. Then they had planned a day when Mrs. Blackmon was taking Troy to one of his head-shrink sessions in Anchorage, and Amy made an excuse to Ma about not working at the restaurant because of a group homework assignment. So the big day came, but with everything planned and the pressure to perform, Amy felt so nervous she had to run to the toilet and hurl before she even got to Spence's bedroom. She washed her mouth out and pretended she was fine. Then they kissed for a while, trying to get in the mood, but Amy could sense that Spence was just as nervous and uncomfortable. It wasn't all romantic like in the movies. Spence poked and prodded around and Amy yelled, "Ow!" and then finally "Okay, stop!" before they just ended up lying next to each other, staring at the ceiling. Spence seemed more relieved than anything else.

But it wasn't the memory of their failed deflowering that made Amy pull back. It was something else that came hurtling through her mind at that moment.

There's nothing like the image of a head in a refrigerator to ruin the mood, but more than that was the thought that whoever had killed that man probably lived in the Dave-Co, and in all likelihood, that someone knew who Amy was and where she lived.

CHAPTER TWENTY-ONE

CARA

BY THE TIME J.B. AND CARA HAD DECIDED TO CALL IT A NIGHT, the storm was dumping pixelated sheets of snow that undulated with the wind, while the building began making a chorus of moans and groans, not unlike the first night Cara had spent there.

She was grateful, at least, that the kitchen was outfitted with basic cooking pans, cutlery, and even spices for the temporary seasonal workforce. Being able to cook even a simple pasta dish with canned sauce and crumbled sausage lifted Cara's spirits.

Looking at another bumpy, disruptive night ahead, she decided to take one of her rationed Xanax pills. Before she knew it, she found herself dozing on the couch. It was a deep and dreamless sleep, and when she awoke again, she looked at the digital clock on the stand to see that it was just past eleven. She was about to get dressed for bed when there was a knock at the door. The late-hour disturbance was starkly reminiscent of her first night in town, but this time she was sure the knocking was real.

Cara sprang for the door and practically ripped off the handle in the process. This time, there was no WD-40 required, and she could see, clear as day, that a living, breathing teenage boy and not a specter was responsible for the knock.

He had a look of surprise on his face and said, "Uh . . ." before he tore down the hallway in the direction of the stairwell. Cara pumped after him.

The boy was quick, running down the stairs. Cara flew after him, determined. She chased him down to the level below, where he sprinted down the hallway. He fumbled on the thread-worn carpet, which allowed her to catch up to him and tackle him. He grunted as she put him down to the ground, grabbing one of his arms behind his back.

"Uncle!" he yelled. "Okay, okay, you got me."

She eased up on his arm.

"What's your name?"

"Joel. Joel Camacho. I don't wanna go to jail," the boy said. "Please don't tell my mom. She'll send me to some kind of Catholic boarding school or something."

"Why were you trying to scare me?" Cara practically yelled.

"It wasn't my idea, I swear." The boy was starting to tear up.

Cara could see this was just a mischievous kid who was scared out of his wits now. She let him sit up so that she could look him in the eyes.

"Whose idea was it, then? Chief Sipley? Ellie Wright?"

Joel looked down toward the floor before barely speaking. "Mariko

Ishida. The bar lady. It was just supposed to be a game. She was paying me."

The pitifully sad lady on the record album was such an unlikely suspect to Cara. "Why? Did she tell you why?"

"No, ma'am. I don't know. Maybe you can ask her yourself. She's always at the pub."

His efforts to deflect worked. Cara got up, letting go of the boy. "All right, Joel Camacho. I may have further questions for you, but you go home now and stay out of trouble."

Joel didn't need any more prompting to hightail it back to his unit.

THE SALTY PUB was the only establishment outside the walls of the Davidson Condos that was open year-round. People could do without the overpriced, tourist-driven shops and restaurants lining the pier, but the flow of alcohol was almost a necessity in a town like Point Mettier.

Cara had managed to avoid another trip to the bar since her first visit, but it was the only way to "have a conversation" with Mariko Ishida without needing a warrant, so she braved the vertigo-inducing enclosed stretch of tunnel to the pub, trying to ignore the tightening in her chest and the anxious beating of her heart.

Inside the pub, the scent of stale beer and the eye-watering cigarette smoke assaulted her senses. A gaggle of patrons was assembled inside, drowning the cold, bitter wind and whatever else ailed them. She recognized a couple of the barflies from her first visit, sitting in the same seats, seemingly nursing the same drinks and fingering the same cigarettes, as if they were permanent parts of the decor. For some, the Salty Pub probably provided a respite from isolation—a way to idle away the time in hibernation while they waited for the next season to come around.

Mariko was up on the stage, again giving it her all, sashaying as if she were the star at a sold-out arena. The Japanese words were incomprehensible to Cara, but the tune was a bouncy bossa nova filled with *ba ba ya ba*s between words.

Cara ordered a club soda and lime and sat waiting for Mariko's set to be over. When Mariko noticed her, she lost a bounce or two and put a little less emphasis into her hip rolls.

At the end of the set, there was no place for her to retreat to, and no way for her to leave without passing Cara, so she sauntered to the bar and sat down. She wiped away the perspiration that was starting to dissolve the heavy eyeliner around her eyes. The tattooed bartender poured her a whiskey sour over ice. Cara got the feeling it was her usual.

"Why are you hiring kids to scare me?" Cara asked, straight to the point, still roiling with the effect of Mariko's pranks.

The Japanese lounge singer gave her a sideways glance as she daintily lifted her drink, with pinky finger extended. "Kids scare you?"

Cara rolled her eyes. "Joel Camacho told me everything, Mariko."

"What did he say?"

"You hired him to come knocking on my door to scare me."

Mariko batted her fake caterpillar lashes. "Why would I do such thing?"

"Why indeed is what I'd like to find out. Perhaps it has something to do with the body parts?"

Mariko laughed. "Do you think I'm murderer? I don't have a gun. I don't even know how to use it."

"How did you know he was shot?"

"Small place. Everybody know everything fast."

Cara decided to grill her on what she had recently discovered. "I know you were a famous singer back in Japan. Why did you give that up to come here?"

A dour look passed over Mariko's face as she swished the ice in her glass. "I am not so popular in Japan anymore."

"You were at the height of popularity when you quit singing. You were engaged to a baseball star, but then something happened, the engagement was called off, and you moved here."

Cara could almost feel the heat from the fire in Mariko's eyes. "That is not your business."

"There was a lot of press. Rumors that you were pregnant before you were married, and then you disappeared off the map. But my records show you later got married in California to an American. In fact, you're still legally married to him."

"This is my life. Not your business," she repeated.

"It is when I'm trying to find out what reason you would have to scare me by knocking on my door."

"You are crazy! I don't do any of this."

"Where is your husband now?"

Mariko put her drink down with a gesture of finality. "I go now. Cat needs food."

Cara almost growled her warning. "Just remember, Ms. Ishida, if you ever try to scare me again, I can and will press charges against you."

Mariko got up and left, her heels hitting the floor in pointed *clacks*.

There was a laugh from the stool at the end of the bar. Cara turned to see the tollbooth operator, Jim Arreak. He tipped his baseball cap toward her. "She doesn't have a cat, you know."

"I didn't think she did," Cara responded. "I'm allergic to cats, so I can usually tell if someone has cats or not." She moved to the seat next to Jim. "You, for instance, have a dog."

Jim's eyes widened. "Okay, Sherlock."

Cara pointed to the fur on his shirt. "It's not making me sneeze, so I'm assuming it's a dog."

Jim brushed the fur off. "So am I a murder suspect too? I hear you've been grilling folks."

"Everyone's a suspect and no one's a suspect until I find out who this Charles Dodger is. Which reminds me, I've been meaning to ask whether you got a glimpse of this guy." Cara held up her cell phone with the photo of the head.

Jim spit out his drink. "Jesus, give me some warning next time, will ya?" He braved another glance. "Probably not his best mug shot, but I don't remember the guy—*Charles Dodger*, did you say his name was? Then again, I see a lot of people come in and out, and not everyone makes an impression."

Cara tapped her phone off. "You strike me as a no-BS kind of guy."

"Thanks, I think?"

Cara looked him in the eye. "The last time I saw you, you said I'd better leave because of what's coming. What did you mean by that?"

"Did I say that? I must've been drunk as piss." Jim tried to hide his expression by taking a long swig from his drink.

"Were you just trying to scare me, or was there something else behind the comment?" Jim was still nursing his drink, so Cara added, "Listen, I'm just interested in making sure the least number of innocent people get hurt here. And I'm going to find the information I need one way or another."

Jim finally put his drink down. "Well, I know you're focusing on a killer inside Point Mettier, but a lot of us are on the lookout for external forces."

"External forces?"

"From all this research you've been doing, you already know that a lot of people are holing up out here for a reason. Sometimes they're bad reasons; sometimes they're good."

"Which is it for you?"

"That's a story for another time." Jim smiled wryly. "Back in the day, when the Point Mettier tunnel hadn't been converted to allow car traffic yet, the only way in was by train. Some women found that a convenient way to keep their exes out. Even if they had restraining orders, you know the law ain't gonna be doing their due diligence."

Cara knew this was true enough. There wasn't much police could do unless and until a crime was committed. They couldn't be personal bodyguards.

"Sometime in the nineties, a disgruntled ex came barreling through the building with a machete. He didn't do no harm, thank goodness, and was arrested. But that's when they came up with a system where the conductor wouldn't allow anyone on a list of no-gooders onto the train, and that worked out real well for the people who came out here to hide out."

"What about now?"

"Now that people can drive through here, there's not as much we can do. Still, I was given a list of people to keep an eye out for when I started. Sometimes I stop people who look suspicious—if they're traveling alone and I can't picture them spending any time in a gift shop. I ask for their ID and sell them some story about a tunnel shutdown and I gotta have their info in case they aren't outa here by a certain time. That's about all I can do, really."

"Can I see the list?" Cara asked.

"It'll cost you."

Cara raised her brows.

"Another gin and tonic."

Cara smiled and raised her hand to the bartender.

"Got the names emblazoned in my head by now," Jim said. "No *Charles Dodger* on the list, though."

Cara slid her napkin over and took out a pen. The night was turning out to be productive after all.

CHAPTER TWENTY-TWO

AMY

THE ORIGIN STORY OF POINT METTIER SCHOOL'S HYDRO-
ponic vegetable garden began a few years back, when a man named
Mr. Fitzbar in Unit 623 had been caught growing marijuana. The
tip-off was his electricity bill, which suddenly skyrocketed because
of the high-powered lights he needed for his homegrown cannabis.
It was legal in Alaska to have a few plants for personal use, but
Mr. Fitzbar had turned an entire bedroom into a pot farm that spilled
over into his living area. Plus, he was illegally selling buds to the
kids, so he ended up with a prison sentence after one of the parents
caught him dealing in the hallway. Rumor was that he finished serving his shortened sentence but decided not to move back to the
Dave-Co because he was starting an ayahuasca retreat deep in the
woods of Washington State. And no one was surprised by that.

The kids were naturally bummed because it meant that their local supplier was gone and that they had to go to Anchorage to score some puff. But Amy had to hand it to the teachers of Point Mettier, who came up with the idea to use Mr. Fitzbar's confiscated lights for an indoor hydroponic garden. As poetic justice, the free labor for growing and harvesting the garden was supplied by the students—the same students who had been buying weed off Mr. Fitzbar.

Truth be told, Amy didn't mind tending the hydroponic garden. They had rigged up a drip irrigation system snaking through beds of lettuce, kale, spinach, cucumbers, tomatoes, radishes, and even strawberries, all basking under Mr. Fitzbar's four-thousand-watt lights. The dirt-filled buckets and irrigation hoses were configured in a kind of jungly mess. They weren't the pristine greenhouse plants, all lined up and symmetrical, that you see in science fiction movies where the future consists of sterile, dystopic, nothing-out-of-place hospital-white spaces. But still, it was cool in a world-building-app-like way to see seeds turn into sprouts and sprouts turn into actually edible vegetables that people were willing to pay money for.

The harvest was sold to residents in the Dave-Co, but there was a limit per customer because of the high demand, especially during the winter months. Ma had been growing her own herbs and green onions for the restaurant since long before the hydroponic garden. Turned out there were a lot of things you could grow in glass jars with LED lights pointed at them. But Ma appreciated that she could now get fresh produce instead of defrosted, cardboard-flavor vegetables, so in the hour after school, Amy picked up some tomatoes, cucumbers, and radishes from the mini farmers' market. Of course, when she got back with her bounty, Ma had to criticize her picks: "This too small" or "Not yet ripe." Ma was pretty much back to being her usual angry Asian-mom self. Then she said, "Order for 812." There was no "How was school?" or "Thanks for picking up the vegetables." It was just "Do my bidding." That was Ma.

Amy stormed to her room. "Jeez, let me at least put my books away, Ma!" she yelled, then slammed her books on her table and made a racket opening and shutting her closet before calming down, remembering again that Ma had made a lot of sacrifices for her. She sighed, held her tongue, grabbed the blue cart, and took the order for 812.

After all these years, Ma still preferred room numbers over names. This was all because of one little snafu Amy had made two years ago, when she accidentally left food at the door of an empty apartment, which she thought was the Wilsons'. When they didn't answer, she figured she'd just come back some other time to collect the cash. There was all hell to pay after that, and now Ma always used numbers instead of names, but Amy obviously knew who lived in 812. It was Mariko's unit.

Mariko rarely ever placed an order with Star Asian Food. Amy knew she was a good cook and Star was probably beneath her standards. Besides that, Mariko was at the bar most nights, doing her sad lounge act, so she could always get free food there if she didn't feel like cooking.

Amy knocked on her door with the order of grilled salmon and pepper soup in disposable containers, all packaged with napkins, rubber-banded, and stacked in a thin plastic bag.

"Amy-chan, come in, come in." Mariko waved her in. She wore a long, flowing mauve robe with a flower pattern, and a turban-like wrap was around her head. Amy knew the turban was a substitute for the wig she usually wore. She reluctantly stepped into the foyer.

Ma didn't accept credit cards, so Amy always had to stick around to get paid. If Amy had things her way, she'd rather just knock, leave the food at the door, and skedaddle, but the credit card companies charged a 3 percent processing fee and that was just plain robbery, according to Ma.

"Please sit down," Mariko said. Amy placed the plastic bag on the kitchen counter and sat down on the doily-covered sofa. She was disappointed that Mariko didn't seem like she was immediately going to get the cash to pay her for the delivery.

"I can't stay long," Amy said, lying. "I've got to make other deliveries." Members of the creepy doll collection stared out at her from their glass case.

"I have present for you," Mariko said.

Amy was caught off guard by that. "That's okay. I don't need any presents," she said. A Victorian doll with painted eyes that was going to haunt her in her nightmares was the last thing she wanted. But Mariko excitedly went back to her room and reemerged with a daintily wrapped box in a tiny gift bag.

"Open!" Mariko commanded, clapping her hands together.

Amy took the small box out of the bag and peeled off the wrapping. Then there was tissue paper in the box to get through. It seemed like a lot of effort for a non-birthday / non-Christmas gift. She finally tore through the tissue to find a Japanese hair comb. It was made of lacquered wood, painted black, with a picture of a gold crane etched into the ribbing. The feathers of the crane fluttered gently over the top of the spine of the comb. Stones colored red and blue filled the wing patterns. It was very detailed and pretty, but there was no way in hell Amy would ever be caught wearing anything like that in her hair, unless it was for a costume party.

"Thanks," Amy said, trying her best to make her smile not look fake.

"My mother gave to me. Very special hair comb," Mariko explained. "I wanted to give it to my daughter." Mariko paused for a guilt-ridden second. "But I give to you instead."

Amy felt slightly sorry for her in that moment, seeing the way that her shoulders sagged a bit. "What happened to her?" Amy finally asked.

"She died long time ago."

Amy had suspected this much. She dared to press further. "How did she die?"

"Accident." Mariko paused, leaving Amy hanging. She doled out some bills and handed them to Amy for the food.

But then there was a glaze in Mariko's eyes as if she had slipped into some distant past. "I wanted to keep her safe . . ." Tears began streaming down her cheeks. "I sang lullaby every night."

Marco, who was into Japanese anime and pop culture, had told Amy once that it was pretty scandalous in Japan, even today, for a woman to have a child out of wedlock. Most of the time, the unwanted pregnancy ended in abortion, and that would be especially true if the woman was a celebrity. Amy wasn't sure whether Mariko had terminated her pregnancy or if she had given up her career to have the baby and then it ended up dead in some tragic accident anyway. Whatever the case, it was some sad, Dickensian-spinster-level of tragedy, and now Mariko was cradling an imaginary baby in her arms. In a whispery voice that made the hair on the back of Amy's neck stand up, she started singing. *"Nen, nen korori yo, Okorori yo. / Akane wa yoi koda, Nenneshina."* Her voice cracked as if she could see her dead child in her arms. It was creepy as shit. And it was definitely time for Amy to make her exit.

"Thanks for the present," Amy said, getting up and stuffing the comb in her pocket. "But I really have to get to my next delivery before the food gets cold." She didn't wait for Mariko to acknowledge her and instead practically sprinted out the door like a bat out of crazy-lady hell, back to the safety of her unit.

CHAPTER TWENTY-THREE

CARA

OUT OF THE DOZEN OR SO PEOPLE WHOSE NAMES JIM HAD scrawled down on the napkin, Cara had expected a few of them. Shane MacCullum had been Ellie Wright's partner in crime. Mariko Ishida's husband, David Collins, was also on the list, as well as Lonnie Mercer's mother's boyfriend, Jake Winston. But there was one name on the list that Cara hadn't come across before—Michael Lovansky.

Lovansky was the ex-husband of the schoolteacher Debra Blackmon. And Cara's digital sleuthing revealed very little about him after his divorce. Lovansky seemed to have disappeared off the face of the earth a number of years ago. Not even a bank account. That raised some red flags.

"Did you know about these people?" Cara asked J.B. after bringing him up to speed on her conversations with Mariko and Jim.

"Sipley told me that Point Mettier's supposed to be a safe haven from domestic abusers, but I hadn't been given an actual list. And I hadn't thought of a possible connection to the body. You really think one of the women here shot up her ex and then cut him up?"

It seemed as if Cara learned something new every day about the town, which was both literally and figuratively shrouded in fog. The knowledge that women were in some way protected here gave her a new perspective as well as inner qualms about whether she was kicking up something she shouldn't be. "I don't know if I'm ready to go that far." At this point, Cara was just trying to get an ID on the body. "I'm going to check with Chuck to see if he keeps receipts of sales. Maybe one of the men on this list purchased something with a credit card there."

"Roger that."

CARA HEADED TO the shop, where Chuck was at his usual perch on his stool and had his newspaper laid out before him. His inanimate zoo of stuffed wildlife peered down at her from the walls.

"Out of provisions already?" he inquired when she came to the counter.

"I need to check to see if you made any sales to any of these men on the dates of October twenty-fifth through the twenty-seventh. Do any of the names ring a bell?" She slid over a copy of the list to Chuck, who looked at it for only a beat.

"No, I'm afraid not. I don't notice names—or faces, for that matter."

"This guy had an arrow tattoo on his cheek."

Chuck gave a shrug of the shoulders. "You know, I'm just not a people person."

Cara had thought that they had developed a friendlier rapport, given that she was probably his best customer. In the five days that she had been stranded in the town, not only had she purchased meats and basic toiletries from him, but she had also raided his clothing racks and now sported a men's long-sleeve shirt from the shop; thankfully it had only a little embroidered POINT METTIER logo on it instead of some of the tackier advertising that adorned most of his collection. Chuck's noncommittal answers now made him seem as frosty as the rest of Point Mettier's residents.

"How about receipts? You got those?"

"A lot of people pay by cash. For credit cards, I'd have to have Marge pull them out. She's better with the digital stuff. I'm a strictly analog kind of guy."

"Marge?"

"Marge is my wife."

Somehow, Cara had pictured Chuck to be a bachelor. "All right, give Marge the list and let me know what you find," Cara said.

Chuck went back to his newspaper, signaling that the conversation was over, but just as Cara was about to leave, his seventies-style rotary phone rang.

"Yellow," Chuck answered. He listened for a beat, then put the phone down. He stiffened and his demeanor grew dark, as if he had just been told his dog had died. He looked up at Cara. "You got a weapon?" he asked; then he grabbed a twenty-six-inch-barrel hunting rifle off the rack behind him.

"What is it? What's going on?" she asked, alarmed.

"Men on snowmachines approaching. Ellie says they are armed."

"Maybe they're Anchorage PD," Cara offered.

"I don't think so, Ms. Kennedy," Chuck said with leaden gravity, opening the latch behind the counter. "Excuse me, ma'am." He moved around her, holding on to his rifle.

Cara felt for her Glock in her holster before following him. "Now, hold on," she said.

When they got to the lobby, the elevator doors opened and Ellie stepped out with an AR-15. Chief Sipley and J.B. both came from the direction of the police office, also armed.

Cara's alertness was heightened. "Whatever's going on, police should handle this. Ellie and Chuck should go back to their rooms."

"There are seven men out there," Ellie said. "You're gonna need some backup."

"Now, Mrs. Wright—" J.B. began, but Chief Sipley interrupted.

"These two can shoot blindfolded better than either of you," Chief Sipley said. "They can stay."

"Are we shooting people now? What is it you're not telling me?" Cara demanded.

"Ready or not, here they come," Ellie said.

As if on cue, a low buzz, like the drone of bumblebees, started to fill the air. Everyone seemed to hold their breath for a moment. They turned their attention toward the snowy landscape outside the glass doors.

Cara squinted, making out dots approaching in a line in the distance, like black ants, kicking up powder as they moved. As they got closer, it became clearer that they weren't ants but snowmobiles, steadily approaching the building. The noise grew from a buzz to a rumble to a ground-trembling thunder.

There were four snowmobiles, three of them carrying tandem

riders, descending toward the snow-covered lot in front of the Dave-Co's main entrance. All seven men were unrecognizable beneath their neoprene masks and reflective sunglasses. They were a post-apocalyptic band of *Mad Max* snow bikers bundled in fur and leather boots, and as Ellie had said, all of them were armed—with semiautomatic weapons, no less.

CHAPTER TWENTY-FOUR

CARA

THE AIR STUNG LIKE A SHARPENED RAZOR, CUTTING AT CARA'S face and nipping at her clothes. She hadn't prepared to leave the building and hadn't brought her coat with her. Once she was outside, her teeth chattered of their own accord.

A few of the men got off their vehicles, and now Cara wasn't complaining about the extra firepower Ellie and Chuck provided. Everyone except Cara lifted their weapons, ready to engage in an all-out battle.

"You men mind telling us what business you got here?" Chief Sipley yelled out to them.

The man in front, clearly the alpha, swung off his snowmobile and pulled off his mask. From his neck sprang a tattooed garden of vines and foliage spiraling upward to his chin, while over his left ear, leading to his cropped hairline, the image of a wolf growling with its teeth bared was inked in bold black strokes. "What kind of welcome is that, Chief?" he asked.

"I don't recall ever sending you an invitation, Wolf. Now, why don't you head back to your village?"

Cara swiveled toward Sipley. "You know these men?" She looked back at the unmasked snowmobiler and didn't see a trace of any Native features. She knew from her experience in Anchorage, though, that there were a lot of bad seeds who married into tribes and lived in Native villages where policing forces were virtually nonexistent.

"There's no law against us being here," Wolf said, and sucked his teeth.

"What do you want?" Sipley asked.

"We want to pick up provisions and then stay here the night."

"We're all full up," Ellie said with a near growl.

"Now, that hurts. I know that ain't true." Wolf's gaze was laser-like, reading each person's expression as well as the weapons they carried.

"I have the right to refuse business," Ellie responded, unfazed.

"I don't know if you've noticed, but we're in the middle of a fucking storm."

"That didn't keep you from getting here, did it?" J.B. chimed in. Cara wasn't sure whether he was familiar with Wolf as well, but his tenor wasn't any less hostile than Ellie's.

"Listen." Wolf spoke slowly, as if he were trying to explain to a group of grade schoolers. "We're shit out of propane, and since the tunnel's closed, we need to buy some from you. Storm wasn't bad when we left the village, but now it's a fuckin' blizzard. Not our fault. You know, it'd look real shitty if we were to be found like goddamn frozen Popsicles in your jurisdiction."

Cara looked at Sipley. This man named Wolf had a point. She didn't like the look of these men, but they couldn't exactly deny them shelter on the basis of appearances in the midst of this snowstorm. They hadn't, as far as she knew, committed any crime.

"We'll fuckin' pay for the rooms," Wolf added, making it even harder to come up with a legal reason to turn his posse away.

Chief Sipley had to mull for a moment. "You're going to have to hand over your weapons first," he finally said. "This is a condo residence, and if you stay here, you gotta abide by house rules. All nonresidents need to check their weapons."

Ellie gave him a sour look. Cara got the feeling she would have preferred the frozen-Popsicle version of these men.

"We ain't gonna give you our weapons, but how about we keep 'em outside?" Without waiting for an answer, Wolf turned to one of his men. "Leon, lock up the weapons." A squat man with a graying handlebar mustache and goatee got off his vehicle. He walked with a stiff limp, gathering the men's weapons and putting them in a black box. Then he made a show of locking the box. "Satisfied now?" Wolf flashed a crooked-toothed smile.

Sipley, J.B., Chuck, and Ellie relaxed their holds on their guns.

"Not 'til we give you a proper pat-down," Sipley said.

"Only if she does the patting," Wolf retorted, pointing his gloved finger at Cara.

"Fuck off," Cara responded. J.B. and Chuck stepped forward instead.

Cara didn't wait for whatever smart-ass words came out of Wolf next. She headed back into the building to shake off the cold and the general vibe of creepiness that Wolf emanated. She took a deep inhale to settle herself, and for once she felt more comfortable behind the enclosed walls of the Dave-Co than outside them.

CHAPTER TWENTY-FIVE

LONNIE

LONNIE HAD TWO HAT TREES FULL OF BERETS. SHE DIDN'T like the ones that people had given her with patterns, stripes, snowflakes, plaid, flowers, decorations. She put those on the tree away from the door. She preferred the hats that had one solid color. Her first beret was one she had made herself when she was still at the Institute, on one of their craft days. It was a tan-colored one, but it got dirty and Chief made her throw it out. Now Lonnie had blue ones, yellow ones, pink ones, orange ones, gray ones. Each beret had its own special place on the tree. Once, Chief bought her a maroon-colored beret and tried to put it where her orange beret was supposed to go. That made her very upset.

Today was a green day. Green like asparagus, limes, leaves, moss, celery, grass.

Lonnie ate her oatmeal. Then she put on her green beret and went to feed Denny his oats. She gave him a good brushing and petted him on his muzzle. She cleaned his stall, put fresh bedding and fresh water in the trough. The voices in her head were quiet when she worked.

When the weather was good, she went to Star Asian Food. Today was a green day, but the weather was bad, so after Lonnie walked Denny around the paddock, she went back to her room and prepared canned soup. *Chunky chicken soup. Soup for brains. Soup's on. Super mart. Super saver. Save her.*

After lunch, Lonnie worked on her jigsaw puzzles. Lonnie loved puzzles. *Questions. Mysteries. Riddles. Mind bogglers. Brainteasers. Head games. They found the head. Off with his head!* She liked touching the pieces, feeling their shapes, matching the colors. The straight-edged ones were easy, so she always started with them. The inside pieces were harder. They looked like nothing—just paint swirls. But when everything was fitted together, it was like a surprise. Pretty houses on pretty islands. Or sometimes they were fluffy dogs or cats. Some were cities she had seen on TV, like San Francisco or New York or London. All these cities were nothing like Point Mettier. They had so many colors and lights and roads. Lonnie had a good eye for matching shapes and colors. She could see how the pieces fit. *Bits. Fragments. Scraps. Slices. Cuts.* She saw an arm, a leg, a foot, a head. They were sawed off. In pieces. Lonnie worked on the pieces of her jigsaw puzzle.

IT WAS TUESDAY. Tuesday nights were therapy nights. At the Institute, Lonnie had to take pills every morning. White ones. Blue ones. Pink ones. "Lonnie, be a good girl and take your medicine." But after Chief got her out, he told her she didn't need to take any "dang pills" anymore, because they "kill your brain," but she could go sit in the women's circle and talk with Mr. Marino instead.

Mr. Marino used to be a doctor, before he came to Point Mettier. He didn't look like any of the doctors at the Institute. He didn't wear a white coat. He just wore the same normal clothes he wore in the shop—jeans and a flannel shirt. He led the talking. People were always talking about her.

They used the space on the first floor where there was church on Sundays. Pastor Wilson used to lead church, but then he got tired of living in the Dave-Co, like a lot of the other people who came and left. Lonnie knew the minister wasn't going to last because of the way he was always saying "Blessed this," "Blessed that," and "Praise God," with a smile on his face. Everybody pretends about something, but Lonnie knew that when people pretended too hard to be nice, they couldn't live very long at the Dave-Co. "Eventually, people are gonna have a mental catastrophe," was how Chief described it. Lonnie didn't even bother to remember the names of people she knew would be gone after winter.

Lonnie didn't go to church. Once, Chief brought her to church and she started saying "Praise the Lord" and "Amen" after every sentence, like she saw on TV, and then Pastor Wilson got really angry, so then Chief said it was better for her to "commune with God" from her room.

Since Pastor Wilson had left, a new minister had driven out from Anchorage every Sunday while they looked for someone else. Last Sunday, though, there was no service because the tunnel was closed.

Tuesday nights they could use the church space for the women's circle. Everyone who came was a woman, except, of course, Mr. Marino. He asked all the questions. "How are you sleeping?" "What have you been thinking and doing since our last session?" "How'd it make you feel?" "Is there anything you want to talk about?" Mr. Marino wanted to know everything. The women in the circle talked about their husbands. *Yelling. Screaming. Punching. Slapping. Kicking. Hitting. Bruising.*

Mariko and Mrs. Blackmon were usually in the circle, and the lady in 304. Lonnie knew she wouldn't last long, so she didn't bother to remember her name. The lady in 304 cried a lot and then laughed afterward. Lonnie knew she was one of those people having a mental catastrophe and would be gone soon. The women talked and talked. Sometimes they cried.

Mr. Marino always wanted Lonnie to talk about Jake. He wanted her to remember things, like the time Jake hit Lonnie with his belt and afterward there were red welts on her leg. But Mama had told her to keep her mouth shut about those things.

At the circle, Lonnie insisted, "I'm not saying a word. You're gonna send me back to the Institute. I'm not talking to you, goddamn it."

"We're not sending you anywhere. You can talk to us. This is a safe space. It'll be our secret," Mr. Marino had said. There were lots of secrets. Mr. Marino always wanted to know everybody's secrets and everybody's feelings. *Angry. Scared. Frightened. Terrified. Cowed. Licked. Guilty.*

Lonnie was expecting to go to the women's circle, but then Mr. Marino called on the phone.

"Sorry, Lonnie," he said. "We have to cancel tonight."

Lonnie didn't like changes. Tuesday nights were supposed to be for therapy. Eight o'clock. "Why are you canceling?" she demanded.

"There are bad men in the building, Lonnie. Stay in your unit and don't go out," Mr. Marino said.

Bad men. Malicious. Vicious. Evil. Evil eye. An eye for an eye. People were always watching.

CHAPTER TWENTY-SIX

CARA

CARA WATCHED THE BAND OF SNOWMOBILERS GO THROUGH a thorough pat-down outside while she vigorously rubbed the warmth back into her hands. When they were done, Wolf and two of his cohorts headed for Chuck Marino's for supplies, while Chief Sipley and J.B. escorted the rest of the men up to the Cozy Condo check-in. Ellie, with a tight grip still on the AR-15, cursed her way toward the elevator after them.

Cara felt it was her duty to have Chuck's back, so she loitered behind, eyeing the trio and standing by the door, acting as an impromptu security guard.

"We're gonna need five tanks," Wolf announced, leaning his arms on the counter.

"I've only got two left," Chuck responded.

"Well, I guess we'll take what you got, then."

Chuck went into a back room behind the counter for the tanks, careful to take his rifle with him.

Wolf's two cohorts—the one named Leon, who was older and had a limp, and a lean, younger man whose features were a mix of white and Native—perused the store, picking through things that looked edible. They were an odd pair of opposites wearing similar duds. Cara wasn't familiar with all the tribal designations and geography of the hundreds of disparate Native villages in Alaska, but if she had to guess, the mixed-race man was possibly part Alutiiq. She noticed a tribal art tattoo on his wrist.

While he waited, drumming his fingers on the counter, Wolf glanced back at Cara and gave her a lewd grin that made the hair on the back of her neck stand on end. Then he sauntered toward her.

"You're not a resident here. I can tell. You a cop from Anchorage?"

Cara wondered how he had figured this out. Perhaps it was her gun belt, which she made sure he could see. "And if I am?"

"Heard about a murder here on the radio. Isn't that right, boys?"

Leon let out a "Yup." The other remained silent.

"What exactly did you hear?"

"Something 'bout a body washing up. Fuckin' chopped into pig slop's what they said."

"Did you know the guy?" What Cara really wanted to ask was, "Did you kill him?"

"You got a name or a photo?"

Cara pulled up the grim photo on her cell phone and showed it to him.

"Holy shit!" She couldn't tell if Wolf was grinning or grimacing at the sight of the severed head. He stepped in closer, putting his ungloved hand over hers so he could move the phone closer. She instinctively pulled back as if she had just been seared by hot coals, and he chuckled.

"I ain't gonna bite," he said. He smelled like an ashtray mixed with sweat, making her recoil even further. "What do I get in exchange? A little tit for tat?" he asked.

"Maybe it'll save you a trip to an interrogation room in Anchorage," Cara responded, unable to disguise her disgust.

"What room was he staying in?" Wolf asked, referring to the photo.

Odd question, Cara thought. "How did you know he was staying here, and is that supposed to affect whether you knew him or not?"

Wolf smiled. "I like you, little lady," he said, showing his yellowed, drug-slanted teeth. "You got cheek."

Cara restrained her impulse to slap him. "It's Officer Kennedy."

"I didn't know he was staying here, but I guess now I do." He called the other men, "Hey, Leon, Willie, come take a look."

The other two came over, putting Cara in an uncomfortable corner. She held the phone screen as far away from her person as possible.

Leon looked at the human head with as much equanimity as he viewed the animal heads mounted on the walls of Chuck's store.

The man named Willie, on the other hand, winced and said, "Fuck!" The color seemed to drain from his face and Cara wondered whether it was a reaction to the gore or because he knew the victim.

"Do you recognize him?" she persisted.

"Hard to say. It's not his best face, if you know what I mean," Leon said, then laughed at his own joke. Willie was silent.

Chuck reemerged and rolled out two propane tanks. The three

men turned their attention back to their purchases, but not before Wolf winked at Cara and said, "I got my eye on you, little lady."

CARA FELT LIKE she needed to take a shower to wash off the odor and vile aura of her encounter with Wolf and his men. She marched into the police station and confronted Sipley.

"You need to stop fucking around with me and tell me who those people are. Did they kill Charles Dodger, or whatever the hell his real name is?"

J.B., who usually took a courtside seat to their interchanges, chimed in this time. "Chief, is there something you haven't been telling us?"

Sipley frowned at the chorus of distrust and rubbed his chin. "Now, hold on. I don't want those men here any more than you do, so don't make me out to be the bad guy here. I can't say whether Wolf or any of his men killed Mr. Dodger or not. It's possible. He and his gang have a reputation. Smuggling drugs and dealing in nefarious operations. But they've got Native protection, so they're out of our hands."

"Why didn't you tell me about them before?"

"Never think about them much. They settled in Chugach Village not too long ago. They've only come once before and they weren't armed to the teeth back then."

"Given the proximity of the village, they should be questioned for information regarding the murder," Cara said.

"You'll have to get the *AST* involved, then." There was obvious disdain in Sipley's voice when he referred to the Alaskan State Troopers.

AS A BLUSTERY night curtained down on Point Mettier, Cara lay awake in her bed, eschewing the blue pills to remain lucid in case Wolf and his men were intent on causing mayhem.

The storm contributed to her unease as the building audibly shivered, and Cara felt unsure at times whether the wind was howling or the men down the hall were breaking into ungodly laughter. There were thumps and creaks that suddenly startled her, keeping her in a half-sleep state, questioning whether every noise she heard could be attributed to flying debris or the shifting bones of the building. At times, she felt certain that someone was actually walking in the hallway past her door.

A sound like something rolling finally caused her to bolt upright. She wasn't sure if the rumble had been real or some part of a troubled dream, but it made her think of little Susie on her scooter. If she was out there while Wolf's men were on the floor, it could spell trouble. With her eyes now wide open, Cara got dressed. As she pulled on her jeans, the combination of grogginess and the listing building gave her the sensation of being on a swaying ship.

She strapped her holster on and stepped into the hallway. It was lit in an unearthly yellow glow.

Susie was nowhere to be seen, but a scraping sound, followed by a muted crashing sound from down the hall, immediately caught her attention. She'd started to make her way toward the noise when a high-pitched cackle behind her startled her and she instinctively put a hand on her Glock.

She saw two of Wolf's men loitering behind her in the hallway, both Caucasian and heavily tatted like their leader. One had blond hair and the other had dark hair and eyes to match. "What are you two doing?" she asked.

"Why? Do we need a hall pass?" the blond one taunted. He had a gruff voice that sounded like cigarettes and metal. He had bloodshot eyes and his teeth were as ugly and decayed as Wolf's from drug use. "We were planning on playing hooky, Teach. 'Cause there's so much to do here in this fun little town."

Dark Eyes preferred to stay quiet, staring at her while he picked something from his teeth.

Cigarettes and Metal pointed a jittery finger at Cara. "Maybe you can tell us where to find some action," he said, then planted a hand on the wall behind her and leaned in toward her.

Cara pulled her Glock out and held it to his stomach. "Back the hell off," she said through gritted teeth.

At that moment, a door opened down the hall and Wolf stood in the doorway. He regarded the three for a moment before saying, "Leave the little lady alone." Cigarettes and Metal immediately backed away and the two men grew silent.

Then Wolf cracked a tobacco-stained smile. "You know I've got dibs on her." There was something about Wolf that frightened Cara more than the other two. It was the way he seared her with his fathomless eyes and the indisputable command he had on his pack.

Just then, J.B. appeared in the hallway and paused when he saw the assembly there. Wolf pointed an imaginary gun at Cara and fired it at her. It sent shivers down her spine. J.B. shot a knife glare his way, but Wolf simply chuckled and motioned for Dark Eyes and Cigarettes and Metal to enter his suite before he shut the door.

"You okay?" J.B. asked.

"I'm good," Cara responded. "Is something up?"

"I just"—he stammered for a moment—"wanted to make sure that you weren't being bothered."

Cara smiled. She had to admit that she felt reassured there was someone in the building looking out for her in a sea of antagonists. "I'm fine," she said.

"Okay, well, you just holler if you need anything."

IT WAS AN uneasy night, with the door both locked and bolted, and Cara keeping sentry on the sofa, her Glock within easy reach.

In the morning, she was somewhat surprised to see that the rented rooms were empty, their doors gaping open, the spaces clearly vacated.

As she turned the corner toward the elevators, she saw Sipley and Ellie engaged in a heated discussion in front of one of the Cozy Condo rooms. Ellie seemed especially irate. Her red wig looked slightly askew as she admonished Sipley.

"I told you it was a bad idea renting the rooms out to those men. Who's going to pay for all the damage?"

"What damage?" Cara asked, approaching the pair.

There was no need to explain once Cara took a peek inside the room. A land-spouting tornado seemed to have struck through the room. Closets were rifled through, drawers upturned, and lamps toppled over. The mattress was gutted, with its innards littering the floor. Even the sofa looked as if it had been murdered and disemboweled. It was Room 42. Charles Dodger's room.

Now Cara realized that the noises she had heard were not from the storm but from the men destroying the room, and that Dark Eyes and Cigarettes and Metal had probably been keeping watch.

"Did you rent this room out to them?" Cara asked.

Ellie gave her a searing look. "I'm not that stupid. Even I know this room is a possible crime scene. They found their own way in."

Cara eyed the door lock, which seemed to still be intact. "Were the keys stolen?" she asked.

"No, but anyone with a good set of bump keys would be able to get in, I suppose," she said, as if she had some firsthand knowledge of this subject. Cara knew from her time on the force that "bump keys" would be part of a Robbery 101 course, if such a thing existed. Any determined thief could pick a lock with a standard tumbler-and-pin mechanism if they had a set.

"Is there anything missing here? I mean besides the soaps or the towels . . ." Sipley asked.

"Well, nothing's usable anymore. But nothing's missing."

There must have been something specific they had been looking for. Something that Charles Dodger had been carrying. The real question was, had they found what they were looking for? Regardless, Cara suspected that she hadn't seen the last of Wolf and his men.

CHAPTER TWENTY-SEVEN

AMY

THE RUMOR THAT THERE WERE BADASS TATTOOED MEN SPEND-
ing the night at the Cozy Condo spread like wildfire through the
Dave-Co. The "Village Men," as Amy called them, sometimes came
to town when the tunnel was closed and they were willing to subject
themselves to the jacked-up prices and slim pickings at Mr. Marino's
general store. Technically, they didn't live on a federally recognized
reservation. Amy had learned in history class that the Alaska Native
Claims Settlement Act of 1971 designated Native townships as "villages." Villages had the same tribal sovereign governance rights, but
Native leaders didn't want the creation of Indian reservations like
in the lower forty-eight and came up with "corporations" instead. So
Alaska villages were owned by for-profit "corporations" and the people who lived in the villages were supposed to be shareholders of the

corporations. Amy always associated the words "corporation" and "shareholders" with manicured men in suits and ancient-computer-era ticker symbols on Wall Street, so it was hard for her to imagine Natives who lived below the poverty line and without working plumbing as shareholders. Clearly, whatever they were holding shares of wasn't making them rich and they were still being screwed by Uncle Sam in some way or another. The Village Men who came to Point Mettier weren't even indigenous, or at least none of the ones who Amy had glimpsed were, which was why she didn't feel bad calling them "Village Men." She didn't know the exact history of why they were living in the village, but she had read in her Anchorage news feed once that most villages couldn't afford their own police force, so nefarious people sometimes married their way into villages or rented land from them. Amy supposed that's where she would hide out too if she were a criminal trying to get away from the law.

Amy was eager to exchange any 411 about the Village Men with Spence at school in the morning, but he was a no-show. Mrs. Blackmon was gone, as well as Troy. "Mrs. Blackmon is out sick today, with the flu, so I'll be subbing," Mr. Healy said. *Odd that all three of them were out with the flu overnight.* Since Mr. Healy wasn't exactly prepared to discuss *Macbeth* or talk about the philosophy of Socrates, he came up with watch-paint-dry sessions of self-study and quiet reading.

The highlight of the day was when Mr. Healy splayed out a bunch of college admissions material for the seniors to peruse during recess. Brochures of faraway places with medieval-looking buildings, but probably expensive as hell. Everybody's plan was to get out of Point Mettier, of course, but few of the students had the money, or the grades for a scholarship. So getting out usually meant getting a job. Mr. Healy had to try, of course, and sitting prominently in his display of brochures was the University of Alaska Anchorage. UAA had a pretty good acceptance rate, 80 percent, because, obviously, not a lot of people think about attending college in Alaska, not even Alaskans.

Marco and Celine made a lackluster attempt at looking through them. They and Amy might still take the SATs just in case they could land a scholarship.

"If anyone should apply, it's you," Celine said to Amy. "You've got the best grades."

Amy supposed Ma's homework-overlord attitude had paid off in the end.

"There are a lot of diversity grants," Marco said.

"Unfortunately, my kind of diversity isn't really a leg up," Amy lamented. Being Chinese-American did little to boost her chances, she discovered. But she bet that being North Korean would open diversity doors, if only she could legally claim that she was. Demographically, there were only a couple hundred legal North Koreans in the United States, according to some wiki post she had looked up. During another Internet surf session, she discovered that there were probably a few thousand undocumented NKs like herself. The idea that she could go anywhere outside of Point Mettier was probably out of the question. Not only would Ma be devastated, but she would wholly freak out that someone might scrutinize their papers, and then what would happen to them?

"You're gonna apply, though, right?" Celine persisted.

"Yeah," Amy said only halfheartedly. Thinking realistically, she would probably look for a local job. Work at some Chinese dive in Anchorage. They weren't going to scrutinize anyone's papers for a waitress job and she had the right experience.

WHEN SIXTH PERIOD was finally over, Amy went home and took an order for a late lunch delivery to Mrs. Wright.

"More rice, less meat!" Ma critiqued as Amy packed the lunch.

"But, Ma, Mrs. Wright said last time that she wanted less rice."

Ma clicked her tongue, took the spoon from her, and removed some of the meat like a depraved orphanage master of yore. Amy thought then and there that she was going to get out from under Ma's thumb somehow or other.

She had lied to Ma about Mrs. Wright ordering hot-and-sour soup. The soup was for the Blackmons. She figured if they were all sick, maybe they could use it, and it would be an excuse to see Spence. Amy would pay for the soup out of her tip money, of course; otherwise Ma would call Mrs. Wright and she'd be in big trouble.

She used tofu, chicken stock, red chile paste, and egg substitute. Egg substitutes were a staple around wintertime when they couldn't get real eggs. Ma had a case in one of the basement freezers. The soup was packed in containers with the flimsy plastic lids they used for take-out orders. Amy always double rubber banded the lids when there was soup because once, when she hadn't, it had made a royal mess, not only in the blue cart, but also in the hallway, where she had left a trail of garlicky liquid that had dripped in the elevator and down the hall. She had tried sopping the mess up with napkins, but everybody in the building knew who was responsible for the foul smell that had permeated the carpet, and she was razzed for months about it.

Amy knocked on the Blackmons' door and waited, but no one came. She had texted Spence before making the delivery, but he hadn't responded. Amy figured maybe he was too sick or sleeping.

"Hello! It's me, Amy," she yelled toward the door. "I bear thee soup." She tried texting again, but still there was no response from Spence. Amy started to seriously worry. She wondered if it was possible that all three of them were too sick to even come to the door.

She stood there for a beat, contemplating whether to turn back and go home. Then she decided it wouldn't hurt for her to tiptoe in, leave the soup for them on the counter, and head back, so she reached behind the hall light where she knew there would be a little magnetic box with a key in it. She knocked one more time for good measure before slipping the key into the lock.

Everything was space-walk-like quiet. Amy unpacked the soup and placed it on the Formica counter, and the eerie silence gave her the chills. It didn't feel as if anyone was there. "Mrs. Blackmon?" No answer. "Spence?" Again nothing. She went to Spence's room and rapid-knocked before walking in. He wasn't there. The bed was neatly made.

Feeling a kind of unexplained panic, she rushed to Troy's room and flung the door open. Also empty. She knew that Mrs. Blackmon wouldn't be in her room either but checked it anyway.

Amy hastily pulled out her cell phone and dialed Spence's number. "I'm sorry, the number you are trying to reach is currently unavailable," came the recorded message. *What the fuck? Where could they have gone? How could they have possibly taken off with the storm outside and the tunnel closed?*

She paced the hallway with dread-filled adrenaline. She had this terrible feeling that something bad had happened or was about to happen. As a last measure, she checked the coat closet and saw that Spence's heavy down jacket was gone, along with Troy's and Debra's.

She tried reaching Spence on her cell a few more times and left rambling text messages, but to no avail.

Thoughts raced up and down like a roller coaster in her mind. It was unlike Spence not to leave a message and to take off with the whole family. Maybe there had been some kind of medical emergency and they had somehow managed to get a medevac to chopper them out despite the storm. Was Spence or Troy in a life-endangering situation? Or maybe the medevac had picked them up and then crashed in some godforsaken wilderness on the way to Anchorage. Amy's stomach churned and her heart raced. *Please, God, let everyone be okay.* She found herself falling to her knees with her hands folded in a Hail Mary.

Amy picked herself up, forcing more positive thoughts. Why had she inherited Ma's worst-case-scenario mentality? She reasoned that a medevac coming into town would have made immediate headlines on the Dave-Co grapevine. No, probably Spence and his family were at the infirmary and his cell battery had died. Or maybe he was up to some practical joke by not responding to her texts. That was Spence. Full of surprises. He would be back, she reassured herself.

She didn't know how long she had been standing there when she heard a knock on the door, startling her back to life. She looked through the peephole. Obviously, the Blackmons wouldn't be knocking on their own door.

Standing outside were Detective Lady and Officer Barkowski.

CHAPTER TWENTY-EIGHT

CARA

CARA LEFT ELLIE AND SIPLEY TO HANDLE THE WRECKAGE OF the vandalized room and headed toward the police office to check in with J.B. As if she had telegraphed her thoughts, a message from J.B. pinged on her cell.

Breakthrough in case. Making us GOOD coffee. Room 714.

When she arrived at his corner unit at the end of the hall, Cara found his door agape. Inside, J.B. was carefully spooning grounds into a chemistry-lab-like contraption. At the bottom of it, a Bunsen burner flickered, heating a bulbous glass carafe filled with water. Up top, a second carafe was connected at the neck with a metal clasp, forming an hourglass piece that could have come from a vintage science catalog.

"It's a siphon brewer," J.B. said, anticipating her question as she walked in. "It's how they used to make coffee in the eighteen hundreds."

"So, did you pick up this contraption at an antiques shop on a whim?" Cara asked, genuinely curious.

J.B. chuckled. "I got it off the Internet. Siphon brewers are back in style now."

Cara watched in fascination as the water bubbled in the bottom glass and then spewed into the top one in a slowly churning eruption. The only coffeemaker she and Aaron had ever owned was a stainless steel K-Cup machine. There was never much thought put into their morning coffee ritual beyond filling the water container and pushing buttons. If she was running exceptionally late, Cara would resort to drinking the burnt-dishwater-tasting liquid that was considered "coffee" at the Anchorage PD station.

She glanced around the room, which had a similar layout to hers, but the furnishings were less grandma-reminiscent in style. Everything was clearly utilitarian rather than for design appeal. A weathered dark brown leather sofa, a couple of wooden chairs, a walnut bookcase, a simple coffee table, and a television were the only pieces of furniture that occupied the living space, but it still managed a cluttered feel, with books and papers splayed on every conceivable surface, plants on the sill in various stages of living and dying, and framed photos in no logical alignment decorating the walls.

Cara took a closer look at the photos on the walls while J.B. continued to cook up the coffee. Most of the photos were nature stills that could have come from a travel catalog used to lure tourists to Point Mettier—a frosty blue glacier perfectly mirrored in the bay; iridescent light filtering through clouds over conifer-covered mountains; and an orca pod with their fins breaching in Loch Ness formation in the sound.

There was one wood-framed photo of J.B. looking younger, with longer hair, posing with people Cara assumed were his mother, father, and sister, but she asked anyway. "Is this your family?"

J.B. looked up from his science lab. "Yup. My parents still live in Montana."

Cara could see the same jawline features in father and son and the same gentle green eyes. J.B.'s sister, meanwhile, took after his mother, with a similar charismatic smile and a slight upturn of the nose that made them both look youthful.

"We had a small farm, but my parents sold it and retired. My sister, Stacy, lives in Europe now. Portugal, to be exact. She went on an exchange program over there, fell for a local, got married, and never came back."

"Portugal. Huh." It sounded faraway and exotic. Cara herself had never traveled outside of Canada and the lower forty-eight, and she missed the trips to national parks that she and Aaron used to go on before Dylan was born.

Cara continued perusing the wall photos, and another eight-by-ten glossy that had nothing to do with nature caught her attention. She stepped in for a closer look. It was a framed photo of J.B. posing with a group of three men and two women, all holding sniper rifles and wearing camo with US flag patches waving on the sleeves.

"Were you in the military?"

"National Guard," J.B. said. "Still am, actually. We train in Anchorage once a month, and for that, I get all my student loans paid off and a chunk of extra salary."

Cara nodded. "A number of people from APD are also in the Guard."

"Milk or sugar?" J.B. poured his concoction into ceramic mugs.

"Black."

J.B. balance-walked with the coffee and noticed the lack of free space to sit on.

"Oh, sorry, let me just, uh . . ." He landed the mugs on the coffee table and quickly cleared off the books and clutter littering the sofa.

Cara settled onto the couch and took a sip. *Pure heaven.* "You've been holding out on me all this time. You should have been making coffee for us every morning."

J.B. lit up with a smile and Cara had to admit that a little fire ignited somewhere deep inside. There was something charming about the whole overture that warmed her as much as the coffee. She wondered if J.B. used to make his almost fiancée the same concoction of science brew on cold mornings and she felt a twinge of jealousy. She shook the what-ifs off her mental umbrella as J.B. handed her a manila file.

"Here's the main course. I managed to do some deep scouring and was able to dig up some info," he said.

Cara sifted through the contents of the file. They detailed Debra Blackmon and her marriage to and subsequent divorce from Michael Lovansky. Some of the info matched what Cara had already discovered. Court documents showed Lovansky had lost custody due to a pattern of domestic violence and a rap sheet of minors, including possession of drugs and drunk driving.

"Were you able to find a photo of Michael?"

"Arrest photos are there at the end."

Cara's hands nearly trembled with excitement as she flipped to the end and studied the photos. It was Charles Dodger. Thinner, less bloated, more hair, but there was no denying the crossed-arrows tattoo. Here was the key they had been searching for all along. An ID on the body. Proof positive that the man whose head was in the freezer was Debra Blackmon's ex-husband, Michael Lovansky. "This is incredible, J.B."

J.B. allowed himself a smile of acknowledgment.

"Now we can officially start looking for suspects and motives," Cara noted. "And from his history of abuse, we can deduce that Debra Blackmon clearly had a motive for killing him." But when she said the words, it was as if the wind in her sails died. "Maybe it was an act of self-defense. A justifiable homicide." *And nothing to do with my husband or son.*

"But chopping up the body and throwing the parts into the sea . . ." J.B.'s voice trailed off for a moment. "It doesn't exactly scream self-defense."

Cara had to agree. "In any case, we need to talk to Ms. Blackmon."

"How about we talk to her after school's out? She's not going anywhere, so, you know, maybe we can wait. No need to scare the kids." That was J.B., always trying to be thoughtful. And he was right. They didn't have a warrant for her arrest, so it would have to be a "friendly visit" anyway.

"MRS. BLACKMON?" J.B. rapped on the navy blue–painted door but got no answer. He knocked a little more loudly, but there was still no response. After a moment, he pulled out his cell. "I'll call the school to see if she stayed behind," he said, but just as he started punching in numbers, the door cracked open and they found Amy Lin peering out at them with an expression of dread mixed with surprise.

"They're not here," she said in a mouse whisper. Then she stepped aside, making way for them.

How is Amy involved in every aspect of the case? Cara wondered to herself. But then again, with two hundred or so residents, she supposed it wasn't out of the question.

"How did you get in?" J.B. asked.

"I . . . Spence gave me a key," Amy said, stuttering. "I brought soup." She pointed to the take-out tubs on the counter as proof.

"Mrs. Blackmon ordered soup?" Cara asked.

"No, I just brought it by for them because I heard they were sick."

"Spence and Amy are dating," J.B. clarified for Cara's sake.

"Are all three of them gone?" Cara asked, and Amy nodded.

"None of them came to school today." Amy continued to whisper for no apparent reason.

J.B. was already checking the rooms to confirm that no one else was in the apartment.

"Do you know where they went? Was there anything unusual you noticed? When was the last time you were in contact with Spence?" Cara asked, and Amy seemed to shrink inward with the barrage of questioning.

She shrugged her shoulders. "I talked to Spence yesterday, but I haven't seen him today and he hasn't answered any of my calls or texts. I have no idea where they are. I was just . . . kind of waiting to see if they'd be back." Amy bit her lip for a moment. Then her tough-girl facade finally reemerged. "My mom's expecting me. Can I go now?" Then she looked at her phone as if she had better things to do and her time was being wasted.

"If there's anything that you're not telling us, Amy, you need to let us know."

She responded with a noncommittal "uh-huh" and started to head out, but then doubled back for the soup and took the cartons with her.

As expected, J.B. came up empty in his once-over of the unit. "I'll check with the infirmary just in case they really are sick," he said, dialing on his cell.

Cara walked through the living area. There was an eeriness to it. A Pieter Claesz painting of life interrupted. Dishes were still in the sink. An open jar of peanut butter sat next to a still-crudded knife and crumbs on a plate. On the dining table were stacks of papers in the midst of being graded with red pen markings. In the living area, a now-warm, half-filled glass of orange juice had made sweat rings on the coffee table.

"None of them have checked in with Nurse Lindbaum," J.B. confirmed. "I also checked in with Kai Peterson."

"Kai Peterson?"

"He rents out snowmobiles. Nobody's rented anything from him since the storm began."

"Do you know what kind of car Mrs. Blackmon drives?"

"The license plates are registered in the condo's database," J.B. offered. "Although it's hard to imagine that they could drive anywhere with the tunnel closed."

"There was a road I saw when I came in, leading away from the tunnel."

"It dead-ends at the cove. Plus, roads only get plowed on Fridays. That's when everybody makes their Costco runs to Anchorage. But, of course, until the tunnel's reopened, I doubt there'll be any plowing action at all."

None of this news was good.

Out of the corner of her eye, Cara spotted something almost out of view behind a lamp on the credenza near the door. It was a black leather handbag. Cara paced over to it. There was nothing unusual about the purse—practical in size and unadorned with any designer labels or flashy patterns. The only thing that stood out for Cara was the fact that it had been left behind. She rummaged through its contents and pulled out a wallet.

"That's odd." J.B. echoed Cara's thoughts.

"Her ID and credit cards are still here," Cara confirmed. "She wouldn't intentionally go very far without these." Was it just coincidence that the Blackmons' disappearance aligned with the arrival and departure of Wolf and his men? And why did it seem as though there was an element of hastiness or surprise in the way they had left their unit?

J.B.'s demeanor turned grave. "Do you think . . ."

Cara finished his thought for him. "That they could have been kidnapped?"

CHAPTER TWENTY-NINE

LONNIE

TODAY WAS A RED DAY.

Red like raspberries, apples, the barn, Mama's dress, blood on the floor, the whirling lights at the Institute. She heated up some frozen raspberries for Denny. Lonnie put on her red beret.

The storm had passed and the sun was peeking out, so Lonnie decided to take Denny for a walk. She put on her snowshoes and put the leash on Denny. *Schlick schlack. Schlick schlack.* Lonnie liked the crunching sound her shoes made on the packed snow. It was the sound of something *crisp* and *new* and *white* all put together. She liked it almost as much as the sound of unwrapping one of Mariko's gift boxes with the dolls inside.

She patted Denny's fur and coaxed him out of the stall with his leash. It wasn't tourist season anymore and there weren't any hunters out, so she let Denny go free. He got excited, lifting his legs up high to make his way through the snow. He trotted out in front of her, but not too far. He sometimes stopped to chew leaves or branches peeking above the snow. They headed toward the trees. *Schlick schlack.* Toward the woods.

When Lonnie had found Denny in these woods, the hunters were there with their rifles, their camo jackets, their camo pants and camo hats. They carried heavy backpacks filled with lots of things just to kill a poor moose. They had binoculars and giant guns with giant scopes. Lonnie could see the moose plain as day. She didn't see why they needed all that equipment to spot a moose when moose were bigger than people.

BOOM! It was like an explosion. *Blast. Crack. Bang. Burst. Rupture. BOOM!* The bad man with the arrow tattoo fell to the ground, bleeding. He had a funny smile.

Lonnie's ears rang. It was like a high-pitched humming, like the buzz of the electric lights in the Institute. Then the hum grew louder, like angry bees. It was getting bigger and bigger.

When Lonnie found Denny, he was still a baby. *Bye, baby bunting, / Daddy's gone a-hunting, / Gone to get a rabbit skin, / To wrap the baby bunting in.*

Lonnie heard all the voices and other sounds. She didn't know if it was happening then or if it was something she was hearing in her head. Everything was jumbled like the pieces in her jigsaw puzzle.

Yelling and screaming. Red lights spinning.

The humming noise wouldn't go away. A swarm of bees buzzing, but she couldn't swat them away. An electric-saw swarm. A chain saw. A snowmobile. Getting closer and closer.

Denny's mama fell. *Collapsed. Toppled. Tottered. Slumped. Dropped.*

The bad man tumbled to the ground. *"I'll cut you to pieces!"* *"Cut off his head!"* She found the head and buried it in the ground.

Lonnie put Denny's leash back on and decided to go back to the barn instead of the woods. Away from all the buzzing bees. All the voices in her head. Spinning.

It was a red day.

CHAPTER THIRTY

CARA

CARA EXITED THE HASTILY DESERTED UNIT BELONGING TO the Blackmons with an unsettled feeling. She and J.B. had decided to retrieve their heavy winter coats and then reconvene outside to do some impromptu reconnaissance. At the very least, before following up on alternative theories, they needed to check the parking lot to see if the Blackmons had attempted to drive off somewhere.

As they walked down the hallway toward the elevator banks, Cara had an inscrutable feeling that someone was watching them—a faint breath or a sound that she couldn't define but that made the hair on the back of her neck stand on end. She swiveled around and scanned the hallway but saw no one. J.B. turned in the direction of her gaze.

"What is it?"

"Nothing," Cara said, spooked. *Was it her mind playing tricks on her again?* "I thought maybe there was someone behind us."

J.B. saw nothing. "They say there are ghosts that haunt Point Mettier. I heard one story about a spirit of one of the servicemen who used to live here when it was a military base who roams the hallways. Chief Sipley says he swore he heard him stomping around in his kitchen one night, but there was nobody there."

Cara remembered how J.B. had mentioned a ghost on her first night in Point Mettier. She didn't believe in ghosts, but if it was a specter of Point Mettier, at least it meant she wasn't going completely batty.

THE PARKING LOT was a large asphalt apron that wrapped around the west and south sides of the building, clearly paved at a time when the Davidson Condos were bustling with military residents, as opposed to now, when they were only half occupied. As J.B. had predicted, it didn't seem likely that any of the cars had gone anywhere, judging from the layer of white that covered the vehicles like sheets in a morgue. And there was a decided lack of tire tracks in the pristine packed snow.

There was, however, something that caught Cara's eye. "I don't suppose there's another lot?" she asked, pointing to a set of footprints that plotted beyond the concrete curb.

"No, there's always plenty of available spots," J.B. said as he scoured the ground. "There's more than one set of prints," he added.

"The men from last night, maybe?"

"Could be." J.B. paced around with his head to the ground like a hound on a hunt, then backtracked toward the entrance of the building. "Looks like this is where the snowmobiles were parked last night." Cara came to look at the indiscernible hodgepodge of boot prints intertwined with the thin parallel vestiges of the snowmobiles, like endless ticker tapes, disappearing into the east.

"But there are three sets of prints headed in the opposite direction," Cara said excitedly. "Maybe it's the Blackmons."

"Possibly. But those footprints look awfully big for Spence and Troy. At any rate, looks like they're headed toward the dock."

"Can people still take boats out?"

"Wouldn't recommend it. Especially after a storm. Water's probably iced or skim ice."

Cara, of course, was familiar with skim ice. She, Aaron, and Dylan used to drive up to Mirror Lake in winter to skip rocks along the iced surface. With each bounce across the thin, hardened top, a chirping noise like a bird emanated, delighting Dylan. Aaron was an expert at sending rocks out at just the right angle, making them bounce several times across the surface, replicating a twittering songbird flying off into the distance. But all of that now seemed like a different time in a different life.

"Did Debra own any boats?" Cara asked.

"I don't know. I hadn't thought about that. A lot of residents have boats for recreational use, but no one uses them during the winter."

They followed the prints through the snow. What was less than a five-minute drive by car took them twenty minutes on a foot slog. Cara was out of breath once they finally reached the pier. She exhaled in visible puffs.

At first appearance, it didn't look as though the water was iced, but when J.B. picked up a rock and tossed it in, it made a distinct crunching sound before it broke the surface into thin, glass-like shards.

Most of the boats had been winterized ahead of the storm, but there were two empty slips with blue tarps sitting in a pile next to them, gusting forlornly with the wind. *Why would they need two boats?*

"Looks like this one's been stolen," J.B. said, lifting up a shot-off bolt. Then he pulled out his cell. "I should tell Sipley about this, if I can get a signal." He tried patching into the station, but the call didn't seem to go through. He tried pointing his phone in different directions to no avail. "No luck."

Cara's mind raced. Two boats, one of them stolen. Were the Blackmons on one and the tattooed men on the other? The scenario weighed heavily on Cara. "There's no time to wait," Cara said with dread in her voice. If only she had found Aaron and Dylan sooner, they might still be alive. "It'll be dark soon."

J.B. gave his tacit agreement by heading quickly toward the coast guard vessel. "If the water freezes, we're toast." After they'd donned their orange PFDs, J.B. gave Cara the task of clearing the area around the vessel with an ice pole while he navigated the boat. Cara attacked the ice, stabbing as if it were the caramelized layer of a crème brûlée. J.B. eased them slowly out of the slip. The ice could damage the hull if they weren't careful.

The boat put-putted along, with Cara warily monitoring for ice scraping and scratching along the sides. The light had already begun to wane and J.B. had to switch on the headlamps, making it even harder to navigate the ice. Cara could feel the chill of the glacial wind down to her bones.

It seemed an eternity before they rounded a bend and the passageway split between open waters and Hidden Cove. J.B. switched off the motor for a moment. "You hear that?"

Cara listened intently. At first, she heard only the screech of an owl in the distance and the sound of crisp water crackling and rippling. Then she finally heard the faint, shrill scream of a woman.

CHAPTER THIRTY-ONE

CARA

J.B. PLOWED THE COAST GUARD VESSEL AROUND THE BEND, and that's when they finally spotted the muted lights of a small motorboat in the distance—a twenty-footer, sitting stalled in ice. Next to it was a trawler that had moored beside it, with a footbridge tethering the two. Some kind of scuffle was taking place on the smaller vessel. Debra Blackmon was screaming as she wielded an ice pole, trying to ward off a man wearing a neoprene mask and a fur coat. From the way he was dressed, the man was clearly one of Wolf's gang.

Another man, similarly outfitted, remained on the fishing boat with a gloved hand gripping the railing on the bow of Debra's boat, keeping the two boats close together.

J.B. trained his searchlights on the action. The flood of white temporarily blinded the men, who shielded their eyes from the glare. The two men immediately ceased their assault, scuttled back to the wheel of the trawler, then motored away faster than they ought to in the direction of Hidden Cove.

"Should we go after them?" J.B. shouted to Cara.

"We should get Mrs. Blackmon and the kids back to safety first," Cara said. Hypothermia was a danger in this weather.

Mrs. Blackmon stood on the deck, still holding the ice pole. And even with her layers, she looked pale blue and was shivering from cold or fright; Cara wasn't sure which. Cara didn't know whether Debra was glad or upset to see them.

"What are you doing out here?" Cara asked. "Where are the boys?"

"What do you mean? Aren't they at the condo?"

Cara looked at J.B., uncertain if Mrs. Blackmon was covering or telling the truth, but J.B. seemed to think the schoolteacher needed some reassurance.

"They're probably staying with some friends," he said.

Mrs. Blackmon's expression immediately turned dark; she wasn't buying into J.B.'s optimism. "Did those men take them?"

"You mean Wolf's men?" Cara asked, voicing the same suspicion. "Why would they take them?"

"Because . . ." Mrs. Blackmon paused as if summoning all her inner courage. "I killed Michael." Mrs. Blackmon began sobbing hysterically. "And Michael worked for Wolf."

CHAPTER THIRTY-TWO

AMY

AMY HAD TRIED SEVERAL TIMES TO REACH SPENCE VIA CELL, but the message remained the same. "The number you are trying to reach is unavailable. At the tone, please record your message." That probably meant either his battery was dead or he wasn't in the building. She had left at least ten trying-not-to-sound-too-desperate-while-being-authentically-worried messages overnight to no avail. She even called the infirmary, but Nurse Lindbaum had told her that none of the Blackmons had been through.

At school, rumors and theories swirled. That was the thing about Point Mettier. It was hard to ditch or be absent for any reason without everyone knowing why. People were always in your business, so naturally the disappearance of the Blackmons was all anybody talked about that day. Even Mr. Healy stopped Amy as she headed out at the lunch bell. "Have you heard anything from Spence or Mrs. Blackmon?"

"No, Mr. Healy," Amy responded truthfully, and maybe she just imagined this, but the worry lines on his forehead seemed to actually multiply. That, in turn, stirred Amy's stress butterflies. She had already been chewing off her nails through third period so that they were ugly, sandpapery-looking stubs.

She headed to the long tables where the kids ate sack lunches or carried their trays of cafeteria fare. Ma always made Amy take leftovers from Star for lunch, but Amy sometimes tossed her lunch and used her tip money to break the monotony with pizza, lasagna, or whatever other unhealthy food was being served up. Sometimes she would grab something from Mr. Marino's general goods store. Ma would have killed her if she knew, of course. Today, after chucking her prepared lunch, she took out a foam-cup instant noodle pack she had bought from Mr. Marino and used the kitchen's hot water to prepare it. She knew this was complete sacrilege since noodles were on the Star menu and Ma's noodles were probably healthier than the instant, preservative-filled lunch in a cup, but today Amy needed the junk-food comfort.

As Amy distractedly stirred the MSG-filled goodness, Marco sat down next to her. "What do you think happened to them?" was the first question out of his mouth. Celine and a couple of other kids, Anna and Joshua, joined them and leaned in toward her to get the scoop.

"I honestly don't know," Amy confessed. "I can't even reach his cell." It was all she could do to keep from breaking down into sobs in that moment.

"Think it had something to do with those Village Men?" Celine asked. She twisted her blond hair, and Amy's completely out-of-context thought bubble was about how Celine's nervous habit made her somehow look sexy while Amy's own nail-chewing insecurity just disfigured her hands and was anything but attractive.

"Or the murder?" Joshua joined in.

The word "murder" stirred up a new set of stress butterflies.

"Do you think maybe they've been cut up and thrown into the sea too?" Marco had to ask.

The thought had never entered Amy's mind until then. She nearly spit out her noodles. She must have turned positively pale, because Celine said, "Shut up, Marco—you're scaring us. Let's think positive thoughts."

Marco grew quiet, but the frightening image of the Blackmons cut up into pieces was seared permanently into Amy's brain. Now, instead of wondering whether Spence was in a crashed helicopter on a forest floor, she had to wonder if he was somewhere at the bottom of the icy sound . . . in pieces.

Amy couldn't bring herself to finish her instant noodles after that. "I don't feel so good," she said to her lunch group. "Maybe it's the MSG."

"See what you did?" Celine berated Marco, who flushed red with guilt and embarrassment.

"Sorry," he said.

Amy got up from the bench and tossed the rest of her lunch into the waste bin. She said her "see you laters" to her classmates and then went to find Mr. Healy, who was still in the classroom, mid-bite of his homemade sandwich. He took one look at her and said, "Are you all right, Amy? You don't look well."

"Can I have a sick absence for the rest of the day?"

Healy nodded. "You ought to go see Nurse Lindbaum."

"Just something I ate," Amy said, a half-truth.

Mr. Healy looked at her sympathetically and gave her an "I understand" nod. "Okay, Amy, you're excused."

NOW THE THOUGHTS that spun like a washing machine rinse cycle in Amy's head were of things Spence had told her not too long ago. After Mr. Healy's roots-discovering extra credit assignment, when Amy found out she was Korean, she had kept the results to herself, but that didn't mean she wasn't going to nose through everyone else's results. Amy felt envious at the time, seeing all the international origins, like Finland, France, Italy, Iberia, South America, Africa, the Balkans, and other far-off regions of the earth. The colorful breakdowns were so much more exotic and sexy than the nearly monotone graphs of her own results. Her classmates' forefathers were doers, adventurous travelers, and intermarriers, while hers were stay-at-homers.

Spence, on the other hand, who was the only other student who had actually opted out of the assignment, didn't seem the least bit interested. He had never really talked about his dad. His dad was just some typical broken-home statistic whom Spence had never mentioned even once. Until now, they had maybe an unspoken code about not questioning the missing half of their respective parents. But Amy broke the code and dared to ask, "Aren't you even slightly curious? Like, maybe you'll find out more about your dad."

"Fuck my dad," was Spence's answer, and that was the end of that.

Then, right before the body parts were found, Spence had said that his family might have to go to Anchorage for a bit, and Mr. Healy would have to sub for his mom while they were gone, but he had been really vague about it. "A relative died," was his explanation. So Amy assumed it was some funeral they had to go to, but then in the end they didn't even go. "Did your relative get miraculously cured of whatever they were dying of?" she had asked.

"Yeah, sort of," Spence had said. But knowing all his tells, Amy knew he had been lying. The whole thing about the relative was some story to cover for something else, but he never gave her another clue.

She was sure that the dismembered man with the arrow tattoo and the Village Men on snowmachines were somehow connected, and the Blackmons' being dead was now becoming a real possibility in Amy's mind.

CHAPTER THIRTY-THREE

CARA

J.B. LOOKED UNCOMFORTABLE CUFFING DEBRA BLACKMON—
as uncomfortable as anyone would be, sending a neighbor to be
locked up. "I'm sorry, Mrs. Blackmon. Watch your step," he said as
he helped her onto the coast guard vessel, while Cara beamed a path
for them with a flashlight. Mrs. Blackmon had something of a dazed
look on her face, as if she had just been woken from a coma.

Cara was in a similar state of numbness. She had suspected for a
while that this case would have nothing to do with Aaron and Dylan,
and Debra's confession was a proverbial nail in the coffin. A finality,
which made Cara question what she had been doing for the last year.
She had been so desperate to make sense of Aaron's and Dylan's
deaths. To take control over her loss by finding answers to nonexis-

tent questions. To try to solve a crime that had never been perpetrated. Perhaps it was time to let go. She couldn't wind back the clock. She couldn't bring them back.

"Are you all right, Mrs. Blackmon?" Cara asked, finally shaking herself to life.

Debra sat down on a bench, teeth chattering despite the blanket J.B. and Cara had wrapped around her. "I'm fine," she said. "Just find my kids."

Debra was right. Now it was time to focus on Debra and her kids.

"Those two men. Did you recognize them?" J.B. asked.

"No, but I'm sure they were part of Wolf's gang."

"But there were only two of them," J.B. noted.

"Did you see anyone else?" Cara asked. Debra shook her head no.

"What did they want from you?"

"I think it was retaliation for killing Mick."

Cara tried to piece together the story, which wasn't completely adding up in her mind. "So, you killed your ex-husband, cut him up with a saw—"

"Chain saw," Debra corrected.

"And ditched him in the ocean?"

"Yes. I thought he would be harder to identify that way. Lots of parts have been washing up, so that's where I got the idea."

It was true enough; unidentifiable parts were being largely ignored and chalked up to all the possible explanations APD had mentioned—suicide jumpers or drunken cruise passengers who had fallen off the ship were some of the running theories.

"Where's the chain saw?" J.B. asked.

"Somewhere in the sound. I dumped it at the same time."

———————

ONCE THEY WERE docked at the pier, they saw that the slip where the trawler had likely been stolen from was still empty. They checked for signs of life on the other parked boats but came up negative. Most of the vessels had been winterized to prevent pipes from freezing, and in their frosty stasis were both unusable and uninhabitable in Point Mettier winters.

Cara asked Debra, "Where were you planning to go on the boat?"

"I wasn't planning on going anywhere," she stammered. "I thought I had left something in the boat and went to get it. Then I saw Wolf's men and panicked."

BACK AT THE Davidson Condos, Chief Sipley was more than a little shocked to see Mrs. Blackmon brought in with cuffs, and when J.B. explained that she had confessed to the murder of Michael Lovansky, his demeanor turned suddenly dark, as if a wrench had been thrown into his chipper wheel.

"I'll get you a cup of hot cocoa and supper," he reassured Mrs. Blackmon.

Debra was fingerprinted, photoed, and booked before she was placed in the cell that not a week ago Lonnie had occupied. Debra made much less of a fuss, though, stoically staring at a spot on the wall, contemplating the decisions that had put her there.

Once out of earshot, Cara turned to the two police officers in earnest. "I think we should head out to the cove. What if the boys are out there with Wolf and his men?"

"They'd be long gone by now. And I don't think there's much we can do in the dark in sub-zero. We ought to wait 'til morning," J.B. said, rubbing his chin, almost apologetic in his assessment.

Sipley chimed in. "He's right. I don't want to be risking either of you before making sure the boys aren't just hunkering inside somewhere with friends. We'll knock on doors tonight."

Cara reluctantly submitted. But that didn't mean she wasn't going to come up with a Plan B. Time, she knew, was of the essence.

A SOFT, MOURNFUL whimpering caught Cara's attention as she exited the elevator to her floor. It was Susie, sitting cross-legged on the carpet next to her scooter.

"What's the matter, Susie?"

"I fell," she said, tears welling in her eyes.

"Did you hurt yourself?" Cara stooped down to see if Susie had any injuries. Cara couldn't detect any visible cuts or bruises.

"I'm okay." Susie rubbed her eyes with her fists, then stood up to prove she was fine.

"Did you hit your head?"

"No."

"Are you sure? Let's go see the nurse, just in case."

"No," Susie insisted. "I was just scared. I should go back now." She trundled her scooter toward the elevator. Cara looked for signs of a limp or anything else unusual in Susie's gait but saw nothing.

"Okay, Susie, you go straight home. Tell your mom what happened."

Susie nodded and Cara pressed the elevator button for her. The doors clattered open and Susie stepped in.

Cara started to head to her room but paused when she noted a soggy spot on the floor where Susie had been sitting. *Odd.* Susie's clothes had looked dry, so Cara didn't think she had wet herself. Cara put it out of her mind, thinking perhaps Susie had gone outside earlier and tracked snow in on her shoes or on the wheels of her scooter.

CHAPTER THIRTY-FOUR

CARA

CARA BASKED IN A HOT SHOWER, DEFROSTING HERSELF AF-
ter the chilly temperatures outside. But her mind continued racing,
unable to quell the thoughts of possible danger for the Blackmon
boys. Once she toweled off, she gave J.B. a call.

"Have you found the boys?"

"Not yet," J.B. admitted. "But they still haven't searched all the
floors yet. A couple of teachers, Mr. Healy and Mrs. Sandborne, volunteered to help us search the building. Chief Sipley told me I needed
to go get something to eat."

"What if they don't find them? You know as well as I do that the
first forty-eight hours are critical."

"What do you suggest?" J.B. asked.

"Organize a search of the town. And we should also pay a visit to
Chugach Village in case they've been kidnapped."

J.B. seemed hesitant about that. "It's out of our jurisdiction. Even if kidnapping falls under the Major Crimes Act, only the AST can handle this."

"But who knows when they'll be able to clear the avalanche and get the tunnel reopened? Ellie said it took a month last time it happened," Cara said. "It's not illegal to visit the village."

J.B. put down his cautionary foot again. "I don't know, Cara. You saw what kind of firepower they were carrying, and who knows how many more men there are at the village? I think we should wait. Maybe APD can send a chopper."

This wasn't a moment to sit on their hands. They needed to find Debra's kids. Cara was determined not to fail this time. "They won't send a chopper," Cara said with authority. "Like you said, the village wouldn't be in their jurisdiction. It would take too long to drum up enough evidence for the AST to get involved. If those kids are in danger, we have to do something now." Cara had already made up her mind. "I can go alone. Just to sniff the place out."

J.B. sensed her determination. "All right, but I'm coming with you. We can go talk to Kai Peterson in the morning. He can rent us snowmobiles." He paused for a moment. "Have you eaten yet?"

Cara hadn't even thought about supper.

After a beat, waiting for Cara to respond, J.B. added, "Just started cooking stew. If you want, I can bring some over and go over the route to the village."

J.B. WAS AS good as his word. He brought up a delicious-smelling stew along with topographical maps. They unfolded the maps on the dining table to study. Chugach Village didn't look to be too far as the crow flies. It was just across the bay on the east side—a point along another jutting finger of the land mass surrounding the sound. It was probably a quick boat ride through the passage and down the bay during summer, but now, in winter, it would take an hour and a half on a snowmobile.

"This area is mountainous, so we'll want to stick to the flatlands here," he said, drawing an invisible route with his finger. "It'd be best to bundle up and bring some protein bars with you."

"And some firepower," she added. J.B.'s demeanor grew dark at that, but he didn't disagree. Cara didn't realize how hungry she really was until she dug into the hearty stew. It hit the spot and J.B. was not a bad cook. "I think Star Asian would have some competition if you ever decided to open up a joint here."

"Not part of my five-year plan," he said, but smiled just the same. After he gave her a sideways look that made her blush, he added, "You've got some on your lip." He pointed to the side of his mouth and it seemed like a cliché move as he wiped the corresponding side of her face with a napkin. But instead of following up, he turned his attention back down to the map, his cheeks suddenly glowing red. Cara had to admit she was slightly disappointed. Or was the wine she'd drunk on a mostly empty stomach making her feel heady? J.B. had been her only life raft since she had landed in Point Mettier and his charm had steadily grown on her.

When they next leaned into the map at the same time, J.B. pointing out a tricky narrow curve that rounded the inlet, Cara gave in to abandon, turned her face toward him, and could hear a slight intake of his breath as she kissed him on the lips. She felt the blood rush to her cheeks and the little fires in her belly flamed. She was certain they were both red as beets now. It was the consent he needed to finally break the tension that had been building between them, and he responded with a harder kiss back. Then things were fuzzy as to exactly what happened next and how she found herself dipping into the couch. It had been such a long time since she had felt this way.

CARA AWOKE IN the middle of the night with J.B.'s arms still resting on her naked stomach. She gently disentangled herself from his embrace and got up. She had always been a light sleeper, but it took her a moment to gain her bearings and recognize that it was the soft buzzing from her cell phone that had woken her up. She carried the phone into the living room before she answered the call from the unknown number in an almost whisper. "Hello?"

"Cara," the voice on the other side said.

Chills went up Cara's spine. The voice sounded instantly familiar, even if it was a voice she hadn't heard in more than a year. The slightly scraggly baritone caller was unmistakable to her. It was her husband. Tears came to her eyes. "Aaron?" she asked in a half plea, half question. Was he still alive? Among the tumbling thoughts that ran through her mind were that he had somehow survived the woods and been lost and was now living a nomadic life. Or perhaps a fall during that hike had left him in a state of amnesia, and it was only now that he finally remembered her.

"Aaron? Where are you?"

"Don't worry. We're fine. We'll see each other again," the voice said before the line clicked.

"Aaron!" It was all she could do to keep from yelling at full voice, and it came out like a hoarse cough. She quickly dialed the incoming number, but it led to a robotic recording. "I'm sorry. The number you are trying to reach has been disconnected or is no longer in service."

Cara tried to call back again but was answered with the same prerecorded voice. *Was it real?* Was it a message from the afterlife giving her reassurance? Or was it all in her mind? Maybe one of the kids was playing another prank on her. The stress of the case, being holed up—everything was messing with her head. She steeled herself to look down at her phone—the unknown number was still there, proving to her that at least the call had been real. Before she could try calling it back a third time, J.B. walked in.

"Who is it? Is it about the boys?" J.B.'s groggy voice came from behind her.

Cara quickly put her phone away. "It's nothing. A wrong number," she said, trying to hold her voice steady.

After J.B. headed back to the bedroom, Cara slumped down onto the floor and began sobbing softly. She was somehow distorting things in her mind. The chances of a prankster knowing what Aaron's voice sounded like were nil and she had seen her husband's DNA-verified remains buried. She glanced down at the gold band around her finger—such a small thing but it kept a massive hold on her. When she had finally decided to put the past behind her and allow herself to open the door she had kept locked, some deeper mechanism inside was slamming it shut again. Maybe she could never really be whole again.

CHAPTER THIRTY-FIVE

LONNIE

"LONNIE, HAVE YOU SEEN SPENCE OR TROY?" CHIEF ASKED. He was standing at Lonnie's door.

"Of course I've seen them," she replied.

Chief's eyes grew wide. "Where are they?"

"I don't know where they are now, but you asked if I'd seen them. I see them all the time when we pass in the hallway or in the elevator and lots of other places."

Chief sighed. "I mean, have you seen them today?"

"No."

"Okay, but if you do see them, you call me. Do you remember what Mr. Marino told you about why the therapy session was canceled?"

"Because of the bad men," Lonnie answered quickly, as if this were a quiz.

"That's right, Lonnie." He scratched his beard. "Now, we have to be careful because we don't know when those bad men might come back here. So you look into that peephole before answering the door, and give me a holler if there's someone you don't recognize. Understand? Don't open the door."

Lonnie nodded. But she knew how to defend herself.

AT THE WOMEN'S circle, Mr. Marino sometimes had guests come and talk. They'd had a lady from Anchorage who came and talked about money. She talked about banks and credit and a lot of other things that Lonnie didn't care about. Chief paid for all her things, so she didn't have to worry about money. Lonnie thought it would be a lot more interesting if they had music sometimes or let Paws 'N Love bring dogs and cats, like at the Institute.

Once, the Anchorage Choir came to Point Mettier. Everybody gathered in the gym to hear them sing Christmas songs. Their voices weaved in and out, high and low, loud and soft, and Lonnie could feel everything warm and humming inside. It was like blue skies and stars and magic.

But in the women's circle, they didn't have music or games. In June, they had a guest speaker named Angie Cisco. Lonnie really liked Angie Cisco. She had nice brown hair and looked real pretty, but she was a tough lady.

"Ms. Cisco is a self-defense instructor and she's going to show you some moves," Mr. Marino had said.

Angie Cisco got up in front of the women's circle. "Alaska is the deadliest state for women. Fifty-nine percent of women here have experienced violence, and we have the highest rate of females murdered by males in the US," she said. The women gasped. Inhaled. Took a breath. Looked at one another. "But I'm here to tell you that we're not just defenseless women," Angie continued. "We can better equip ourselves, increase our self-confidence, and feel better about our bodies, just by learning some basic techniques that can save our lives."

Lonnie noticed that when Ms. Cisco talked, she waved her hands around a lot, like the conductor directing the Anchorage Choir. She had lots of energy.

"Okay, first I'm going to demonstrate with the help of Mr. Marino, and then I'm going to have you all practice."

Everyone, including Lonnie, watched closely. Mr. Marino looked really funny because he was covered up in knee pads, elbow pads, a cushion that covered his chest, and a motorcycle helmet.

"We'll do it once quickly, and then I'll show you again in slow motion. Chuck, just come toward me from behind and grab me around the waist."

Mr. Marino did as Ms. Cisco asked, and then the lady bent forward, elbowed him, and kicked him. Mr. Marino fell to the floor. Lonnie got scared for Mr. Marino and stood up out of her chair. "You hurt Mr. Marino!"

But Mr. Marino got up quickly. "It's okay, Lonnie. It's just a simulation. We're pretending so that you know what to do if something like this happens."

"Okay." Lonnie sat back down and shut her mouth.

Mr. Marino and Ms. Cisco pretended again, but in slow motion.

"First thing you do is bend forward. Then throw your elbows from side to side toward the attacker's face. Turn and then kick him in the groin!"

Mr. Marino pretended to be hurt again, but Lonnie stayed quiet.

"Bend forward. Throw your elbows. Turn. Kick him in the groin."

Everybody practiced. Bend. Elbow. Turn. Kick.

Then they all got their turns with Mr. Marino. Mrs. Blackmon went up first. Bend. Elbow. Turn. Kick. You could tell she was being careful not to actually hurt Mr. Marino. It looked like they were dancing.

Next was Mariko. When she did her bend, elbow, turn, kick, she let out yells. "Hya! Ai! Yo!"

Ms. Cisco praised her. "Good!"

Then it was Lonnie's turn. "It's just pretend, now, Lonnie," Mr. Marino said when it was her turn. "You don't have to really kick me."

"I know what 'pretend' means!" Lonnie said. She wasn't going to really try to hurt Mr. Marino, but his cushion didn't go below his waist and he covered his balls with his hands just in case. Bend. Elbow. Turn. Kick.

CHAPTER THIRTY-SIX

CARA

MORNING BROUGHT STILTED AWKWARDNESS. AN UNCOMfortable exchange of words.

When Cara awoke, she found J.B. staring at her. "Oh, sorry," he said. "I just like the way you look with drool hanging out of your mouth."

Cara put on a paper smile but felt herself withdraw. The phantom call had put a damper on things. J.B. pulled her close for a deep kiss but sensed her stiffen. The previous night, she had welcomed the warmth of another human stirring a long-dormant part of her, but now the extra body heat was almost stifling under the layers of thick blankets. She felt as if she couldn't breathe.

J.B. sat back and looked into her eyes.

"It's been a while," was her excuse as she moved to get off the bed. "I think we ought to take it slow."

J.B. nodded as if he understood, but from the way he looked, Cara might as well have slapped him in the face.

"UH-HUH," SIPLEY SAID when they walked into the station together. He gloated as if he were replaying a voyeuristic reel in his head of what had happened the previous night and had been expecting it all along. "Looks like you two had a good night."

Cara wondered what the tell was. The flush in their faces? Or the fact that J.B. was wearing the same shirt as the previous night?

"Have the Blackmon boys been found?" she asked, trying to deflect.

Sipley's demeanor turned dark. "No, they've done a Houdini number. No one's seen them in the past twenty-four hours."

Cara telegraphed her thoughts to J.B. with a look and he nodded his acknowledgment that Plan B was now in effect.

They decided that Sipley would stay at Point Mettier to organize a search party and scour the surrounding area for the Blackmon boys, while Cara and J.B. would head over to Chugach Village. Although Sipley wasn't exactly happy about them heading to Chugach Village, his stance had changed after the previous night's search had come up empty. The safety of the boys was paramount. Cara did feel a modicum of apprehension when Sipley told her that there would be a cell phone signal void once they left the Dave-Co and he wasn't sure what kind of service there was out in the village. But at least they had snowmobiles at their disposal instead of having to risk a boat ride.

KAI PETERSON'S UNIT was on the sixth floor. Kai, J.B. explained, not only rented out snowmobiles, but also owned a watercraft operation. In the summer, people zoomed through the relatively calm turquoise waters on Sea-Doos at fifty miles per hour to get an up-close-and-personal view of the glaciers. With the popularity of his Sea-Doos during the high season, Kai had decided to invest in a handful of snowmobiles to operate during the off-season, but the winter tours hadn't managed to pick up steam. With no powdery ski slopes, Alaskan husky–led sled rides, or frozen lakes suitable for ice fishing, Point Mettier remained a dead zone in winter and Kai's snowmobiles generally sat idle except when they were occasionally rented out to local residents who were bored enough to pay his outrageous prices.

A transplant from California, Kai was once a pro surfer, but after paddling into a twenty-footer at the Banzai Pipeline off of Oahu's North Shore, Kai wiped out, hit a reef, and nearly drowned. He suffered a concussion and "saw God," then decided to put the kibosh on his surfing career and retire. Now in his forties, he still sported his requisite shoulder-length blond hair. When J.B. and Cara walked in, his room was hazy with vapors emanating from a large glass bong on a table. He was wearing flip-flops and board shorts—something that was possible when you never had to leave the Dave-Co.

"Who's the lovely lady?" Kai asked, waving away the smoke. Cara knew the question was an act for her benefit, because surely, by now, there was no one in the Davidson Condos who didn't know who she was.

"This is Detective Kennedy," J.B. said.

"Oh, right, you must be the one looking into the dude who was shark chummed."

Cara perused the room. It was a contradiction of surfboards, tiki-themed decor, and posters of blue island waters pitted against the snowy landscape outside the windows. "J.B. tells me you were a surfer. Alaska seems like a far cry from California."

"What can I say? You gotta transform. Go with the flow. Become the butterfly. If I can't use my board to ride the waves, gotta find another way." He chuckled out a surfer's laugh.

"We'd like to rent a couple of snowmobiles," J.B. said once the intros were over.

"We'd like to get started soon," Cara added. She hoped they could get to Chugach Village and back before the sun went down.

"No problemo," Kai answered. "I just need you to sign some stuff." He sandal-flopped over to a stack of ready-made forms. "Waivers and shit, so you don't sue me," he said. Then he laughed again for no good reason.

THE SNOWMOBILES WERE parked in a garage between the Dave-Co and the pier. Kai hadn't skimped on the machines, which had heated seats, large fuel tanks, tall wraparound windshields, and electric power steering. Cara and J.B. both had experience driving snowmobiles, so his standard orientation session was bypassed. They set off, deciding to first inspect the cove, where the two men had headed the prior night. The stolen fishing boat was beached there, left tilted and abandoned in haste. Its ignition had been hot-wired.

"Snowmobile tracks," Cara said, pointing down at the ribbon imprints similar to the ones they had spotted the day before. "These aren't ours. They're headed in a different direction from the condos."

"Chugach Village," J.B. confirmed. "I guess we could just follow their path," he said as they remounted their machines.

After her being cooped up in the Dave-Co for a week, the crisp open air felt refreshing and freeing to Cara despite the cold. J.B. moved ahead, carefully navigating the curves and valleys. His snowmobile kicked up a wake of powdery snow, leaving a mystical white trail behind him. The vast blanket of white in the backcountry and the thrumming whir of the engine were strangely hypnotic. Cara understood the high from riding waves that Kai couldn't let go of, whether they were on water or snow. His rentals included safety helmets outfitted with Bluetooth speakers they could communicate through. "I've never seen anything so beautiful!" Cara said through her headset.

"I forgot how fun this was," J.B. chimed in. "Maybe I'm in the wrong profession. I should be working for Kai," he joked.

In the vastness, it felt to Cara as if they were the only two people in the world. Forgetting for a moment the gravity of their task, they each couldn't help letting out a whoop of joy now and then, whenever there was a rise and fall into a valley.

Their demeanor turned serious, however, when they spotted Chugach Village ahead. They could see wooden houses rising on stilts. There were maybe twenty-five similarly sized rectangular houses in all, with wood frames and blue tarps used as ad hoc patches for leaky roofs and side panels. A steep set of stairs off one end of the village descended to an inlet, where a dozen or so boats were lined up along a small dock like blades on a fern frond.

They decided to park their vehicles just outside the perimeter of houses.

As they dismounted, Cara could see their breaths meld into the air. J.B. seemed suddenly focused as he lifted his rifle from the rear cargo area of his snowmobile. It felt like a moment when Cara needed to say something to him. "J.B., I just . . . want to thank you for having my back through everything. I know you didn't have to do any of this."

J.B. turned back to her and squeezed her hand. "Don't worry—we'll get through this."

Maybe it was the adrenaline, but Cara felt that fire flare again. She'd never noticed until now how intense and mesmerizing his green eyes were or the way his dark hair curled ever so slightly on his forehead.

"Do we have a plan?" he asked.

Cara paused. "We knock on doors and start asking questions."

CHAPTER THIRTY-SEVEN

CARA

THE OVERT STARKNESS AND POVERTY CARA WITNESSED IN Native villages always stunned her. Brown clumps of scrub sprouted above the snow line between islands of discarded items—a rusted motor, the skeletal remains of a fishing boat, an ice chest toppled on its side, an ancient satellite dish—everything half-buried and decaying into the landscape. Other than a dog testily barking in the distance and a screen door squeaking open and shut in the wind, it was eerily quiet. It felt like a ghost town with snow swirls forming mini tornadoes in the wind. But as they walked in closer, Cara could see smoke rising from chimneys and they could hear the sound of a TV blaring.

J.B. looked at Cara. "Which door do we knock on first?"

As if on cue, a woman emerged from one of the houses, hefting a bag of trash in one hand while cradling her bawling toddler in the other arm. Her long charcoal black hair went down to the middle of her back. When the woman noticed them, she glared, giving apprehensive looks toward J.B.'s rifle. "What do you want?"

"Point Mettier police," J.B. said, showing her his badge. "We're looking into a possible kidnapping."

"Police have no business here," she said bluntly, and was about to scurry back into the house.

Cara stepped forward. "Please, ma'am." Cara looked toward the woman's baby. "There are kids involved. They could be in danger."

"Haven't seen any kids I didn't recognize," she responded with ice in her tone.

Cara decided to try a different tactic. "Look, AST're gonna get here eventually if it turns out someone's kidnapped a child. Then everybody goes through the whole wash-and-rinse cycle. I can guarantee they won't be half as pleasant as we are. Or we can point them in the right direction and nobody else gets bothered."

The woman paused for a second. She looked both ways, making sure no one was outside to see her, then ushered them in.

The interior of the house was best described as "orderly chaos." The lack of space necessitated bins full of clutter—baby toys, blankets, diapers, and bottles—to be stacked one on top of another. On a weathered couch, a boy of about eight sat on the sprung, sagging cushions, watching a wrestling show on the television. He looked up at them, wide-eyed to see people he didn't recognize.

"Jason, go to your room," the woman said. He looked reluctant but plodded down the hall. She put down her toddler in the crib, and a pacifier worked to momentarily placate the crying child. The TV was left on, perhaps acting as a white-noise distraction.

The woman didn't offer them a seat, leaving them to mill by the door. She told them her name was Nikki.

Cara jumped in with her questioning. "Can you tell us about Wolf and his men?"

She grimaced with disdain. "I stay out of their hair. Wolf's married to an elder's daughter, so I don't butt into their business, but he and his buddies have been up to no good ever since they got here. Personally, if it were up to me, we'd kick them out, the whole lot of them."

"What exactly do you mean by *no good*?" J.B. asked.

Nikki pursed her lips. "I don't know. But we can't afford a police force, so they do what they please. They have guns and snowmachines, which make for good hunting, I guess. Plus, let's just say they pay 'rent' to the village."

"Who are they dealing to?" Cara assumed that the money to pay "rent" came from the drug dealing Sipley had alluded to, but she knew Chugach Village and even Point Mettier would be small potatoes.

"Like I said, I don't know and I don't ask questions. I got a family to tend to, so are we done here?"

"Can you just tell us which house is Wolf's?" Cara asked.

Nikki was hesitant.

"You tell us where to go, I promise no one will know we've been here," J.B. coaxed. "I don't think you're the only one who wants Wolf and his men out of here."

Nikki exhaled. "The house on the north end with the animal skulls. You can't miss it." Then she opened the door and held it for them as a not-so-subtle cue that they were no longer welcome.

AS NIKKI HAD said, the house was hard to miss. It sat throned upon a promontory overlooking the inlet, looming large over the village and leaning a tad askew. Everything in the village, it seemed, was slightly off-kilter. Like the yards outside the other houses in the village, this one was a virtual dumping ground, with trash strewn haphazardly, rusted mechanical parts and stacked tires tucked into the snow. The wind rocked an open glass bottle that was clearly a recent addition to the heap on the ground. What was most striking about the house was the collection of animal skulls and horns that covered the entire front wall. Most were caribou skulls with protruding antlers, but there were several moose skulls as well as those of foxes, a bear, and, of course, a few wolves, with their unfleshed faces and hollowed-out eyes making a macabre display.

Before knocking on the door, J.B. hesitated. "You sure you don't want to rethink this?" Worry filled his eyes. "Like Nikki said, there's no other law enforcement out here."

Cara realized it was a risk. But what was the alternative? To go back to Point Mettier and file a crime report with the AST? Would the state even intervene without credible evidence? If the boys were in there, Cara would never forgive herself for not at least investigating. "The first forty-eight hours . . ." she said, almost mouthing it to herself, and J.B. nodded that he understood.

He rapped at the door. "Hello? Joe Barkowski here from Point Mettier police station. Just want to talk to you."

There was no answer and Cara gave J.B. a slight nod. He slowly twisted the knob, which gave way, unlocked. In this tiny village, Cara supposed locks were unnecessary for a house where all the probable criminals were assembled inside. The door squeaked open, and then only the sound of the TV was heard. It was the same wrestling show Nikki's TV had been blaring. Was there only one TV station in Chugach Village?

They entered cautiously, as if treading on a rooftop edge.

"Hello?" J.B. repeated. He proceeded in one direction, while Cara headed in the other.

She held her breath as she came upon a living space and looked into the open doorway, but she could see no one. On a table, three freshly stubbed cigarettes were still snaking smoke into the air.

She heard the first shot before feeling the wood near her shoulder splinter with the bullet. It was one of Wolf's men on the stairwell. A skinhead with sunken eyes, aiming his pistol at her. She reached for her Glock and ducked just before a second explosion ripped a hole in the wall where her head had just been. A third shot went off and she was sure her luck had run out. But this time, it was from J.B.'s rifle. His sniper-trained accuracy sent the bald man tumbling down the stairs. *One.*

With the occupants clearly in a shooting mood, Cara slid behind the door of the living room. J.B. took cover in the nook beneath the stairwell. They froze in anticipation for a beat before a chirp-like creak along a floorboard alerted Cara to the presence behind her. Then she found her air cut off—a piece of cloth used as a makeshift rope wrapped around her neck. Cara felt herself being dragged backward. She tried to cry out, but it came out as a weak gasp. J.B. was no longer in her line of sight. Despite the instinct to pull the cloth away from her neck, she mentally willed herself to hold on to the Glock in her right hand. She gagged, trying to steady her hand long enough to pull the trigger, aiming at the arm cinching the cloth around her neck. Pain in her lungs. Her vision washed white. Her finger finally found the trigger. "Fuck!" the voice behind her said, and the death choke finally abated. Cara swiveled to face him, then shot him in the leg as well for good measure. "Son of a bitch!" he yowled, falling to the ground. *Two.*

J.B. rushed toward her, forgetting about keeping his cover.

"I'm okay," Cara rasped, trying to regain her composure and frisking Number Two for weapons.

"I'm going to kill you, you goddamn bitch!" he yelled through clenched teeth, but it came out weakened by pain, and his complexion was turning pale from the blood loss. Cara recognized him as Dark Eyes—the man she had seen in the hallway the night the gang had descended on Point Mettier.

"Where are they?" Cara asked.

"Eat my dick," was his response before passing out.

CARA AND J.B. cleared the rest of the first floor, moving softly and swiftly through each room, weapons drawn, but finding no one. "Spence? Troy?" Cara called out. Muffled clomps coming from the upper floor confirmed that there was at least one other person in the house.

J.B. nimbly stepped over the body of Number One on the stairwell and crouched his way up. Cara had moved to follow when Number One suddenly came back to life and startled her by grabbing onto her ankle with an octopus grip. She resisted the urge to scream and boot-kicked him back into unconsciousness. J.B. paused, but seeing she was okay, he continued up with his rifle raised to eye level, monitoring a row of doors, while Cara aimed her Glock at the other end of the hallway.

The air became stiflingly still. Nothing but the sound of their own breathing. A shadow flitted across the threshold of a partially open doorway. It was enough warning for J.B. A succession of shots rang out, and at first Cara wasn't sure who had shot whom, until she saw the ripped splinters in the frame of the door and a voice behind it yelled, "Motherfucker!" *Three.*

"Okay, okay," Number Three said, clearly in pain. A gun dropped to the floor and Number Three slowly emerged with one hand up, the other trying to stop the blood gushing from a side wound.

"Who else is up here?" Cara asked, her gun pointed at him.

"Nobody."

"Where are the boys?" J.B. asked.

"What boys?" Number Three had greasy, unruly hair framing a pudgy face and large, bulbous eyes. He was less full of brawn and brute than his cohorts, but made up for this lack of muscle with an excess of intensity. Despite the disadvantage he was at, he seemed to be grinning at them internally, as if he controlled the helm, which unnerved Cara, in the same way that Wolf had.

J.B. cuffed him while he protested. "This is Native land. You can't arrest me."

"Take it up with your local law enforcement," Cara quipped. "Where are the others?"

"I don't know what the fuck you're talking about."

"There should be at least four more of you somewhere. But we can do this the hard way."

"The hard way, please," Number Three said, smiling. Cara regretted that J.B.'s bullet hadn't struck higher. J.B. grabbed him by the back of his collar.

They swept the second floor, cautiously entering each room and using Number Three as a shield. All the while, Number Three spewed inflammatory words and leaked a trail of blood. They found no one else, until they got to the last door, which opened into a bathroom.

A rustle from behind the shower curtain put Cara and J.B. on the alert, with their weapons ready. She mouthed, "One, two, three," before yanking the curtain open. A woman screamed. Cowering in the shower were an Alutiiq woman in her late thirties, one barely out of her teens, a child who looked about five, and a baby. They sat huddled together, fear in their eyes.

Cara relaxed her hold on her gun.

CARA DID HER best to patch the three men with gauze and alcohol she found in a medicine cabinet, and she made tourniquets out of ripped sheets to stop their bleeding. Both Number One and Number Two were still passed out, and they propped Number Three on a chair.

A deep search of the premises revealed a cornucopia of drugs stashed in a dresser drawer—methamphetamine, cocaine, and two kinds of heroin, all neatly weighed and uniformly bagged. No clever hiding places were needed in a remote outpost that was normally out of reach of the law. In another drawer, rubber-banded stacks of twenties and hundreds were piled in mini towers. The AST would have a field day if Cara and J.B. decided to inform them about what they had found. But for now, it seemed more advantageous to proceed with their own questioning first.

"Where are Wolf and the rest of the gang?" J.B. tried again.

"I don't know," he said.

Cara tied the cloth around his waist a little too tightly, until Number Three yowled in pain.

"Fuckin' bitch!" He glared at her with his bulging eyes. "All I know is Wolf's gonna have his way with you when they get back."

J.B. punched his face then, which Cara hadn't expected but secretly appreciated. Number Three simply laughed, reminding Cara of a croaking toad. She knew they weren't going to get far with Number Three, so she asked J.B. to keep an eye on him while she saw to the Alutiiq women and children, who were in the next room huddled together on the bed. By now, the baby was wailing, so Cara turned to the older woman and said in the most comforting voice she could muster, "Does the baby need changing?"

"She needs her formula," the younger one said.

"Let's go down to the kitchen."

The younger Alutiiq woman, who said her name was Hanna, went down the stairs holding her child. She was slim, with a high forehead and large, doe-like eyes. She glanced down at Number One lying at the foot of the stairs, where Cara and J.B. had left him instead of trying to carry him to a sofa or bed. Cara felt the onus of gravely injuring someone who might be a husband or father. But the young Alutiiq woman nudged the body with her foot, and when he remained unconscious, she spit on him. She wore an expression of triumph and vindication as she raised her head toward Cara.

Once they were settled in the kitchen and the baby had been quieted with the formula, Cara sensed she would get further in questioning this young woman.

"Do you know where Wolf and the men are?"

"The others haven't come back yet," she said. "And I don't care whether they ever do."

"Have you seen two boys? About age seventeen and thirteen?"

"No, we haven't seen them. Joey, Bill, and Victor didn't bring anyone with them. The one in the other room, that's Bill. The guy up-stairs is Victor. Victor is Wolf's brother. Even though Wolf thinks he's the boss, I think Victor's the one who really calls the shots. The one at the stairs is Joey. He's"—she hesitated, then looked down at the baby—"Nona's father." Cara knew the details wouldn't be good, so she tried to avoid the subject.

"Do you know Michael Lovansky?"

"Mick? He joined a little over a year ago. Mick's father worked on the trash barge that comes out every month, and that's how Mick got introduced to the gang. He was crazy. Always talking about cut-ting people up into pieces."

That made Cara freeze and sent shivers down her spine. "Did he? Cut people up?" Was there a connection? Was it coincidence?

"I don't know. I thought it was all talk. He was supposed to go out on a drug run or something and never came back. Wolf went crazy. And then Wolf got a tip from someone that his body was at Point Mettier."

"He got a tip? From who?" Cara bristled with alarm.

"They don't tell me anything. It's just from what I picked up. The less I knew, the better."

Cara's disquieting thought processes were interrupted by the sud-den whir of an electric motor from the hallway. Had they missed someone? Cara instinctively felt for her gun.

All senses on alert, she peered into the corridor but saw no one. She followed the sound to a console table on which sat a nineties-era fax machine egesting a piece of paper. Cara hadn't seen a fax ma-chine in years but she supposed in an area devoid of cell service, this was still a useful commodity. She picked up the facsimile and was alarmed to see the simple printed text. "Pigs on their way."

It was a warning bell. Too late for Wolf's men. But who was sending them the message? There was no originating fax number printed anywhere on the page. No signature. No clues as to where it had been sent from. Were there other messages? Cara looked in a nearby trash bin and unfolded a wadded piece of paper. Printed on the page was another fax message: "Point Mettier. Search Room 42." The room number was familiar to Cara. It was the room rented by Michael Lovansky, aka Charles Dodger, which had been ransacked the night Wolf had arrived.

Clearly, someone who had inside knowledge was feeding the men info.

CHAPTER THIRTY-EIGHT

AMY

AMY RUMMAGED THROUGH THE CABINETS OF THE BLACK-mons' kitchen, looking for anything edible—granola bars, cans of soup and chili, half a loaf of not-yet-moldy bread, and peanut butter. Luckily, the Blackmons were well stocked for the winter and had been ready to go into hibernation like the rest of Point Mettier's ready-for-doomsday residents. Everything went into her backpack. In the fridge, she found some bologna and cheese. That went in too. Then she filled a couple of water bottles from the filtered fridge dispenser. But when she tried to lift her now-heavy-as-a-ton-of-bricks backpack, she had to rethink her "everything at once" strategy and decided that the cans of soup and chili had to stay. She would return for them later.

She had kept the spare key that was typically hidden behind the light because she didn't want Detective Lady to take it away permanently, and thank goodness, the usually sharp-as-a-tack Detective Lady hadn't even thought to ask for it. Maybe Amy had overestimated her. Anyway, keeping the key seemed like a wise decision. She would have tried to siphon food from Star deliveries, but it wasn't easy getting things past Ma, who was hawkeyed when it came to keeping track of supplies, and that's why Amy found herself raiding the Blackmons' pantry. She wasn't exactly stealing. She was just delivering.

AFTER SHE'D BEEN excused from school the previous day, Amy hadn't immediately gone home. Instead, she had found herself inexplicably drawn to the Blackmons' unit again, despite knowing that none of them would be there—just like how characters in horror movies are always compelled to go alone to the places where they are most likely to be decimated by monsters or axe murderers.

She had half expected Spence to text or call with a "Ha ha, had you all going there," just to prove his sardonic sense of humor. But absolutely zilch had been heard from him, and since Joshua and Marco had planted their terrifying theory of murder, she couldn't help thinking that maybe there was something she was missing—some kind of clue as to what in Dante's *Inferno*'s universe had happened to the Blackmons.

In Spence's room, everything was still in the same state of mid-disappearance clutter as it had been the previous day. Amy sat on the bed for a moment, hugging his pillow and inhaling the slightly bitter scent of men's shampoo from it. She picked up from the nightstand the plush toy that she had given him last Christmas—a zombie version of Winnie-the-Pooh she had found online. Pooh's innards hung out of his belly and blood-colored wax poured from Pooh's decayed teeth. Spence had reacted in exactly the way she had expected, smiling with one corner of his lip raised slightly higher than the other. That expression killed Amy every time. She wondered if he was making the same smile from whatever pearly-gate nirvana cosmos he was looking down from. *Holy crap, he's only been gone for one day and I'm already thinking of him in the past tense!* Outside, the gray light was beginning to glint off the snow. It would be dark soon and Ma would be wondering where she had gone off to. Plus, Amy had managed to thoroughly creep herself out with her own morbid thoughts.

Amy had never explicitly told Ma about her relationship with Spence, but Ma was no dummy. They had a "don't ask, don't tell" kind of situation. Amy was certain, though, that Ma had spies working for her, because every now and then, she would yell at Amy for something she wasn't supposed to have known about, like the time when Amy went with Spence to the big entertainment center in Anchorage that housed a bowling alley, arcade, and ice-skating rink, instead of on a school-sanctioned-educational-boring-museum field trip that they had made up. Ma found out about it, and not only did Amy have her cell phone taken away for a week, but she was also punished with some kind of North Korean–style torture where she had to scrub all the grout in the bathroom with a toothbrush until everything was sparkling white. But overall, Amy was certain Ma just held her tongue because at least Spence was someone she could keep an eye on. Some of the other girls at Point Mettier struck up scandalous relationships with otters or temporary summer people.

CHAPTER THIRTY-NINE

LONNIE

THERE WAS A GHOST IN THE DAVE-CO. HE DIED, CROAKED, expired, a long time ago, before Lonnie ever got there. She didn't know his real name, but she called him "Mr. Mettier." Mr. Mettier had started making noises after Chief came the night before. Mr. Mettier made a goddamn racket upstairs. *Creak. Squeak. Groan. Scrape. Bump. Scratch.* He was making so much noise that Lonnie couldn't even hear the voices inside her head. There were always voices.

There were voices upstairs when Pastor Wilson and his family used to live there. Lonnie could hear footsteps, music, singing, chairs moving, and at night the *thump thump thump* above her bedroom. But after they got tired of living in Point Mettier, they left and it was quiet. *Quiet as a mouse. The mouse ran up the clock. Hickory dickory dock.*

Lonnie liked the quiet because she could watch her TV shows in peace. She liked watching the show about the psychic medium who helped people with their problem ghosts. Ghosts always had messages. Maybe Mr. Mettier had a message. He had something to say. People were always talking.

Lonnie's favorite show of all was the one where people wore masks. *Obscured. Disguised. Veiled. Secret.* So many secrets. She liked the singing, the dancing, and all the costumes. Animals. Fancy dresses. Cartoon monsters. Like fairy-tale characters that Mama read to her about. Then *Bang! Clatter! Clang!* The noises Mr. Mettier made ruined the show. It made Lonnie upset. "Goddamn it, Mr. Mettier!" He had interrupted just when Sad Turtle was singing a song about dancing in the sea.

There was a knock on the door and Lonnie was not happy, since it was almost time to watch her show *Sarah the Psychic*. She remembered what Chief had said about not opening the door to any strangers, so she looked through the peephole and saw it was Chief again.

"Brought you some fried rice," Chief said when she opened the door. He was holding a take-out box from Star Asian Food in his hand.

"I like stir-fried rice," Lonnie said. She liked the sound of the word. *Rice. Ice. Nice.* "*Roll the dice. Don't think twice.*" That's what Mama used to say.

"I know you like fried rice, darling. That's why I picked some up for you while I was at Mrs. Lin's place," Chief said. "Now I gotta come in and have a look around in your unit."

"What for?"

"Just want to check to make sure the Blackmon boys aren't around."

"I already told you I haven't seen them, and why would they be in here?"

But Chief was already looking around, walking into the bedroom. *Hunting. Searching. Exploring. Inspecting.*

"Have you seen anybody else since I came by yesterday?" Chief asked from the bathroom.

"I saw Denny and Mr. Marino. And I heard Mr. Mettier."

"What do you mean, Lonnie?" Chief came back into the living room. "Who's Mr. Mettier?"

"Mr. Mettier's the ghost upstairs. I could hear him stomping all around."

Chief raised his eyebrows at that. "When did you start hearing him?"

"Last night."

Chief got all serious then. "You stay here, Lonnie. I'll go upstairs and check it out."

"But you can't get rid of a ghost without doing an exorcism or a cleansing. I need to go upstairs and burn my sage there," Lonnie insisted. She had seen it on one of her shows. To get rid of a ghost, you needed to do an exorcism, but since Pastor Wilson was gone, the next best thing was to do a cleansing. That's how she saw it being done on TV.

"You're not going anywhere," Chief said. "If I'm not back in ten minutes, call Chuck Marino."

So Chief left while Lonnie waited and waited, and when ten minutes was up, she was about to call Mr. Marino, but then her phone rang.

"Hello?"

"Nobody's up here," Chief said. "I'm sure it was just a mouse, Lonnie." *When the cat's away, the mice will play.*

"It wasn't a mouse," Lonnie said with conviction. "I need to do a cleansing," she told him again. Lonnie heard silence on the phone and wondered if Chief had hung up. She heard a sigh on the other end.

"All right, but come up and do it quick."

Lonnie needed sage. Mariko had given her an indoor herb garden for her birthday, but most everything had died except the basil and chives. The sage was wilted, but Lonnie decided it was okay because the sage they used on TV was dead and dried up anyway.

"MAYBE YOU CAN just ask Mr. Mettier real nice to be quiet and we'll call it a day," Chief said when Lonnie got to the room.

She waved the wilted sage, still in its pot, inside the room. It would be better if she could burn it, but Chief told her she couldn't do that, and she didn't have a lighter anyway. The room smelled like must and sweat mixed together, like Denny's barn after it rained.

Lonnie thought she saw a shadow outside the window. She got scared and closed her eyes. *Three blind mice. See how they run.* When she opened her eyes again, she saw it was just trees. "Please, Mr. Mettier," she said as she walked around the space, "please move to another unit. Or if you're going to stay here, please be quiet between seven and ten so I can watch all my TV shows in peace," Lonnie said. She walked all around the living area and then around to the kitchen. There were empty bottles and cans on the back counter. "Mr. Mettier's been eating chili and drinking Red Bulls," she said.

"What?" Chief looked alarmed as he came over to the kitchen where Lonnie was looking. His eyes grew wide as saucers. He picked up a knife that was on the counter. *They all ran after the farmer's wife, who cut off their tails with a carving knife. Three blind mice.*

CHAPTER FORTY

CARA

"WALK ME THROUGH HOW YOU KILLED YOUR EX-HUSBAND,"
Cara said to Debra Blackmon.

The fluorescent lights of the "interrogation room" cast a sallow
yellow glow on the schoolteacher. Without makeup, she seemed to
have aged overnight, with rings around her eyes and a general mal-
aise from fatigue and sleep deprivation.

DURING CARA AND J.B.'s trek to Chugach Village, Chief Sipley
had organized a volunteer search party to comb the area surrounding the Davidson Condos. Twelve men, four women, and six teens
had combed the pier, the boats, the cove, and the woods on foot but
found no evidence of the boys. Two snowmobiles, however, match-

ing the vehicles that Wolf and his men had rode in on, were discovered hidden within a grove of spruce trees. "Wolf and at least some of his pack must be circling the wagons before they go in for the kill," Sipley said, making the hair on the back of Cara's neck bristle with his unsettling analogy. Alarm bells went off when he told them that he had found evidence of Wolf's men hiding out in the room above Lonnie's.

Not wishing to wait until the following morning, Chief Sipley had decided to embark immediately on a door-to-door search of the building, including the unoccupied units, to find the men or the Blackmon boys or both, and he would notify the residents to be on the lookout for possibly armed and dangerous intruders lurking in the building. J.B. was now joining the probe.

Cara, meanwhile, felt that Debra Blackmon was still holding back some pieces of the puzzle. She had handed the schoolteacher a deposition form to sign and convinced her that it was really about getting clues to the whereabouts of the boys.

"You have to find them, Detective," she said. The desperation in her voice was all too familiar.

"J.B. and Chief Sipley are scouring the building as we speak," Cara reassured Debra, then added, "Would you like some coffee?"

"I'm good," Debra replied tersely, almost as a declaration that she viewed Cara as the enemy.

"Let's start at the top." Cara studied Debra's countenance as she laid her arms on the rectangular plywood table that separated them. It wobbled unsteadily. "Why did you and Michael get divorced?"

"I don't know. Why don't you ask half the couples in America?" Debra took the question as judgment.

Cara pursed her lips. She could tell that the schoolteacher was on edge. Cara ripped a page from her memo pad and folded it neatly into a square. Then she calmly placed the folded paper under the short leg of the table. The wobbling stopped. Meanwhile, Debra thought better of her answer.

"After Mick came back from his tour in Afghanistan . . . he was a different man. I'm sure you know the drill. PTSD, drinking, abuse . . . Police and social services didn't lift a finger. You can take a look at the records. They never did anything. You know, it's not as easy as they make it seem in the movies to uproot your entire life with two kids in tow, but I finally got out."

Cara had covered many domestic abuse cases in the past. They were an all-too-familiar theme in Alaska. How little could actually be done to address the issue frustrated her to no end. "So, after you left your husband, you came here?"

Debra nodded. "I had heard a tip from someone that Point Mettier was a haven for women like me. That didn't stop him from trying to come through the tunnel, though. Jim Arreak already knew not to let him through. Chief Sipley helped me file a restraining order that forbade him from entering. Didn't hear from him for a while. Thought he had finally disappeared. Then I got the scare of my life when Ellie Wright told me he had checked in. He must've come in by boat. I told her I could handle it. Maybe that was my first mistake. I gave Mick warning to leave us the fuck alone or I was going to have him arrested. But then he said he had connections now and they could hurt Spence and Troy and I needed to keep my mouth shut."

"Connections?"

"I didn't know exactly what he was talking about, but it frightened me, and then I found out that he had joined those goons at the village."

"What did he do when he found you?"

"He said that all he wanted was to see Spence and Troy. Wanted to go hunting with them. I wasn't going to let that happen, but I told him I'd bring the boys to meet him in the woods because I didn't want him in my unit. I brought my rifle with me just in case, and went to see him alone. He got upset, of course, that the boys weren't with me. We started fighting, and then when I thought he was going to hit me . . ." A deep inhale and her eyes started to water. "I shot him."

"How did you shoot him?"

"What do you mean?"

"Was it a struggle? Were you facing him and he was advancing toward you? The details would be helpful for a self-defense case."

Debra hesitated in her recollection. "He didn't have a hold on me. I was facing him and, yes, he was advancing toward me, so I shot him. It's all kind of blurry."

"Then what happened?"

"I got scared. I didn't want anyone to find the body, so I went back, got a chain saw, and cut him up. Like I said, I thought with all those body parts washing up recently, people would just think it was more of the same."

It was true that had Cara not decided to meddle, the story might have faded. "Do you still have the weapon?"

"You mean the hunting rifle? No, I motored out and threw it into the sound with everything else."

Debra's leg convulsed in a nervous tic while Cara made notes in her pad.

"Why were they going after you?"

"Revenge? I mean, why else?"

"How did they know it was you who killed Michael?"

"I don't know. When I was at the boat I just saw them coming after me."

"Mrs. Blackmon, we want to find your boys, so anything you can tell us to help us find them . . ."

Debra buried her head in her hands.

"Do you have anything of Michael's?"

"No. Everything happened so fast, and like I said, everything's a bit fuzzy, so I can't be sure, but I think he had luggage. It was dark. I was nervous . . . The reason I went out to the boat was because I thought maybe I had forgotten it when I was . . . disposing of the body. But there wasn't anything there. Then those men found me and I took off."

Cara tried to get a read on whether Debra was being truthful. "Do you remember what it looked like?"

"No." Then Debra suddenly broke down in tears. "Just get them back in one piece."

Cara thought for a moment how unfair life could be. Despite the endless precautions parents took to keep their children safe, any one of infinite variables of chance could thwart them all. Cara had spent hours analyzing car seats that protected their occupants from frontal, side, rear, and rollover crashes. She had stood suspended in grocery aisles, reading labels to make sure food was organic and allergen-free before serving it up in BPA-free cups and melamine-free dishware. The crib she had purchased for Dylan was void of VOCs and came with a mattress firm enough to prevent suffocation. But at the end of the day, Cara knew from her time on the force that more often than not, when tragedy strikes, it's nothing a parent could have had control over, prepared for, or read about in a parenting tip blog. And that was the cruelty of it all.

CARA ESCORTED DEBRA back to her cell, where she deflated onto her bunk with a clouded countenance. There was no veil of hope Cara could offer her for her sons other than that Sipley and J.B. were doing a building sweep to find them. Debra's testimony had not shined any further light on where the boys had disappeared to, but it did confirm something for Cara.

She thumbed through evidence photos to revisit Lovansky's gunshot wound. His floating head and eerie smile had always been telling her something, whispering from the beyond. The fatal bullet had clearly entered his right jaw and exited his top left cranium. Debra, standing in front of him, face-to-face, would have to have been left-handed for that to happen, but Cara had watched Debra carefully when she signed the consent form with her right hand.

Debra was lying.

CHAPTER FORTY-ONE

CARA

THE SCENE OF INFLICTED CHAOS AND MASSACRED FURNITURE was similar to how they had found Michael Lovansky's rented room. With the Blackmons' unit, however, the destruction of family photos, memorabilia, carefully considered furniture, and collected belongings somehow seemed more offensive than the dismantling of Ellie's rental decor. Sipley had called, sounding breathless, to alert Cara that the apartment had been "B and E'd."

J.B. was continuing the door-to-door search, so it was just Sipley and Cara surveying the damage. Cara had brought her camera and evidence kit in case there was some clue she could ferret out from the destruction. Sipley hemmed and hawed, pacing back and forth. "We haven't found them, but they're still in the building," Sipley said, referring to Wolf and his men, as if he hadn't been certain before.

They exited into the hallway, with Cara, unfortunately, not having gleaned any further clues to where the boys might be, although it continued to add fuel to her suspicions that Wolf and his men must have been looking for something—possibly a missing shipment of drugs or other contraband items. Something that Michael Lovansky had with him and Debra perhaps now had.

The mouse squeak of wheels rolling down the carpeted hallway alerted Cara and Sipley to Amy with her blue cart. Amy promptly froze when she saw them. It seemed to Cara that the "deer in headlights" look was Amy's standard reaction to seeing her.

"Don't tell me you have a delivery for the Blackmons."

"No." Amy faltered. "It's for the Hammonds down the hall."

"I thought I told your mother to keep to your room and hunkered down," Sipley said with genuine concern. "Those thugs could still be around."

"Oh, I must have already left the unit when you came," Amy said. "I'll go back now."

"Do you still have the extra key to the Blackmons' unit?" Cara asked. "This is a crime scene now, so we'd like to close off access."

"Holy shit!" Amy said. "A crime scene? Did something happen in there?"

"It's just been vandalized."

Amy's face turned a bluish gray and Cara grew concerned for her. Certainly everything that had happened was a lot for a teen to take in. Cara put her hand out for the key. "Do you have that key?"

"I think I lost it. I can bring it by later if I find it," Amy said in an obvious lie. Then she hovered for a while as if she were waiting for some kind of tidbit. She finally started pulling the cart again. "I'll take the stairs," she said. Cara and Sipley headed toward the elevators, Sipley glancing at his watch. "I need to check in on Mrs. Blackmon. Get her some supper and follow up with J.B. on the search," he said.

Cara couldn't shake the feeling that there was something Amy was hiding. "You go on ahead. I think I left my camera flash in the unit."

The camera flash was just an excuse to check on Amy, since it seemed odd to Cara that she would prefer to take the stairs while hauling a cart behind her. She suspected that Amy's real intention was to enter the Blackmons' apartment despite the warning that it was off-limits.

Cara went back and entered the unit, but there was no sign of Amy or the blue cart. She wondered if her hunch that Amy would double back after they were gone was wrong. While she stood there reassessing, she felt a sudden flush of cold air on the back of her neck, as if someone had just switched on an electric fan. She gasped at the unexpected sensation.

Cara swiveled on her heels, but there was no one behind her in the hallway. Down the dark corridor, she could hear the sound of wheels sliding on the carpet, different from Amy's squeaky cart. *Was it Susie on her scooter?*

Cara hastened down the hallway and saw neither Susie nor Amy, but she glimpsed a tall, hooded figure disappear through the stairwell entrance.

CARA PEERED DOWN the flight of stairs. She caught sight only of the back of the hooded person descending soundlessly, like a shadow.

She thought her eyes were deceiving her when another, similarly dressed person dashed down the stairwell. There were *two* of them!

Cara followed carefully, treading lightly so as not to be seen or heard by them, which was made difficult by the extra weight of the evidence kit she carried. Down. Down. Down. To the bowels of the building. Cara could feel the air start to get thicker and heavier on her. She knew it was all psychological, but it felt like a real, physical attack on her entire body. She white-knuckled the railing for support.

In her hesitation she lost her bead on them. She reached the basement level and scanned the space but saw no one. It was almost as if the men had disappeared into thin air. How was this possible? Cara began to question all her senses—what had she really seen, what had she really heard, and what had she really felt? Was any of it real? Or was this just part of another nightmare? Finally, her eyes spotted Amy's blue cart. Her heart skipped a beat. The cart sat abandoned in a corner. Cara peered into the cart and saw that it was empty.

She stopped to concentrate for a moment, feeling as if she were part of an escape-room challenge, trying to figure out what clues she was missing to find the exit—a seemingly invisible one that had allowed Amy and two men to vanish into thin air. It was the sound that caught her attention first. Just a drip of water falling on the concrete floor. It was coming from a wooden panel that seemed ever so slightly askew, covering some kind of hole or tunnel. Cara put her evidence kit on the floor and tested the plywood, seeing if she could pry it off, and to her surprise, it gave easily. It was a trick door. But the black hole beyond was more than daunting and she couldn't help but inhale sharply at the sight of the airless abyss, even darker and more confining than the tunnel to the bar. She cast a light using her cell phone, but the disappointingly small cone of visibility made the space seem even narrower, if that was possible. She remembered the manual camera flash in her evidence kit and retrieved it. Paving an intermittent path of light into the tunnel, Cara was grateful that she had thought to load a fresh set of batteries. Then she headed in.

CHAPTER FORTY-TWO

AMY

AMY DRAGGED THE CART DOWN THE STAIRWELL. *THUMP THUMP thump* down the concrete steps. But then she thought she heard a stray sound out of sync with the cart, or maybe it was just an echo. Amy looked up but couldn't see beyond a flight up. Was it Detective Lady? She stood perfectly still, holding her breath, listening for the sound, but heard nothing. Definitely an echo.

WHEN AMY HAD followed the clue to the City, she had found Spence and Troy hiding out in the Walcott Building in a space with four intact concrete walls that she and Spence had only recently discovered. It had been hidden away all these years behind an elephant-size pile of debris. Moss covered and bunker-like, it was a tiny room—a ten-foot-square safe room, or whatever it had really been during its wartime heyday. They were going to clean it out sometime and bring an inflatable mattress over to use it as a "make-out room." But now Spence and Troy were using it as their refuge, clearly not as concerned about cleanliness and hygiene as Amy was, given how much dirt there was still on the floor, although they had done a half-decent job of cleaning out the debris. They had brought their sleeping bags and battery-operated lights, but regardless, it had a serial-killer secret-basement-room vibe and it was cold as fuck, despite the four walls.

Spence had told her that the reason they were hiding out was because they were afraid of the Village Men. He finally came clean about his deadbeat dad, who, the story was, had gotten involved with the thugs, but because of some kind of botched deal that probably had to do with drugs had become their target, and now the whole family was in jeopardy, even though they had been estranged from him for years.

"Were those body parts we found . . . were they your dad's?" Amy's eyes had widened.

"I don't know," Spence faltered. "Maybe. I never saw the head."

"Why didn't you go to the police?" Amy asked.

"Mom doesn't trust them. Thinks maybe there's someone on the inside, probably at APD, getting payoffs from the Village Men."

"Whoa." Amy had to process this info.

"You don't know who you can trust," Spence added.

The whole thing sounded like some kind of Scorsese gangster flick, but Amy was just glad that Spence wasn't at the bottom of the sound like she had thought.

Mrs. Blackmon had planned for them all to escape together, but then when she never came back, Spence decided it was best for him and Troy to hightail it.

Amy let Spence know that his mom was being detained at the police station, which everybody at the Dave-Co knew by now, and when he looked freaked-out at the news, she added, "Maybe they'll let her go eventually, like they did with Lonnie, once they find out the Village Men are the real killers."

Spence nodded in agreement. "That police lady, Kennedy—wasn't that her name? She's just grabbing for straws."

Then, when Amy had planned to swing back to the Blackmons' unit to restock on canned food and some clothes Spence and Troy had asked for, it was just Amy's luck to run into the speak-of-the-devil detective lady and J.B. again in the hallway. Amy wondered if she had some invisible magnet for police—some kind of Spidey-sense radar that drew her to where the police action and gruesome evidence were.

Amy had wanted to turn back around, but Detective Lady had already spotted her and Amy quickly had to come up with some lie about a delivery to the Hammonds three doors down. That was the second fabrication she had come up with in the space of an hour, because when Ma had told her to hold any deliveries because of police activity, Amy had told her, "But this is for the police station."

Ma had looked conflicted about that.

"It should be fine to just take the order to the police station. And it's for chow mein, so I heated the leftovers from yesterday." She had hoped to God that Ma wasn't actually going to inspect the cart, because there was no chow mein in it, just her gray backpack, a charged USB power pack, D batteries, and a yellow plastic flashlight. But Ma had relaxed and nodded in approval at Amy's economic leftovers mentality and let her leave. She knew she would have to make up another excuse to Ma about the length of time she needed to get to the Blackmons and back, but she'd deal with that later.

AMY SHOOK OFF the feeling that someone was following her and continued down to the basement. At the entrance to the tunnel, she pulled out her backpack and the flashlight and left the cart behind. Despite her failure to retrieve the extra food and clothes, at least she could bring the boys the extra juice they needed to power their devices. She carefully unhinged the trick door and closed it behind her. She had to hand it to the older kids who had rigged the plywood covering to make it look as though the tunnel was still boarded up. The water splashed against her shoes as she plodded through the cold and dankness that nipped at her. She had been through these tunnels so many times in the past that she probably could have made her way even without a flashlight. But one of her worst fears was to be stuck down there alone in the dark with a dead light, so the spare set of Ds in her backpack was a comfort.

When the kids had discovered the tunnel many years ago, they had decided to mark the path to the City with symbols instead of arrows so that it wouldn't easily be discerned by adults who might stumble on their markings. One of the kids had been all into Egyptology and hieroglyphics. He had seen some old movie about an action-hero archaeologist and become one of those I-know-everything-about-Egypt dorks, so it was his idea to mark each tunnel split with different symbols—a bird, a stick-figure man, a circle with a dot depicting the sun. He also came up with a rhyme that was supposed to help them remember the way:

> We traveled far away from the sun.
> Into the secret tunnel we did run.
> Nary will a chirp be heard.
> From a fine or feathered bird.
> We'll do all our deeds in the dark
> And stealthily we'll leave our mark.

Following the right cues—a sun or a stick figure of a man running—they would arrive at the City. If they followed a false cue, like a picture of a house, then they would end up at a dead end, or a flooded passage.

Having run the rhyme in her head in the early days, Amy had it down to sun, man running, ear, bird, black box, and "X marks the spot." But now, of course, she didn't even need to reference the symbols, because the path was all in her physical memory.

Amy was already far into the tunnel where the water rose to the ankles of her boots when she distinctly heard sloshing behind her. And then there were voices, like distant murmurs. A shiver ran up her spine. *Were they ghosts?* No, not ghosts but men. The men who were after Spence. She quickly flicked off her light, and the sudden switch to black was blinding. Her worst fears were coming true in this creepy-as-hell lair of darkness. She resisted the urge to immediately turn her light back on and waited for her eyes to adjust, then began to make her way, with one hand on the slimy wall. But the noise her boots made in the water telegraphed her presence. There was no way to stifle them.

Behind her, she could hear the *slosh slosh* of possible-gang-assassins' boots coming nearer to her. She decided, instead of trying to outrun them, to get to a fork and stay perfectly still behind one of the walls, holding her breath.

The men were coming ever closer and closer. Right behind the bend. She could see their lights bouncing along the walls.

Amy resisted her urge to scream and instead closed her eyes and willed them to be gone.

CHAPTER FORTY-THREE

LONNIE

THERE WERE BAD MEN IN THE BUILDING. BUILDING UP TO
something.

Bad men in the hallway.

In the hallway at the Institute, when the red lights started blinking, the men came running. *Charging. Sprinting. Darting. Dashing.*

There were bad men dashing in the hallway with fur coats and
leather boots. One was older and had a funny limp. The other was
young and had a tattoo on his wrist. The difference in their sizes
kind of reminded Lonnie of the funny magicians she saw on TV,
where one was short and the other was big and tall. But Lonnie
knew these two weren't funny magicians. They were bad men, like
the ones who killed Denny's mama. Like the men that the women
talked about in the Tuesday circle. Bad men were everywhere.

Lonnie was on her way to make sure Denny was warm. Covered with a blanket. Safe and cozy. That's when she saw them. They carried guns. *Gun the engine. Gunga Din. Gung ho.*

Jake was gung ho about guns. He had lots of them. He tried to teach Lonnie how to shoot when she was ten, but Mama didn't like it. Like the time Jake took Lonnie out to shoot empty cans. Canned soup, canned tomatoes, canned beans, canned peas. Lined up like birds on a wire. *Boom. Bang. Crack.* Jake shot 'em up. Lonnie didn't like the sound of guns but Jake said, "Your turn," and he put both of Lonnie's hands on the warm grip. "Keep your feet wide. Look through there and aim at those peas in front of you," he said. "Then you pull the trigger, but be ready, 'cause it's got a bite."

Lonnie pulled the trigger and the gun bit her. It sent her sprawling on her butt. Lonnie cried and Jake just laughed. "Didn't I tell you?" he said, and when Lonnie kept crying, Jake told her to "Shut up!" and "Stop yer bawling!"

When they got back home, Mama scolded Jake. "What the hell were you thinking?"

"I'm not gonna let her grow up to be a goddamn sissy ass who doesn't know how to shoot a gun!" Jake said.

"She's just a kid," Mama yelled back. Then there were bangs and screams and things flying and Lonnie went to her safe space in the closet.

Mama had told her that Chief wasn't a good father 'cause he abandoned them when Lonnie was still in jumpers. "He wasn't cut out to be a family man," she said. Lonnie didn't know what a good father was because she had known only Jake and Chief. She preferred Chief. He pretty much left Lonnie alone most of the time, but he always bought her a cake on her birthday, just like the way Mariko made her pretend daughter a cake. *Piece of cake. Cakewalk. Have your cake and eat it too.*

Most of all, Lonnie preferred Chief because he wasn't like Jake. He didn't want Lonnie to have a gun and told her to stay away from them. "Don't be shootin' a gun. Don't be holdin' a gun. Don't even be lookin' at a gun."

Lonnie couldn't help but look at the guns the bad men in the hallway were carrying. They were gonna do something evil. *Malicious. Dreadful. Villainous. Criminal.*

Chief said to keep away from the men. That she should go straight back to her apartment. That's what he told her. "Lonnie, you stay away from them. Hide if you see 'em." Run and hide. *See how they run. See how they run. They all ran after the farmer's wife. Three blind mice.*

Lonnie closed her eyes. In the woods, the bad man fell and Lonnie found his head. The red lights whirled at the Institute. Bad men in the hallway. Lonnie should run. Hide. Hide in the closet or Jake would have her hide.

Lonnie opened her eyes. Now the bad men were kicking open the door where Chief's office was. Holding their guns. In fur coats and leather boots. She should help Chief.

What do I do? What do I do? The voices in her head started yelling. They were telling her to *Run, Lonnie, run!*

Lonnie ran.

See how they run. See how they run. The mouse ran up the clock. Hickory dickory dock.

CHAPTER FORTY-FOUR

CARA

CARA HAD ADVANCED NO MORE THAN TWO TIMID STEPS into the tunnel when a voice from behind her caused her to nearly fumble the camera flash she was trying to use for light.

"Cara?" It was J.B.

"J.B., what are you doing here?" Cara retreated out of the enclosed space to steady her breath.

"Keeping you from disappearing down a hole along with the Blackmon boys," he joked. "The basement was the next stop after coming up empty on our unit-to-unit search."

"Did you know about this tunnel?"

J.B. peered through the hole. "No. Pretty clever. I mean, I've heard rumors, but I thought everything was supposed to be flooded."

"I think this may be the kids' secret back door."

J.B.'s demeanor turned serious at that. "Hang on." He rummaged through a nearby storage rack overrun with plastic bins, rags, toolboxes, and cords, and produced a metal flashlight. "I don't think the maintenance crew will mind my borrowing this." Then without another word, he hopped in. Cara followed suit. Feeling the frigid draft of the tunnel, J.B. took off his coat and put it on Cara, who was without her jacket. She would have rejected this gesture had they not shared the previous night of intimacy. She had to admit she was relieved to have the backup and the extra warmth in the underground tomb that embodied all of her fears.

J.B. lighthoused his beam back and forth in front of him, but it seemed to Cara that it did little to lift the veil of darkness. Still, it was better than the intermittent pulses her digital flash afforded, so she pocketed it away. "What have you heard about the tunnels?"

"Back when Point Mettier was a secret military base crawling with servicemen, they dug all these underground passages to connect the whole town. Not just 'cause of the weather, but also to keep their movements hidden from enemy aerial surveillance. They say there are tunnels between this building and the Walcott Building, to the sea, and maybe even an underground bunker. This whole place was a marvel of engineering back in the day, I suppose. But that's before the 9.2 earthquake and tsunami of 'sixty-four brought it to its knees and the army closed shop here."

Listening to his voice kept Cara's mind off the darkness and the pressure on her lungs. Still, as they got deeper, she could feel the walls of panic enclosing her and her heart beating faster. It was almost as if the inky blackness was a living, predatory entity, waiting to pounce at the right opportunity, staved off only by their feeble beam of light.

After what seemed an eternity, they came upon a split. "I think that's just going to double back to the other end of the Dave-Co," J.B. said a bit hesitantly, pointing in one direction. "So probably this way."

Cara had to admit that she was clueless in terms of compass directions, given that her claustrophobia overpowered her focus. They continued, with the water level rising at their feet. Ever present in the background was the echoey sound of water dripping—the slow melt of snow above, seeping its way below. Ten minutes went by before they came to another split.

"Your guess is as good as mine," J.B. admitted. He sent his light down each artery as far as it would go, but there was no clue as to what each led to other than pits of darkness. Cara could see only kids' graffiti spray-painted over each entrance. "I imagine one way is to the sea and the other is to the Walcott Building."

Being trapped in the tunnels was a fate worse than death. Cara thought back to something her father had taught her when she was a kid and they went through a haystack maze at a country fair—the right-hand rule. If you kept your hand out to the right and followed the wall, turning right at every intersection, it would eventually lead you out of the maze. This is what they would do. "Let's go to the right," Cara said, trying to control the trembling in her voice. Another fifty yards and a cool draft seemed to penetrate the space. Perhaps they were nearing an exit or a passage to the Walcott Building. Regardless, Cara welcomed the circulation of air that alleviated the oppressiveness.

They came upon another fork, and following the maze rule, Cara again directed them toward the right. But after a few minutes the water level rose to knee-deep and seemed to get deeper the farther they traveled. "I think this section is impassable. We need to turn back," J.B. said. Cara agreed. They backtracked, and when they got back to the fork, Cara pointed toward the right again, leading them to the artery they had bypassed earlier.

They continued through the tunnel, wading through the eerie wash. Cara focused on the sloshing of their steps echoing against the walls and she noticed there was something off tempo about the discordant noises she was hearing. She knew it was just her mind playing tricks on her, but with every drop of water that echoed through the tunnel, she thought she could hear a little girl's voice whispering, "Watch out! Watch out!" Cara halted suddenly.

"What is it?" J.B. asked, turning back toward her.

"Listen," Cara said, and held her breath. For a moment there was nothing but water dripping, and blood pulsing in her ears. The anxious feeling of being swallowed into the darkness intensified. Another childhood memory, which was more a sensory recall than a vivid memory of an event, flashed through her. It was the fear of her dark closet at night, of being unable to see what was inside but certain that someone or something was lurking there, just waiting to pull her into some otherworldly hell full of monsters. She had the same uneasiness in her gut now. If she could have sat down and balled into a fetal position, she would have.

Then a distinct swish of water in front of them seemed to validate her dread and caused J.B. to swivel. He cast his light toward the sound just as explosive bursts reverberated through the entire tunnel system like firecrackers, making Cara's heart leap out of her chest. The panic-induced fog in her brain made her slow to process what the noises were, but she finally realized they were *gunshots*.

J.B. crumpled into the shallow water at her feet, dropping his flashlight, which sizzled into darkness.

CHAPTER FORTY-FIVE

AMY

THE WAY THE VILLAGE MEN GRABBED HER BY THE ARM, PRESSING their fingers into her flesh, caused Amy to cry in pain. She knew there would be a black-and-blue bruise in the morning, and oddly, her first thoughts were *Ma's gonna kill me when she sees this* and *I'm gonna have to explain it to her.* But then the reality of the situation hit her and she started trembling, wondering if this was the end of the road.

"Spence!" she screamed, before a hand muffled her mouth. She thought she was going to hyperventilate when a chilling voice growled in her ear.

"Where are the boys?"

By "boys," Amy assumed he meant Spence and Troy. She couldn't see the men's faces, both because it was dark and also because she was trying very hard not to look at them.

One of the men grabbed her backpack to search it. When he saw there was nothing but batteries in it, he tossed it.

"Lead the way, or we'll blow your pretty face off."

Who the hell says, "We'll blow your pretty face off?" The man sounded like a badly written goon in a black-and-white movie. Amy kept silent. Her teeth were chattering like crazy in a combination of cold and fright, and tears rolled down her cheeks. Her legs felt as stiff and heavy as cinder blocks, but she willed herself forward. She didn't want to show them where Spence and Troy were, but she also didn't really want to have her face blown off, and most of all, she didn't want to die alone. At the very least, she wanted there to be a witness to her demise. So she plodded through the water on her own private death march, keeping her eyes on the bouncing white circle her flashlight made in the black void.

With the men focused on the path in the darkness, Amy deftly moved her hand to her pocket where her cell phone was. She knew, however, that it was a futile attempt because there was absolutely no signal in the tunnel or in the City. You could get a bar or two if you got to one of the top floors of the abandoned building and pointed your phone toward the Dave-Co, but the basement was a dead zone. Was there something else she could do with a phone? Throw it at one of the men? It seemed like nothing but a sure path to getting shot. She thought better of the whole idea and instead began reflecting on the sum of her existence. All the things she hadn't done. All the things she hadn't seen. If she were to die, her life wouldn't be even a paragraph. Maybe just a sentence. "Here lies the daughter of the owner of Star Asian Food, who delivered bad takeout to its customers."

Amy pulled her hand back out of her pocket when something sharp poked her fingers. It was the prong of something. *The hair comb that Mariko had given her.* Amy had completely forgotten about it. She wrapped her fist around it. If either of the men tried to touch her, she decided she would do her best to poke his eyes out.

The sound of echoing voices caused all of them to stop in their tracks. It sounded like a man and a woman. *J.B. and Detective Lady?*

"Fuckin' pigs!" the Village Man with the gruff voice said.

"Watch the girl," the other one said, and Amy finally turned, to see one of her captors slosh back in the dark, with his gun out in front of him.

Now's my opportunity, Amy thought, fingering the comb. *All I have to do is stab this guy and run.* But she was too chickenshit. She was trying to muster up the courage to either scream or comb-prick the man and run, when two loud *pops* reverberated through the tunnel and she let out a gasp.

"Shit!" the guy who was supposed to watch her said. He turned to her now, with the whites of his eyes showing, looking crazy. "Don't move, or I'll kill you," he said. He grabbed her flashlight for good measure, then went to help his buddy.

Amy remained still only for a moment, then put her hand against the wall and headed for Spence and Troy's hideout.

CHAPTER FORTY-SIX

CARA

"J.B.!" CARA GASPED, PRAYING THAT HE WAS STILL CON-
scious. She had dropped to her knees in the icy water and was blindly
clutching at the warm body in front of her, but she couldn't see J.B.'s
face or assess his wound. There was no response.

A round of *pops* clipped the tunnel wall above her, and she knew
there was no time for wallowing. She felt her way around J.B.'s body,
making sure first that his head was above water, then hooked her
forearms under his armpits and, with all the effort she could muster,
dragged him backward, retreating into the flooded tunnel they had
just come from.

As the water level rose, he became easier to maneuver, with buoy-
ancy on their side. Hypothermia, though, was working against them.
Cara could feel the ice-cold water stabbing her ungloved hands.

Two reverberating voices caught her attention. She instantly recognized the gruff voice as belonging to the man she had dubbed Cigarettes and Metal their first night at Point Mettier. "I think you popped one of the fuckin' pigs," he said excitedly. The other voice, which Cara instantly recognized to be Wolf's, said, "The little lady's still alive." He said it with such calm and equanimity that it was conversely frightening. Still, there was a modicum of relief when she determined that it wasn't an entire posse in the tunnel with them. She couldn't see them beyond the fork but could hear the hurried *swash* of their steps.

Cara continued to caterpillar backward, dragging J.B. as quietly as possible into the flooded pathway. It was dark as pitch. She still had the digital flash in one pocket and her cell phone in another but didn't dare use either.

The water was almost to her knees. She knew she couldn't go much farther without the danger of J.B. drowning, let alone succumbing to the cold. This was where she had to take a stand. She halted and propped J.B. up against a wall. She tore off the waterproof jacket he had lent her and wrapped it around him. He made a soft groaning noise, which both frightened and relieved her at the same time—she was frightened that he would give them away, but relieved that he was still alive.

"Shit! Did ya fuckin' hear that?" the gruff one asked. Cara knew the deceptive echoes and the constant trickle of water made it difficult to pinpoint from which direction the sound was coming.

"Take that tunnel. I'll take this one," Wolf said.

They had now switched on their flashlights to navigate, and Cara could see their beams just around the bend. She flattened herself on the wall opposite J.B., doing her best to blend in with the shadows.

"Come on, little lady," Cigarettes and Metal said. "I promise I'll be gentle." Cara could almost imagine him giving a toothy, repulsive smile. She carefully drew her gun. Despite her attempts to rack the slide to the cocked position as quietly as possible, there was no way to silence the click of metal.

A spray of bullets erupted as Cigarettes came in blazing. He wasn't really aiming so much as recklessly firing. Bullets plowed the water and plastered the ceiling and walls. His light beamed up and down like a deranged disco strobe, searching the interior, but he wasn't far enough in yet to get a bead on them. Cara held her breath as Cigarettes continued advancing and shooting, with water exploding in mini fountains.

Not a moment more and his light would find them. The bullets were closer to the mark. J.B., against the wall, was in a precarious position. She needed a distraction. Cara took a deep breath, pulled the digital camera flash from her pocket with her free hand, and pressed the button. An atom-bomb blast of light filled the tunnel, startling Cigarettes, who was momentarily blinded, and he instinctively held up his hands to parry the attack of light. It transpired in a matter of seconds, but to Cara it felt like slow motion as she saw that Cigarettes was moving his AR-15 back into position. Her pistol was no match for his assault weapon. She aimed for his upper torso, knowing she had one shot to make it count. It did.

Cigarettes held his chest with a shocked expression before dropping his weapon and his flashlight and dipping to his knees, not quite dead. His fallen light, which must have been waterproof or at the very least water-resistant, remained on and cast an ambient glow on his pained expression.

Rapid boots on water followed. "Fuck! Skinner?" Wolf's voice yelled from the corridor. Only a groan emerged from the man whose name was apparently Skinner.

Cara flattened herself against the wall again. Just like Skinner, Wolf entered the tunnel launching a haphazard spray of bullets, accidentally finishing off his partner. Skinner wore a look of shocked betrayal before he fell face forward into the water. "Fuck!" Wolf said again when he saw whom he had shot, but he stepped over the man without another thought.

Cara tried to use the same trick with Wolf, sending another blast of light, but Wolf was quicker than she was. He never stayed still for a second, and Cara fired off a shot that missed. But luckily, Wolf's blind and random blasts of ammo were missing their mark as well.

She was certain she and J.B. were done for as Wolf moved in for the kill; then she heard the empty-ammo *click* of his weapon. Cara shot her pistol again, just as Wolf swiveled back away from her. "Motherfucker!" he yelled as the bullet hit his arm, but he continued running into the depths, back to where the gun battle had begun, and beyond.

Cara used her cell light to check on J.B. He was still breathing, although his pallor was an unhealthy blue. She could finally see that he was holding his torso where he had been shot. She was debating for a second whether to get J.B. to safety first or go after Wolf when J.B. seemingly read her thoughts.

"The kids," J.B. managed to gasp.

Cara's mind raced as she tried to calculate who was in more danger. Finally, she stood up. "Don't die," she commanded. "I'll be back for you." Then she grabbed Skinner's still-working flashlight and his rifle and took off after Wolf. She wasn't sure whether the weapon was as watertight as the light, but it was worth the risk.

CHAPTER FORTY-SEVEN

LONNIE

LONNIE RAN TO THE BARN. AWAY FROM THE BAD MEN. AWAY from Chief. She had to hurry. *Scurry. Hustle. Bustle. Jack be nimble. Jack be quick.*

Quickly through the school, to the back, and to the barn. Denny was there. He lifted his muzzle and looked at her, hoping for raspberries, but she had none to give him, so she just petted him. She petted the space between his eyes. It made her calm. Steady. Staid.

"Gotta stay away from the bad men," she said to Denny.

WHEN JAKE KILLED Mama, Lonnie hid in the closet. It smelled like mothballs and moldy bread. There were coats. Hats. Gloves. Boots. Scarves. She could hear Mama screaming and Jake yelling. She closed her eyes tight and covered her ears. *Racket. Discord. Wailing. Sobbing. Crying. Bang. Thud. Quiet.*

Lonnie couldn't save Mama. She couldn't save Denny's mama. Denny's eyes were brown and sad. He snorted at her. He looked at Lonnie kind of like the way Lonnie looked at Mama that day when they had packed their bags.

"We are leavin', Lonnie," Mama had said. "Today's the day. We are outa here and we're not coming back." She emptied all the drawers and started putting her clothes in a suitcase. She packed Lonnie's storybooks, her pajamas, and her teddy bear. "We're gonna drive to Seattle. I'll find a job and everything's gonna be fine." After she packed all of their stuff, she grabbed Lonnie's hand.

They went to the front door. Mama's heels click-clacked on the floor like she was ready. She put her hand on the knob and started to turn. But then she stopped, paused, halted. Then her hand went back down in slow motion. She put down the suitcase and the duffel bag. She went to the couch. The couch was sagging. Mama was sagging. She started sobbing. "I'm sorry, honey," she said. Lonnie felt disappointment. Maybe it was the same disappointment Denny felt and the same way Chief would feel if she didn't do anything to help him.

If the bad men killed Chief, she would have to go back to the Institute, where the red lights whirled and the white-haired man with the long, dirty beard was always yelling about a hole in the floor. Lonnie steeled herself. She picked up the shovel.

LONNIE POKED HER head into the police station. Too late. Chief was lying on the floor. On the ground. Knocked out. Out like a light. Lights out. Blood spilled on the floor.

Tears came to her eyes. She wanted to go back. Back to her unit. To her safe space in the closet. But then she heard a woman scream. *Screech. Shriek. Cry. Wail.* It was Mrs. Blackmon.

The two bad men were gripping Mrs. Blackmon. In their coats and leather boots. "Where is it?" the short, older one with the limp was yelling.

Lonnie's breath grew faster and louder. People were yelling. Screaming. "I don't know! I don't know what you're looking for!" They twisted Mrs. Blackmon's arm behind her back.

Yelling and screaming. Yelling and screaming.

Lonnie knew what they were looking for. "I buried it!" she said. *There's a goddamn hole in the floor. They found his head. Head for the hills.*

Everybody looked at her with their eyes wide, and Lonnie ran in with her shovel, the shovel she dug the holes with, the shovel she used to clean Denny's shit. She hit the man with the limp hard over the head. He fell to the ground.

"Watch out!" Mrs. Blackmon yelled.

The bad man with the wrist tattoo grabbed her from behind just like in the self-defense class in the women's circle. *Bend. Elbow. Turn. Kick.* She had practiced it so many times. Lonnie bent forward, but the bad man didn't let go. This wasn't like they had practiced in class. He was supposed to let go so she could throw her elbows from side to side, but he just gripped her tighter. Lonnie felt pain in her wrists. She dropped the shovel. *What to do? What to do?* The man slammed her to the ground. Pain in her knee and her chin where it hit the floor. Mrs. Blackmon screamed. Or was it the voices in her head? *Run to the closet! Go to your safe space.* Sobbing. Crying. Bang. Thud. Quiet. That's how it went with Mama.

Lonnie tried to shut out the voices. She remembered Angie Cisco's class and the way Mariko was when they practiced their moves in the women's circle. She could be strong, mighty. Mighty Mouse. Superman. Wonder Woman. Lonnie got to her knees, and this time, she bent her legs like a spring. Then she screamed, *"Ayeee!"* and kicked her feet backward with all her might, like the way Denny would have kicked his hind legs, right into the man's nut sack. He yelled, *"Awoooo!"* Then Lonnie turned, picked up the shovel, and hit him over the head. *"Hya!"*

The bad man fell to the floor. Debra's mouth fell open. She looked down at the two bad men. She looked up at Lonnie. Then she grabbed their guns.

CHAPTER FORTY-EIGHT

CARA

CARA PRESSED THE WALL, MOVING THROUGH THE UNDER-ground passage, armed with Skinner's flashlight and his AR-15. As she advanced farther, thin slivers of moonlight began to illuminate the tunnel, signaling that she must be near an exit. A modicum of relief. The rapid pulsation through her veins now had less to do with claustrophobia than with the thought of J.B. sitting in the frigid water, possibly dying. If she didn't find Wolf and the kids in time, she would fail J.B. or the kids or all of them. A prospect suddenly far more frightening than a dark tunnel.

Cara quickened her pace and found steps to an opening where a door must have once stood but which was now just a gaping mouth with rusted-off hinges. Accumulated slush melted and dripped from what she assumed was a floor of the Walcott Building and into the tunnels. She gingerly made her way up to the landing. Snow had drifted in through blown-out windows and covered the space, painting an homage to Dr. Zhivago's abandoned Varykino. Seeing the snow made Cara realize that she ought to be freezing, but in her heightened state, she felt strangely unfazed by the cold.

Footprints bread-crumbed an instant path to follow Wolf. But there was also a set of smaller boot prints, probably made by Amy. If Amy was the Little Red Riding Hood of the equation, Cara had to be the hunter after Wolf.

The expansive hallways and hollowed-out rooms spoke of a grander time, when the place teemed with life as a military base for servicemen and their families, but now it was only a weather-eaten spook house for bored teens to get their adrenaline kicks. Graffiti was scrawled over practically every inch of drywall that hadn't chipped or peeled away. Icicles of frost hung from the ceiling, dripping into toxic puddles. Cara had to be careful not to trip over metal and wooden debris that littered the floors—parts of pipes, chunks of drywall, and pieces of furniture that spiked above the snow. Fallen-in ceilings were testament to the fact that the building was decaying from the inside and was a possible death trap for vandals.

Cara continued tracking the prints until they seemed to end in a slushy mess at one of the puddles. She halted for a moment, trying to decide which direction to take, before the squeak of a door shifting open sent shivers down her spine and she swiveled her light toward the sound. There was no one there, just the wind or some invisible hand showing her a path up a flight of stairs.

Cara jogged up to the next level, then through a series of open doorways that had a creepy, fun-house-mirror look, with doorframe after doorframe down the long passageway extending into infinity, leading her into the bowels of the building. She stopped when she thought she heard a soft whimpering—the eerie sob of a teenage girl. *Amy!*

Wolf stepped into the light. "Well, now that the lady detective is here, I guess we can start the party." His voice echoed in the hollows.

Cara could see through the dust particles filtering the light that Wolf had Amy wrapped in his bloody left arm. In his right hand, the empty rifle gone, a Glock was pointed at the teen's head. The canine tatted on his cheek looked ready to devour his captive.

Cara had to stall. "How do I know it's loaded?"

Wolf shot at the ceiling, causing Amy to scream and concrete to shower down dangerously.

"Okay," Cara said defeatedly. "I'm going to put the gun down." She slowly deposited the weapon she had picked off of Skinner and raised both her hands.

"I'm not stupid, lady," Wolf said. "Where's the pistol you were taking potshots at me with earlier?"

Cara weighed her options. She was not the quick draw that J.B. was. Wolf definitely had the advantage. "All right," she said, inching her hands toward her back pocket.

"If you try that light shit on me again, I swear, this girl's brains will paint the walls red."

Amy's eyes showed a new level of fear.

Cara decided to try a new tactic, knowing that giving up her Glock meant certain death. "Only one of us knows where the stash is. If you kill either of us, you may never find it." Cara was taking a stab but it seemed to strike a chord.

"I'm betting it's this one," he said, but Cara detected just a hint of uncertainty.

"That's a big bet." Cara was alarmed to see Amy slowly moving her hand into her pocket. It seemed like a dangerous move. All she could do was keep Wolf distracted. "You don't want your friend's death going to waste, do you?"

"Fuckin' bitch! Throw your fuckin' gun down or, I swear, I'm just gonna shoot you and her both!" He was turning red with anger, his eyes practically bulging. Even the foliage that had been inked into his neck seemed to change color, growing more vibrant. His hold on Amy loosened with his aggravation.

It was at that moment that Amy sprang to life. She pulled a curved hair comb out of her pocket, an intricate and innocuous-looking weapon, and stabbed Wolf's arm at the bullet wound. Cara heard the puncture of flesh like a knife slicing a dead fish.

Wolf let out a howl that befitted his name. Amy screamed and pulled out of his grasp. It transpired in a matter of seconds, but to Cara, it felt as if time had suspended. She dropped her flashlight, grabbed her pistol from her back pocket, and felt her breath slow as, with both hands on the gun, she locked her aim just above Wolf's flashlight. She knew she had only three bullets left in the magazine. At the same time, Wolf, still in pain, aimed his weapon. *BLAM! BLAM! BLAM!* Her shots reverberated through the building as Amy retreated down the hall. Cara held her breath in the aftermath. If none of the bullets had hit their mark, she was certainly dead.

Wolf finally crumpled, his gun tumbling out of his hand.

Cara retrieved her light and rushed forward, kicking away Wolf's pistol before checking him for other weaponry. It was clear, however, that he was in his last throes. "Fuck me" were his last words before his eyes glazed and rolled into his head.

"Amy? Are you all right?" Cara called out. She flashed her light down the tunnel. Everything beyond her weak circle of white, however, was shrouded in darkness.

"Amy?" she called out again.

"We can trust her," a voice whispered.

Then finally, not one but three silhouettes emerged into the light. Amy, Spence, and Troy.

CHAPTER FORTY-NINE

LONNIE

LONNIE KNELT NEXT TO CHIEF, WHO WAS LYING ON THE floor. Everybody ended up on the floor. Lonnie's mama. Denny's mama. Bad men. Chief. All falling down. *Ring around the rosie, a pocket full of posies.* Lonnie touched Chief's arm. Without Chief, they would send her back to the Institute, where people were always yelling and screaming.

LONNIE REMEMBERED WHEN there was yelling behind the barn. "I'll cut you to pieces!" That's what the bad man with the arrow tattoo on his cheek said. He was yelling at Mrs. Blackmon. "I'll cut you to pieces!" *Cut. Carve. Slash. Slice. Cleave.* Mrs. Blackmon yelled back, "Stay away from us!"

She heard a *BANG* in the woods. In the woods, there were always hunters in camo pants and camo shirts like the ones who killed Denny's mama. Lonnie had to be careful when she walked Denny during hunting season. She kept him on his leash and stayed away from the woods. But there weren't any hunters that day.

Mrs. Wright came outside with her binoculars. She must have seen something, because she and Mrs. Blackmon were talking outside the barn, all agitated. Then Chief showed up and Mr. Marino came with a chain saw. All gathered round like a flock of crows. *Four and twenty blackbirds baked in a pie.* Lonnie followed them to the woods, where the bad man with the arrow tattoo was on the ground, blood spilled from his head. He had his eyes open and he was smiling crooked. Everybody was around him. Like busy bees buzzing, hovering. They were cutting him to pieces.

"Take an arm." That's what Chief said. Mr. Marino held the bad man. Chief was using the chain saw. Buzzing. Like busy bees.

"Cut off his head!" Mrs. Wright said.

Mrs. Blackmon went to throw up in the trees.

The man with the tattoo grew smaller and smaller. Pieces in a Hefty bag.

Mrs. Wright picked up a hand. *They found a hand on the beach.*

"Lonnie!" Mrs. Blackmon yelled when she looked up and saw her. Lonnie knew she wasn't supposed to see. She started running back to her unit. Lonnie was afraid Chief was going to send her to the Institute because she saw a bad thing.

"Now, Lonnie," Chief said later, "that was a bad man. He was going to hurt Mrs. Blackmon."

Lonnie kept her head low, but she nodded. She had heard the arrow man say, "I'll cut you to pieces!" outside the barn. But funny, now he was the one cut into pieces.

"Bad man," Lonnie repeated.

"Now, you just keep your mouth shut. Don't talk to anyone. Don't tell anyone. Understand?"

Lonnie nodded. *Hush, little baby, don't say a word.*

"Because if you talk to anyone, they're going to send me away, and if I'm gone, they're going to send you to the Institute. You don't want to end up back at the Institute, do you?"

"No, sir," Lonnie said. She didn't want to go back to the Institute. That's where she got backhanded. *They found a hand on the beach.* Then she found a head. Then she found a bag. She buried them both. *Don't tell anyone. Keep your mouth shut.*

SHE OPENED HER eyes to look at Chief lying on the floor. "I didn't say a word. I didn't say a word." She cried as she rocked back and forth, making Chief's shirt all wet. "Please don't die, Chief." Lonnie knew that he was the only one left who loved her besides Denny.

"Lonnie!" Mrs. Blackmon came to her side now. She checked Chief's wrist and put her ear to his mouth. "He's still alive," she said.

"Wake up, Daddy!" Lonnie said. And then Chief listened to her for once. Maybe he was so surprised to hear her say "Daddy" instead of "Chief" that he opened his eyes, looking dazed. Lonnie felt relieved. "Daddy," she said again, giving him a hug.

CHAPTER FIFTY

CARA

IN THE MORNING, A MEDEVAC CHOPPERED IN—A METAL-GRAY
Black Hawk helicopter provided by the National Guard, kicking up
fierce snow gusts as it hovered to land. J.B. was already on a stretcher,
wrapped like a mummy in thermal mylar. Leon and Willie were escorted into the chopper in cuffs, morosely realizing that their leader,
Wolf, and their cohort Skinner were also making the ride, albeit in
body bags.

Chief Sipley, on the other hand, declined to fly to Anchorage, in-
sisting he was fine. "People're always telling me I got a head as hard
as a rock," he said. "I guess they were right." He agreed to be monitored by the resident nurse, Sara Lindbaum—a five-foot-two bundle
of energy with fiery red hair and an apple-pie personality.

Nurse Lindbaum had also been in charge of stabilizing J.B. Seeing Cara's distraught demeanor, Lindbaum had reassured her, "No one's going to die under my watch, hon. We got this." She worked through the night, with the assistance of Chuck Marino, who, it turned out, had a medical degree, although it was in psychiatry. There seemed to be no end to the surprising details of the long-bearded storekeeper's life.

Cara paced in the hallway. Despite her mental gymnastics to tamp down her feelings, she knew inside how much she really did care for J.B. More than she wanted to admit. The hometown awkwardness. The nonthreatening overtures. His unexpected steeliness in moments of peril. Even the care he took to impress her with a cup of coffee. All of that had taken a hold inside her. So much so that when she saw him fall like a rag doll before her eyes in the tunnel, she thought she actually felt physical pain. Would she lose yet another person in her life? She wasn't sure if she could survive that.

At three in the morning, Cara was encouraged by the nurse's assessment that it didn't appear as though the bullet had hit any major organs. But J.B. had a fractured rib and would probably be losing a toe or two to hypothermia.

"You ought to get some rest," Chuck said at that point. Cara realized then how much she had been operating on the fumes of adrenaline. It had been a very long day from the time she and J.B. had set out in the morning for the village. A feeling of overwhelming exhaustion took over. She dissolved into a seat in the hallway and promptly passed out, but awoke in time to see J.B. off to the helicopter. He was still unconscious, but she squeezed his hand and whispered, "I'll see you in Anchorage." She was battling two conflicting parts of her psyche—one that was consumed with the distress of knowing that despite the nurse's reassurances, J.B. might *not* make it. The other was spinning a protective cocoon of pragmatism, compelling her to focus on the case at hand. If she concentrated on saving someone, in her absurd logic, that might counter losing someone else.

CARA STARED INTO the gaping hole. She was bundled up and armed with a flashlight, bracing herself for what she hoped would be the last time she would have to take a jaunt through a tunnel. After the previous night's harrowing events, she had ordered all the teens to leave their belongings and get back to the safety of the Davidson Condos. She had promised they could come back during daylight to retrieve their things, as long as she was accompanying them. So here she was again. When they were done, she would make sure that someone would make a tamper-proof blockade that would lay this tunnel entrance in the basement to rest.

She let the Blackmon boys lead the way and tried to focus on the light and the rippling sounds their feet made. Now seemed as good a time as any for off-the-record questioning, and Cara needed the distraction.

"When you decided to hide here, did you know your mother had killed your father?" She tried to make her tone seem casual, although there could be nothing casual, really, about a murder involving one's parents.

"She didn't kill him," Spence said. It was a response Cara had expected.

"Do you know who did?"

"Probably one of those Village Men that tried to kill us." Spence was clearly taking the lead in the conversation.

"Did you find anything of your father's that they might have been looking for?" she asked.

"No," was his curt answer. She might as well have been talking to one of the glacier formations in the sound.

"What about you, Troy?"

Troy, who had remained silent, ventured a soft "No."

"I don't think we should be answering any more questions without a lawyer," Spence huffed.

Cara felt she had probably stretched her limit. "Okay," she said. "No more questions." They came upon the spot where J.B. had been shot, and she had to mentally distance herself, trying to erase the instant replay running through her mind.

When they reached the bunker-like space the boys had sheltered in, Spence pulled open a still-intact plywood door with a finger hole. Protected from the elements, it was dry and warm inside. Too confining for Cara's comfort, but for the boys, it had served its purpose. They began gathering the sleeping bags, clothes, battery-operated lamps, and other belongings they had escaped with or that Amy had procured for them.

There were two backpacks, one camouflage green and another sporty black with a neon red stripe. But what caught Cara's attention was a white knitted ski cap resting on top of one of them. She had seen this ski cap before, at Hidden Cove on the day she had arrived in Point Mettier. It belonged to the person who had spied on her and J.B. from the woods. She picked it up. "Is this yours?" she asked, tossing it to Spence. Spence caught it in his right hand. "No, it's Troy's," he said, and then hot-potatoed it to Troy, who caught it in his *left* hand. Cara pretended this meant nothing to her. She lifted the backpacks and held them out for the boys, as if she were offering them assistance. Spence took the black one and slung it over his right shoulder. Troy took the other and slung it over his left shoulder.

"You're a southpaw," Cara noted.

Troy nodded, then looked apprehensive, realizing that he might have just given himself away.

There was a heaviness in Cara's heart. "I know your mother had reported your father for domestic violence. But she's not the only one he abused, is she?"

A momentary silence while Troy looked at his shoes and Spence seemed to be calculating how to answer.

"He beat all of us," Spence answered for Troy. "That's what abusive fathers do."

"There were hospital records." Cara continued to address Troy, keeping her voice soft. "They said you had fallen from a tree. A black eye. A concussion." Troy was thirteen now, but he was only six at the time of the reported fall. It was shortly after that Debra finally left their father. The thought was deeply disturbing to Cara. What kind of person would do that to their own child? She was sure Lovansky deserved what he got. Troy was frozen. Cara drew in a deep breath before continuing. "Was it an accident when you shot your father?"

"Hey!" Spence stepped in again, this time with a threatening glare. "Like I said, it was those fuckin' men from the village, and you can't talk to us anymore until we have a lawyer."

"You're right, Spence. Nothing said here is admissible in a court of law." Spence didn't know what to make of that.

Troy linked eyes with Spence, seemed to gain a new kind of confidence. "It's okay. I want to tell her."

"A lie is often harder than the truth. You tell me the truth and then I'll do the hard part," Cara coaxed.

"Troy . . ." Spence tried to butt in.

"I said I want to tell her," Troy repeated with a conviction that made Spence shut up. Cara could almost see the weight of the burden Troy had been keeping. "It wasn't an accident," he finally said.

"When you saw your father two weeks ago, were you afraid he might hurt you again?"

Troy nodded. "Mom said she was going to meet him in the woods, but she was going alone. I got worried, so I followed and took the hunting rifle. I knew he was going to hurt Mom. When he started yelling and I thought I saw a knife, I came out and I shot him." Tears rolled from his eyes as his voice broke into sobs.

"You were trying to protect your mother," Cara practically whispered.

"It's my fault. Nobody else's."

Cara surmised that this last comment was because Troy's mother had tried to take the fall. She didn't blame Debra. She would have done the same, because when Troy decided to pick up the rifle and shoot his father, she knew it wouldn't exactly fly in court as an act of self-defense. And Cara was certain there were others involved who had helped to cover up the crime, or at the very least were privy to the secret. Perhaps they had even helped to disassemble the body piece by piece and throw the pieces into the sound. She wasn't sure who all the players were. She suspected Chief Sipley and Ellie Wright were part of it, based on their general posture of uncooperativeness. There were probably others. Perhaps if Cara had never come to Point Mettier or been trapped behind an avalanche, the scheme would have worked and the murder would never have come to light. But now, with a trail of bodies, the vestiges of Cara's time spent there could not be erased. Should everyone involved be incriminated? Or should Debra become the martyr she had intended to be? Cara had already deliberated these questions in her mind. "It's all right, Troy," she said. "It will be all right. I promise. Just tell me where the drugs are, or whatever your father was carrying and Wolf's men were looking for. It's all I need to know."

"We don't have his drugs," Spence said. "I swear we don't have anything of his." Troy nodded in agreement.

Cara believed them, but she now had a problem. Because without the object that Wolf was looking for, it was going to be harder for Cara to come up with the lie she planned to deliver to Anchorage PD.

CHAPTER FIFTY-ONE

AMY

AMY RARELY EVER SAW MA CRY. THERE WAS THE TIME WHEN
Amy discovered the universe-upending fact that she was Korean,
and once she caught Ma after school, sitting alone in the dim light of
the TV, watching her favorite get-rich-quick-with-garage-items antiques show, crying for no good reason. But now here Ma was, bawling for the second time in one month. She was in hysterics, hiccuping
and wailing, with her arms wrapped so tightly around Amy she
could hardly breathe. Then Ma pulled back for a moment and
slapped Amy on the arm. Not particularly hard, but still with a sting.
"How can you do such dangerous thing?" she practically screamed.
"You don't go anywhere without telling Ma first, okay?"

That wasn't going to happen, but Amy nodded anyway.

After her ordeal with the Village Men, Amy had done some serious reflection on her life. All she had ever known was the Dave-Co. Not literally, of course. She had gone on shopping trips to Anchorage and school field trips, and there were those times she had absconded with Spence under false pretenses. But she had never been out past the ten p.m. tunnel curfew and she had never known life beyond five hours of sun in midwinter. She had never gone to a party where there were people she didn't know, never attended a major-league sports game, never seen a live concert, and now, having discovered she was Korean, Amy realized she had never even tasted Korean food before. There were so many "nevers" that the thought scared her. Amy stared at the mementos she had collected over the years combing the beach. Plastic and metal buttons, a lipstick case, euro coins, someone's 1985 class ring from the University of Florida, a silver dollar, a plastic lighter, a corroded Omega watch frozen at two twelve, various earrings, and even a gold wedding band inscribed with the words "Always & Forever." They were left by tourists who were sailing, traversing, exploring, and experiencing while she was stuck in forever stasis. She was going to die having known just a piece of what life was—an island in a sea of real-world experiences.

Now was probably not the best time to bring this up with Ma, but Amy was bursting to declare her intentions—a new urgency to her revelation that she didn't want to die in some stuffy, sunless building in Point Mettier.

"Ma," she finally said. "I have to leave here."

"Wha—?" Ma's eyes nearly rolled into the back of her head. "What you saying? Police want to take you to Anchorage? Ma will not let them."

"No, Ma. *I* want to go. I can't stay here in Point Mettier forever."

Ma seemed unable to comprehend the words coming out of Amy's mouth. "I . . . don't understand. Where you want to go? Shopping?"

"I'm talking about after I graduate. You moved us here for a reason. So we could live a better life."

Ma's eyes narrowed; she was finally understanding. "We don't starve. We have freedom. I own my business, work for nobody. This is better life."

Amy had to put it in terms that Ma understood. "We're prisoners in this building. No better than if Dear Leader had put us in jail."

"No, we can go places. We go to Anchorage. We can take trip somewhere."

"We've never gone on a trip anywhere in my life."

Ma panicked. "We go. I promise. On next school holiday. I will hire someone to take care of restaurant."

The desperation in her voice was almost pitiful. "Ma, I need more than that. I want to get out, go to college, do things."

"College?" She hesitated a beat. "Yes. Yes. University of Anchorage."

"I don't want to stay in Alaska. I want to go somewhere else. Maybe California."

"California?" She nearly spit the word. Full of disdain and loathing. "They will find you there. Send you, us, back to North Korea. Then we die." Tears streamed.

"You brought me here to be free. I need to be free. I want to do things." Amy looked in her mother's eyes. There was a kind of slow metamorphosis. A realization that there was truth to what Amy was saying. "I'm going to apply to out-of-state colleges and scholarships for next year. I've already looked up some information and California has a Safe Schools for Immigrants bill, which means they can't ask for my citizenship or immigration status."

Ma, defeated, sat down on a chair. Wiped her eyes with a kitchen towel. Amy knew that she would feel bad about leaving Ma and that her mother would be lonely as hell, but she just couldn't stay at the Dave-Co forever. And someday, when Amy got a job and a place on the outside, she would get Ma out of here too.

"You . . . and Dad. You made sacrifices for me. I want to do something to have made it all worth it."

Ma sighed twice. Big, gasping, revelatory sighs, as if she were exhaling the weight of the world. She finally lifted her head and looked at Amy with bleary eyes. "Yes," she said. "Yes, Amy. You should go away to college in California."

CHAPTER FIFTY-TWO

CARA

"SO, WHAT WAS IT BROUGHT YOU HERE AGAIN?" OFFICER NEW-
orth asked, incredulous that anyone would actually *volunteer* to
come to Point Mettier in the off-season.

It was Cara's turn now in the hot seat, across from the investigator in the tiny, cold concrete room of the Point Mettier police station. Crews had begun working on clearing the avalanche debris
shortly after the medevac airlifted J.B. and Wolf's men out. The tunnel was once again functioning, albeit on a limited schedule. This
was the second time Officer Neworth had been sent to Point Mettier,
after having accepted a noncriminal explanation for the washed-up
body parts. This time, however, there was no doubt about the crimi-
nality behind the shoot-out that had resulted in a couple of corpses

and a handful of injuries. Neworth's colleagues were, at that moment, examining the tunnels beneath them.

"Kennedy . . . that name sounds familiar. Did you work at APD?"

"I'm on disability," Cara said. "I was just visiting here when I got stuck because of the avalanche."

"Uh-huh," he said, looking her up and down, trying to determine what her disability might be, then made some indecipherable notes.

"You can take a look at the report with my findings." Cara attempted to change the subject and slid over a manila file containing freshly printed documents.

Officer Neworth opened the folder and flipped through the pages, only half interested in their contents. Cara wasn't sure if his obvious disdain was because he distrusted her or because he hated having been proven wrong in his initial assessment of the case.

"I'll summarize for you," Cara said, growing weary. "The head of the floater, which washed up later on the cove, was discovered by a resident, and Debra Blackmon was subsequently able to ID it as belonging to her ex-husband, Michael Lovansky. You have the head now as evidence." She glanced at the duct-taped cooler on the table, which had until recently been sitting in Chuck Marino's freezer. Neworth had a slightly horrified look when he realized what was in it. "Mr. Lovansky had heavy violent priors and was connected to a band of ex-convicts that resided in Chugach Village. The leader of the gang went by the name of Wolf. He was the transported DOA with the neck tats who was involved in the shoot-out. I'm sure your office will be able to ID his real name based on his prints. Lovansky had taken an unearned commission from Wolf. He had then planned to get back with his ex-wife and family and run off with them against their will, but Wolf caught up with him, shot him in retaliation, cut him into pieces, and dumped him into the sound. You can see the photo documentation on page nine of the report."

Officer Neworth flipped to the page and winced at the visuals. Then he looked back up at her. Cara wondered if she had any tells when she lied. Officers always looked for tells. She had coordinated with Chief and Debra in advance so that their stories would line up.

"But then what was this man, the one called Wolf, and his gang doing back here? And why were they in the tunnels if they had already dispensed with Mr. Lovansky?"

This, of course, was the last piece of the puzzle that Cara had needed to make her story work.

"SHIT, POOP, DUNG, crap, moose pie," Lonnie had said, pointing to Denny's excrement.

"Yes, Lonnie, we can see that," Mrs. Blackmon said. "We want to know where you hid what you found."

Cara took a stab. "You didn't feed whatever it was to Denny, did you?"

Lonnie rolled her eyes. "Why would I do that? It's in a goddamn hole in the ground, under there."

Cara exchanged a confounded look with Debra before she picked up the shovel. When Cara had confided her plan to pin the murder of Michael Lovansky on Wolf, Debra opened a door of cooperation, but she still couldn't illuminate where Michael's belongings might have ended up. "Do you think Lonnie knows something?" Cara had asked. "She trusts you more than she does me. Maybe you can convince her to talk." And that's what had led them back to the barn, with Cara shoveling manure. Lonnie had eventually confessed to Debra that she had buried something other than Lovansky's head.

After about twenty minutes of strenuous digging, they glimpsed a patch of blue plastic material in the earth. Debra helped her scrape the rest of the dirt away to unearth a large duffel bag. Cara zipped it open and there it was. She had seen things like this in the movies, but it was breathtaking to see it in person. Wads of cash in rubber-banded stacks filled the bag. Unlike in the movies, the bills weren't crisp and new. They were worn and uneven, with some stacks comprising Benjamins while others were of twenty-dollar bills. All told, it must have been at least a couple hundred thousand. She was certain this was what Wolf and his men had been looking for, and now she finally had what she needed for a believable motive in an intra-gang murder.

As a bonus, Cara found a cell phone in a flashy gold case in a side pocket of the bag. The battery had long ago died, so there was no way to confirm that it was Michael's, but Cara decided she would keep it rather than turn it in for evidence. She told Debra she didn't want the police uncovering something that might incriminate her or the boys. The truth, however, was that she intended to dig through the contact list to see if she could discover who Wolf's inside connection had been.

CARA NOW UNZIPPED the duffel bag, which was on the table, and watched Officer Neworth's eyes grow wide at the stacks of money. "Again, this is speculation, of course, but we believe that Mr. Lovansky had stolen the cash from Wolf. Then he had unsuccessfully tried to visit his ex-wife here to try and get her to get back with him, and rented a room under the alias Charles Dodger. The unit he rented had been ransacked. You can take a look at the evidence photos of the destruction. This is where I believe the men ultimately found the cash. Officer Barkowski and I had discovered Wolf and one of his gang trying to abscond through the tunnels with it when they began shooting at us, while Chief Sipley was trying to apprehend two others lurking in the building before he was also attacked, but his daughter was able to fend off the suspects with a shovel."

It all added up. Cara had left out details about Amy, Spence, and Troy. The Anchorage investigator leaned back in his chair and closed his eyes for a moment, mentally adding things up in his head. Then he threw in a wrench. "So, about Ms. Blackmon. I understand she was being held at the police station when Chief Sipley was ambushed. Can you tell me what she was being held for?"

Mrs. Blackmon wasn't supposed to be a part of the story. Cara fumbled. Who could have mentioned her being at the station? Mrs. Blackmon surely wouldn't have confessed to this. Had Chief Sipley mistakenly let it slip after his head trauma? Cara had made it clear that Lonnie was unreliable as a witness because of her mental disability. J.B., she presumed, was still in an unconscious state. To avoid entangling more of Wolf's men in the questioning, Cara and Chief Sipley had decided not to report to the AST the visit to the village, but she couldn't be sure of what Leon and Willie had said in custody. Cara had to come up with an answer. "She was being detained," she said, "because, since we discovered that the body parts belonged to her ex-husband, naturally we needed to question her."

Officer Neworth looked down at his notes and the room suddenly felt hot. He shifted in his seat. Cara bit her lips and wondered if that was her tell. Was there an inconsistency in the story? But then he finally looked up. "Okay, I think we have everything we need here," he said.

Cara felt a wave of relief. She knew she would have to worry about APD questioning J.B. before she had a chance to get to him and bring him up to speed, but for now, she had dodged a bullet.

"Well, everything looks in order," Officer Neworth said, slapping his knees and getting up. "And now you can finally get out of this hellhole." He practically whispered this comment and winked at Cara.

If he had said this to her nine days earlier, she might have completely agreed. But now, something about Point Mettier had grown on her. Not the living in a boxed-in building, of course. She had had her fill of tunnels and cloistered spaces for a lifetime, but even in winter, the natural surroundings were strikingly beautiful, and Cara had come to understand the community of stragglers, oddballs, and recluses who had chosen to live here. At the end of the day, they were a group of people who might not always get along but who rallied together to protect their own. There was something hopeful in that.

AFTER CARA GATHERED her laptop, her ad hoc wardrobe of Point Mettier sweats and tees, and the record albums she had been loaned on her first night, she made her way to the Cozy Condo check-in to square away her bill with Ellie Wright.

"Hope you enjoyed your stay," Ellie said with a smile.

Cara noticed Ellie's binoculars on the counter. "How are the whales today?" She couldn't resist one last jab.

"Oh, I think I saw one maybe alone and lost in the sound. But since the sun's out, I expect she'll find her way out soon."

They gave each other a half grin as a sign of understanding.

"Such a shame about all that cash." Ellie sighed. "I don't think Anchorage PD would have missed what they weren't looking for."

"That kind of money brings nothing but trouble, Ellie," Cara said. "Better in the hands of the police. And you know we needed it as evidence, to make everything hold water."

"Well, maybe you didn't need *all* of it," Ellie grumbled as she handed Cara her receipt.

Cara placed on the counter the stack of records Ellie had lent her the first night. Ellie was about to put them away but then halted. "Why don't you keep this one as a souvenir?" she said, handing Cara Mariko's record.

Cara smiled. "Thank you, Ellie. I'd like that."

As Cara made her way down the hallway, she spotted Lonnie, who gave her a sideways glance. "I'm not answering any more questions."

"It's all right," Cara said. "I'm not going to ask you any more questions. I'm leaving. You did a really brave thing saving Debra and Chief Sipley. Now, you take care of yourself."

Lonnie looked at her feet, then said, "Thanks, Ms. Kennedy."

CHIEF SIPLEY, WHO had clearly recovered from his ordeal, stood waiting for Cara in the lobby. "Come back and visit anytime," he said. "We'll give you the Point Mettier welcome." Cara wasn't exactly sure what that meant, but she returned his gruff shake.

"I wanted to say goodbye to Susie too," Cara said. "But I haven't seen her in a while."

Sipley gave her a strange look. "Susie?"

"The kid who always rides her scooter in the hallways. She must be about eight, with wavy brown hair?"

The police chief couldn't suppress the level of shock in his eyes. "That sounds like Susie McNally." He paused to consider that possibility. "She used to live here."

"Used to?"

"Two years ago, she and some of the older kids were riding their bikes and scooters over near the pier. That's before we put up the barricade. She got too close to the water and fell in. People don't know this about cold water, but most people die before hypothermia even sets in. Cold-water shock can kill a person within the first minute. Even the best swimmers can lose muscle control in ten minutes. We give up 'bout one every year to the sound, but it's usually the fishermen getting caught in the nets. Susie's accident . . . that was a real tragedy."

Cara was dumbstruck. "She can't be dead," she finally said. "I know you're just trying to pull my leg." But Sipley didn't laugh. He pointed to a printed notice on the residents' bulletin board.

"I posted it this morning," he said.

Cara leaned in to look at the flyer, stapled to the cork notice board, that Chief Sipley was indicating. MEMORIAL FOR SUSIE MCNALLY. CHURCH SERVICE TO BE HELD NOVEMBER 18TH AT 7:00 P.M. There was a picture at the bottom, and Cara saw the same expressive brown eyes, the same curly locks, and the dimpled smile of little Susie, whom she had spoken to not just once but several times in the dim-lit corridors of the Davidson Condos.

CHAPTER FIFTY-THREE

LONNIE

PEOPLE WERE ALWAYS TALKING ABOUT HER BEHIND HER BACK. Lonnie knew it. They were saying things. Looking at her, whispering about her. Smiling. She heard them say *Hero. Rescuer. Brave. Courageous. Amazing.* Chief even said she was going to get a medal or something.

She told Chief how she was afraid after the bad man attacked him, that he was going to die and then she would be sent to the Institute. But he told her that all the bad men were gone now and Lonnie didn't have to worry about going to the Institute anymore.

Chief had brought a double order of Star Asian Food's fried rice for her and was sitting in his favorite recliner. He had a big bandage on his head where he got hit.

"And if I die, I made sure there are people here who'll look after you, so they can't send you back there ever again."

Lonnie felt a lot better after that. Now she could go feed Denny, brush his coat, take him for a walk, without having to run into Ms. Kennedy and watch what she did and watch what she said.

At the women's circle, Mr. Marino told everyone to give her a round of applause. Lonnie had never gotten a round of applause. *Why was an applause round instead of square?* She liked the sound of claps, like rain on a rooftop, or Mariko's glass case opening and shutting, or Denny's feet on the barn floor.

Mrs. Blackmon brought her a pie. *Georgie Porgie, pudding and pie. Kissed the girls and made them cry.* "Lonnie saved us," Mrs. Blackmon said. She described to everyone how Lonnie had hit one man with a shovel and kicked the other in the balls like a donkey. "She was a real superhero!" Lonnie wondered why the other women wanted so much to praise. *Commend. Approve. Compliment. Flatter. Hail. Cheer.* Maybe when they were always watching her, they were looking out for her.

They started their session and Mr. Marino asked her, like he did every session, "What are the voices saying today, Lonnie?"

Lonnie paused for a moment, trying to hear what her voices were saying, but she didn't hear anything. "They're not saying a goddamn thing, Mr. Marino. It's all quiet. Quiet as a mouse."

EPILOGUE

THE CRITICAL CARE UNIT WAS BATHED IN STERILE LED LIGHT reflecting off polished vinyl floors. Electronic monitors with a jumble of cords and tubes blipped and chirped, and every so often a gasping noise emanated from the breathing apparatus of a curtained-off patient. J.B. looked helpless and vulnerable as he lay asleep, vested in bandages and connecting wires. Two toes on his left foot and one on his right had been amputated, but as Nurse Lindbaum had said, his broken rib would heal and he would otherwise recover. Still, Cara hated seeing him like this. She reached impulsively for his hand. J.B.'s eyelids fluttered as he woke. When his eyes adjusted and focused on her, he smiled—a grin that seemed to go from ear to ear. She mirrored his smile, content to just feel the warmth of his hand

and the beating of his pulse for a moment. The signs of life proved to her that he *had* to be real, and not a ghost like Susie.

Cara had already brought J.B. up to speed on what had happened and on the story they had told APD, but with the various meds coursing through his veins, she wasn't sure how much he would remember of what she had told him.

"How do you feel?"

"I still have phantom itches on my toes and I have a headache the size of Texas, but otherwise, A-OK," he said groggily.

"Can I get you anything?"

"Just the fact that you're here is pretty good." Another infectious grin.

"J.B., do you remember what I told you about what happened . . . after you got shot?"

"Everything's a bit fuzzy," he said. "Maybe it's post-traumatic amnesia."

Cara studied him anxiously, wondering whether, despite his assessment, his physical and mental injuries were more serious than he let on.

"All I remember is that we discovered Wolf killed Debra's ex-husband and was trying to find something he'd stolen. But all the other details, well, they're kind of foggy." Then he winked at her, letting her know that he actually remembered everything clearly. Cara relaxed. "But there is something about the case I've been thinking about while being trussed here like a Thanksgiving turkey."

Cara's puzzled look was the cue for him to continue.

"That fax at the Chugach Village. Remember my buddy Charlie Wilkes at APD, the one who helped me speed up the warrants?"

Cara remembered the name as that of the person who had also outed her to J.B. when she had first arrived at Point Mettier. "Yes."

"He would've seen Ellie's registry, because I sent him a copy. It was part of the evidence I sent him to justify the warrant. He could have figured out that Lovansky had stayed in Room 42. And when we got back from Chugach, Sipley told me he had called and left a message. Maybe Sipley told him we were headed out to the village and then Charlie faxed that warning over."

"How well do you know Charlie?"

"We're both in the National Guard. We go out for beers after training, but that's pretty much it. I mean, it's only a hunch. All I can really do is keep an eye on him for now."

It was true. As troubling as the thought was that there might be a mole at APD, there wasn't enough evidence to act on. Maybe Lovansky's cell phone, which was currently in the hands of a tech expert Cara had hired, would reveal something.

Then J.B. turned quiet and serious for a moment. "You know, there's something else I've been thinking about with all this spare time and only my thoughts to keep me company." He paused as if it were taking a lot of effort to say what came next. "I'm wondering if I oughta leave the self-exile life in Point Mettier. Maybe I could apply for a transfer to Anchorage." He watched Cara's reaction.

She stuttered in her own thoughts. "I hadn't even thought about that . . ." she replied, and she could tell her hesitation wasn't exactly the response he was looking for. Cara suddenly felt like an ass. Her stilted response made it sound as if she didn't want him to move, that she was hedging.

J.B. quickly tried to cover. "I mean, it would give me more of a chance to advance to detective. Plus, I hate to say it, but excepting for the last two weeks, being a cop at Point Mettier is more like being a building manager than an actual po—"

Before he finished his sentence, Cara silenced him by pressing her lips to his. She was done trying to check herself. It was time to unfetter from the past and her emotional stasis. Everything that had been held back within her and all the pragmatic self-preservation gave way to her most basic of instincts, washing over her like a waterfall. She wanted to throw her heart all in. She wanted to be loved again, fears and practicality be damned. J.B. seemed to shudder before entwining his arm behind her head and bringing her in further, as if he were trying to inhale her very being. Cara felt herself tearing up with relief, almost as if she had been wound into a tight coil in a box until this moment, when she was finally allowed to spring free. She grasped the ring on her finger and almost subconsciously slipped it off and placed it in her pocket.

They gazed at each other, wordless. In that moment, there was no one else but the two of them in the world. Even the inhale and exhale of machines in the background seemed to be a part of something within them instead of something external.

The spell of the planet-aligned moment was broken when Cara's cell phone rang. She was going to choose to ignore it, but she recognized the name on her display.

"I . . . have to take this," she said to J.B.'s visible disappointment, and their hands lingered a moment before she stood up and made her way out of the room.

"Angelo?" she answered, once she was in the hallway. Angelo Fernandez was the Filipino tech whiz she had hired to break into Michael Lovansky's cell phone. "Were you able to get in?" she asked.

"Easy peasy," the voice on the other side said. "I think you're gonna want to take a look at something I found."

IN THE DIMLY lit back room of a secondhand computer shop on Airport Road, surrounded by a sea of computer parts, electric cords, pocket-size tools, an oscillator, and the requisite pizza boxes, Angelo Fernandez sat staring at a bank of LCD monitors, blue light reflecting off his glasses. The tech whiz sported a grizzled, beyond-a-five-o'clock-shadow look.

Angelo had been arrested in the past for hacking into a bank's mainframe computer and had served his sentence for it. He had added an extra zero to his own account, which got him ten years in the holding tank. But time in the pen was slashed in exchange for working for the government on cybercrimes. He sometimes fell into that nebulous gray area of using not-exactly-legal methods to hack into computers, but with police turning the other way. Angelo knew Cara wasn't officially working for APD on this case, but that didn't matter as long as she was paying.

"Want a Rolo?" he asked, offering Cara a piece of caramel candy. Cara always liked his instant-friends demeanor.

"Thanks—I'm good."

"Got his contact list, his photos, calls, text messages . . ."

In the back of her mind, Cara was slightly alarmed at how easy it really was. "Can you transfer all of that onto a flash drive? I'll pay extra."

"You said the magic words," Angelo chirped. "And you need to see the photos," he said, posting images on his big monitor for Cara to see. "Yeah, this guy was a real piece of work." He scrolled through the images on Michael's phone. Various shots of naked and half-clothed women, coke-and-booze-flowing parties, the carcasses of hunted animals intermingled with an occasional contemplative vista of nature. But then, in the parade of pictures, Angelo slowed on a series of idiosyncratic photos. They were one-off shots of ordinary people in the middle of mundane acts. A white-haired woman with a knitted scarf sitting in a coffee shop while reading a book. A thin man, possibly in his forties, chaining a bicycle to a rack. A young woman in her twenties who looked indigenous. All seemingly unaware that they were being photographed.

"I don't know if this guy was into some weird voyeurism shit or what," Angelo commented as he clicked through the one-offs. "But this is what I wanted you to see."

Cara couldn't help but let out a gasp of overwhelming shock. It was a slightly blurry photo, zoomed in from afar, of a family—a mother, a father, and a fair-haired boy—with their backpacks, cooler, and hiking gear. The father, wearing his down puffer jacket, gazed attentively at his similarly bundled son while holding his hand. The mother, facing forward, loaded with packed gear on both of her shoulders, still had in her eyes a mirthful light that was now foreign to Cara. They were just stepping out of their two-bedroom house with the white-trimmed windows and the wooden door they had painted red, about to embark on a journey they could never return from.

It was a photo of Aaron, Dylan, and Cara on the day they left for Talkeetna.

ACKNOWLEDGMENTS

There are many people who encouraged and buoyed me in the process of getting this book to fruition.

My brilliant agent, Lucy Carson, laid her reputation on the line in submitting a partial manuscript from a first-time novelist, got it sold, and then held my hand through the process. She is an absolute wonder with her timely reads and generous notes, and I realize just how fortunate I am that she responded to my work. Thank you for always being so warm and constructive.

I am also forever grateful to everyone at Berkley, including the editors, the legal team, and the publicity and marketing champions. Danielle Perez and the amazing copy editors shot holes out of the manuscript until it was Swiss cheese. Your eagle eyes and questions have enhanced the story in so many ways and saved me from much future embarrassment. Thanks also to Tracy Bernstein, who graciously picked up the baton and made everything work seamlessly for me during the process.

Jimmy Tsai and Daniel Benjamin, I am indebted to you for your charity of time and your invaluable notes. Shirley Eng graciously contributed her insight into and knowledge of Alaska. I am also thankful for the critiques and general mental therapy from my writing group, including Kris Young, Kelly Thomas, David Ariniello, Michelle Krusiec, Kimberly-Rose Wolter, and Weiko Lin. Your affirmations and constructive comments gave me the courage to write this book.

Naomi Hirahara, a fellow Japanese American mystery writer, has shown me such kind generosity, sharing her tips and advice. Thanks for always being there to answer my newbie questions. I look forward to our next get-together.

Thank you to the people of Whittier, Alaska. It is important to note that Point Mettier is a nonexistent place with purely fictional characters. While the city of Whittier inspired the setting, the people there were perfectly welcoming and friendly and bear no resemblance to the characters in my book.

Of course, I would have been completely lost without the support of family. I would like to thank my wonderful husband, John Louis Chan, who patiently listened to countless rants and story ideas, contributed notes, and always had my back through the ups and downs of life as a writer. My sister Satsuki and my extended Chan family members Rose, Michelle, Meg, Betty, and Jesse have always been supportive cheerleaders in my endeavors.